Closeness

Other Bella Books by Y. L. Wigman

Filigrane
Milgrane

About the Author

Emerging from a career in research and public service, Y. L.Wigman has turned her skills to the art of telling heartfelt stories. Her passions for studying the human condition, spirituality and astrology are evident in her novels. With extended family nearby, she lives in *Bandicoot Hollow*, a cottage in the hills above Perth, Western Australia. Website: www. ylwigman.com.

Closeness

Y. L. WIGMAN

BELLA
BOOKS
2021

Bella Books, Inc.
P.O. Box 10543
Tallahassee, FL 32302

Printed in the United States of America on acid-free paper.

First Bella Books Edition 2021

Editor: Cath Walker
Cover Designer: Kayla Mancuso

ISBN: 978-1-64247-184-7

Acknowledgments

To my nearest and dearest (you know who you are)—thank you for taking an interest, and supporting and encouraging me through the highs and lows of scribbling.

To Christine and Annelies who always put up their hands to read that creaky first draft: I fully appreciate your sincere appraisals and well considered suggestions. Every book has been substantially the better for your input.

To the intrepid Cath Walker who edited this work—thank you for your thorough care and attention, ensuring a job well done.

To those who fought for women's suffrage, equality, and liberation from archaic laws and repressive attitudes. Thanks to them we enjoy the current freedoms that we must preserve and expand upon.

To the ordinary lesbians who built decent lives with those they loved, despite patriarchy and social condemnation. The ones who trod a far harder, extraordinary path when they chose not to compromise themselves by marrying for safety's sake. They will always inspire me.

To the Loving Unseen for your constant support and guidance: Gratitude.

CHAPTER ONE

The electric wok did not want to fit into the corner cupboard next to the kitchen sink. Duscha turned the cumbersome appliance every which way until it finally slid onto a shelf, at the selfsame moment as someone hammered on the front door of her newly rented two-bedroom unit.

Distracted, she straightened up, only to smack the crown of her head hard into the bottom edge of an overhead cupboard door she'd left ajar. Excruciating pain swept through her skull, buckling her knees with nausea.

"Ow! *Blyat*! Ow, ow, ow…"

Eyes squeezed shut, she continued to swear in Russian and rued her height for a change. The front door rattled again. Gingerly rubbing her noggin through its thick wavy dark-blond mop, she made her way past the packing boxes scattered down the hall.

On the doorstep, a hesitant man in a business shirt and tie said, "Duscha Penhaligon?"

In suburban Wagga Wagga on a peaceful Saturday afternoon, ties were an unusually officious sight. Was he doing a survey or collecting for charity? Perhaps peddling solar panels? But he already knew her name. Not a cold-caller, then. Even so, she held the door handle firmly. "Who's asking?"

He swapped a manila envelope from his right underarm to his left and held out an apologetic hand. "I'm a private investigator. Name's Aaron Fischer. May I come in?"

With a noncommittal shrug, she closed the door behind him. He followed her into the dining-cum-lounge room. "I'm afraid I'm in the middle of moving in. Find a seat where you can." She straddled a rotating PVC-covered stool that last looked appealing in the 1970s. "What can I do you for, Mr. Fischer?"

He pulled up a pine kitchen chair that creaked in protest as he sat. Deep-set brown eyes blinked and crinkled with dawning amusement. "I appreciate your time, Ms. Penhaligon. This won't take long." Smile tightening, he slid out a single page from the manila envelope. "I'm here at the behest of Fielding and Atkinson, your father's solicitors in Canberra."

Fine hair rose at the nape of Duscha's neck, and she inhaled sharply. Her pale blue eyes narrowed when he looked away, pursed and licked his lips, and then spoke deliberately. "Your father died twelve days ago. It's taken an inordinate amount of time for me to find you, I'm sorry. You've moved around a bit. It's been a while since you've seen him?"

Duscha's heart thudded uncomfortably. She reached for the letter, lifting her chin as she scanned its contents. "Last time was when I was eighteen. Saw him once and never again. How did you find me? I've only just leased this place."

"Police. Death opens doors while privacy goes out the window."

She raised a fair eyebrow. "According to this, they want to see me in Canberra."

"Just so they can talk to you in person. I was told you are mentioned in his will, written long ago, regularly updated and still valid. If you don't mind, Jim Fielding requests your presence." As a foil to Duscha's prolonged silence, he added, "I believe it will be worth your while."

"But you can't tell me why."

"I regret to say I'm not privy to the details. I'm just the messenger."

Two hours later, and with most of the unpacking completed, she relaxed on the unit's back steps in the welcome afternoon sun. The steps led into a meagre concrete courtyard bordered by a stark metal fence less than two metres away. The unit was one of a block of four on Langdon Avenue in central Wagga. It was a brisk five-minute walk to the Murrumbidgee River that snaked its way through the inland New South Wales city. She'd chosen the beige brick building for its proximity to her new workplace, rather than its street appeal or architectural merit, both notable by their absence.

She cradled a mug of freshly brewed latte between her palms. At least the coffee machine was unpacked and working perfectly. Large gulps sent welcome caffeine into her bloodstream, and she brightened enough to muster a sardonic smile.

After all this time, what could her biological father possibly have in store for her?

Last she'd heard, he was bankrupt, yet again. A builder and self-titled architect, he'd risked millions on redevelopments in Canberra's older, more rundown suburbs, and not always profitably. Not that the occasional bankruptcy ever stopped him. Cliff Coxall was a big man with sky-high dreams: charming, persuasive, and a convincing purveyor of his unique brand of morality. One moment he was cheating on his oblivious wife, the next he was conscientiously paying child support to Duscha's mother, her Mamochka, who had naïvely thought him single, barely long enough to conceive.

Duscha had met him just the once. Come her eighteenth birthday, his financial obligations had ceased, and he had insisted he meet her. Against her mother's better judgment, he visited their home in Queanbeyan, just outside Canberra. Duscha remembered the meeting as awkward and confusing.

Although Duscha was already considerably taller than her diminutive Russian-Chinese mother, Cliff had still towered over her, grinning maniacally while patting her on the arm too often. Eagerly he had shown her a photo of her blond half-sister Roxanne who, being three years older, seemed thankfully remote. Yet Duscha had been freaked out by the fact that they could have been twins, were it not for her own flatter cheeks and distinctly almond-shaped eyes. Handing back the photo and unusually tongue-tied, she had plastered on a smile, and hoped he would go away. This much older man to whom she bore an unnerving resemblance seemed more like a circus ringmaster than anyone's dad. Why couldn't he just be normal? Why couldn't her family be just like everyone else's?

In the fading afternoon light, Duscha downed the last of her coffee, acknowledging at least one truth about that day twenty years ago. At eighteen, fitting in with her peers was mega-important, and he had disappointed her. With hindsight, he was obviously delighted to meet the forbidden fruit of his loins and simply proud of a fine young woman who happened to be his illegitimate daughter.

Revived sufficiently, she stepped back inside, unpacked the television and arranged furniture so as to make the lounge vaguely liveable. The bed needed making, but she was fading fast. If necessary she could sleep on the sofa.

Flopping into an easy chair, she rubbed her face vigorously with wide warm hands. There was still so much to do before starting her new job on Monday with the Wagga Wagga City Planning Directorate. Although she'd once studied architecture, she'd ended up with a degree in town planning. She had last worked in Griffith, a distant New South Wales city where she and Noelle had lived for six years. That was until Noelle complained of back pain. The cancer had metastasised into her spine. She was gone in a handful of weeks.

Noelle, born Christmas Eve two years before Duscha, was too young for breast cancer. Or so the statistics said. Duscha thought about her every day, too much every night, and lived with an assortment of keepsakes in plain sight that made her smile, made her weep: a plush toy rabbit, an antique sewing kit and numerous kitchen gadgets. There were no photos of her on display. Duscha couldn't bear to see them. Images of Noelle made her disappear for days at a time down a black hole jammed with anguished memories.

After the funeral, she had immersed herself in work, hating to go home to an empty house. The end of the working week had loomed oppressively. She would lose whole weekends bringing Noelle to life again, talking and weeping with a ghost who was keenly remembered and still deeply loved. Not going out and forgetting to eat real food, drew carefully worded comments from colleagues who pointed out that she was becoming alarmingly gaunt.

When she didn't feel too awful, she phoned Michele, a friend from Karabar High School who still lived in Canberra to whom she said the bare minimum, not wanting to burden another with her abject misery. Michele had a husband, kids, and her own life hours away from Griffith. Troubled by Duscha's censored version of her mental and emotional state, Michele had nagged her to come back and stay with her mother. But Duscha's mother had recently married. It wouldn't be fair to her, Duscha had explained. Then Michele pointed out that Duscha sounded like she had post-traumatic stress. That observation helped her better understand intellectually what was going on, yet did nothing to ease the bone-sapping grief. On Michele's urging, she went to a general practitioner who listened briefly, and reached for his prescription pad. He sent her off with five repeats of the antidepressant Paroxetine. After a fortnight, the medication began to make a positive difference.

It had taken Duscha ten long months to wean herself off the drug and gather the wherewithal to find another job in another town—any other town. The move to Wagga was a godsend—a new start. Although she had a sound professional reputation, she didn't want to blow it by immediately asking for time off. Come Monday morning, how was she going to walk through the Planning Directorate's door and wrangle leave to go to Canberra? Fortunately, it was only a three-hour drive, and she could overnight with her Mamochka. Plus she had a compelling reason. One's father died only once. They didn't need to know he was a virtual stranger.

To the walls, she said too brightly, "Well, Cliffie…Dad. This had better be worth it."

CHAPTER TWO

Ruddy-faced Jim Fielding sat at a sleek Tasmanian-oak desk facing Duscha. He had grown up in the nearby farming community of Harden-Murrumburrah and brought his country sensibility to his share of the Fielding & Atkinson legal practice. A routinely friendly man, he was intractable when necessary.

Jim loosened his tie where the shirt collar strained against a neck thickened by prosperity. Reading glasses teetered as he scanned through sheaves of paper. With a soft harrumph, he slid a large mustard-coloured envelope across the desk.

"You'll need a copy of this."

"Why am I here? What's it all about?"

He whipped off his glasses, leaned back and drummed sausage fingers on the desk. Blinking at her, he said, "Your father was a generous man when he could afford to be. It may surprise you that he was, shall I say, comfortably well off. The full extent of his estate, you don't need to know. However…"

Duscha was tired from the long drive and the stress of the last few weeks. Or was it months turning into years? "You're toying with me. However?"

He chuckled in spite of himself and reinstalled the glasses on his nose. "In front of you is a copy of the title of a house in Ainslie that was his last residence. He wanted you to have it. Now it belongs to you."

A wary hand crept to Duscha's throat. "Are you serious?"

"Absolutely. It seems he was very proud of you, discreetly keeping an eye on your career. In addition to the house, there's five hundred thousand in cash." He took off the glasses and sucked the tip of one arm. "The house originally belonged to one of Cliff's sisters. After his wife died, he chose to live there peacefully, but I believe it's become unkempt. He was a terrific entrepreneur. Not so good on mundane chores." He slapped the desk and leaned forward. "Anyway, you can do what you like with it! And here's a letter from him that you can read at your leisure."

She drew the bulky cream envelope toward her and bundled it with the house title. "No strings attached?"

Jim Fielding hesitated. "Not that I know of. But your half-sister Roxanne resents sharing her inheritance. Or so she told me at the formal reading of her...your father's will. As far as the house goes, legally she hasn't a leg to stand on. Could be just talk." He ran a searching hand under files on the desk and retrieved a zip lock bag that jangled with keys alongside a business card. "These will get you in the door. The address is on the back of my card. Call me if you have any questions."

Driving east to her mother's house, Duscha took the back road past the airport and then, just outside of Queanbeyan, a sharp left turn toward the Molonglo Gorge. It was late afternoon. She was overdue at her mother's, but she needed some peace and quiet to digest what Jim had told her. Once the car was parked, she headed into the pine forest.

As kids, she and her friends would come here during the summer holidays to cool down in the Molonglo River which emptied into Canberra's Lake Burley Griffin, a few kilometres away. Not far down the walking trail, she stopped at a wooden picnic setting in a barbecue area overlooking the river. It was chilling down in the shade. She folded her long legs over the seat, settled on the cold timber and peeled open the letter. Two handwritten pages fell out alongside a curled photo she hadn't seen before.

A man with longish wavy blond hair and sideburns wore a sky-blue body shirt. He held a bundled baby in his arms. She flipped it over and read "1/81" handwritten in a large scrawl. About a month after she was born. If this was her once-young father, the baby had to be her.

> *My Dear Daughter,*
>
> *More than anything else, I want you to know that I loved your mother Valeria. I told her many times but I know she never believed it. I wasn't always honest with her because of my wife and daughter. And I'm not proud of my behaviour. I don't know what she told you, but I want to tell you my side. No excuses, just reasons.*
>
> *I first met your mother when she rented a house from me. She was young, feisty, and irresistibly lovely, so petite and pretty with laughing eyes, always smiling. I decided to collect the rent myself so I could see her. You don't know but my wife was mourning our thirteen-year-old son Phil who had died of galloping leukemia six months before. She was deeply depressed and shut me out. Left me sad and alone. Valeria was warm and lively. She always invited me in, fed me coffee and cake and talked to me. At the time, she was a housemaid at the Russian embassy, wanting a better job. I helped her get work in the Russian church's nursing home where she was much happier.*
>
> *She presumed I was single and I couldn't tell her, couldn't lose her. I refused her paying me rent, brought her food, presents, and loved every time we were together, grew to love her. Some busybody told her I was married. She was very angry, furious, would not see me. All over, all gone, except for you. I have always paid my dues and did not hesitate to pay child support. She never wanted to see me again and did not want me to see you. I pleaded like crazy to see you when you were a baby, again when you were turning eighteen. She's stubborn, your mother. Unforgiving.*

But I believe she suffered because of our association. I'm very sorry because I always admired her strength and courage. I want you to know that I absolutely don't regret for a second that she had you.

I have been told you built a worthwhile career in town planning. You must know I have a passion for building and construction. I like to think you have inherited my better genes! As my daughter, you deserve a portion of my estate. Therefore I've left the old Ainslie house to you because it holds family history. My side of the family. It belonged to my elder sister, Charlotte, who lived there with Sylvia (a close friend) from 1960 until her death in 1999. She knew about you, would have liked to have met you. It was not to be. As she had no children, she wanted the house to be yours one day. I always liked the house and moved in myself. Now I ask you to move back to Canberra, close to your mother, close to my legacy.

By now you will know I have left you some handy folding stuff to spend on renovations. Please come home where you belong, dear Duscha. Your loving father, Cliff.

A cutting breeze came up off the river as the autumn evening closed in. Duscha tugged a tissue from her jeans pocket and the bag of house keys fell in the dirt. Eyes and nose wiped dry, she read the back of Jim Fielding's card where he had written, "21 Hargraves Crescent, Ainslie." Ainslie was one of Canberra's oldest suburbs, very close to the city centre. The blocks were large, which made them ripe for redevelopment, and therefore prime real estate. She could hazard a guess that the house, or rather the land, was worth well north of a million. Never having owned a house with Noelle, her vagabond who hated to be tied down, she felt daunted more than she cared to admit.

But her mother was expecting her. Hurriedly she extricated herself from the barbecue setting and threw back her head, hands up to the darkening sky. "Come home. Seriously, Cliff? Your family, your legacy. It's all about you, isn't it? You've left me a tired old humpy out of guilt, and I'm supposed to be thrilled? Hope it sells fast. Then I'm out of here."

By the time she'd walked back to the car, she was having second thoughts. The downside of her and Noelle moving so often was they had struggled to make new friends. The less-gregarious Noelle had never been close to family, had no lasting friendships and had made an island of them as a couple. Duscha had quietly missed her old mates back in Canberra. Besides Michele she had kept in touch with Emily who she had met through an after-school supermarket job. Both friends now had their own families, yet would help out if need be, not just physically but emotionally. After Noelle died, Duscha had struggled with living alone in Griffith with its rather blinkered mentality that was far from queer-friendly. Conservative Wagga might be even tougher still.

Duscha negotiated her way along Queanbeyan's main street where cars drew in and out of parking spots, their harried drivers picking up takeaways and last-minute groceries. She would have to think carefully about the benefits of a rent-free home, having Mamochka living in the same city and the pleasure of being close to friends again. When she turned off Donald Road, the car's headlights lit up her mother's driveway.

CHAPTER THREE

After dinner, Valeria's husband, Theo disappeared into the kitchen to make a pot of tea, pointedly leaving the women to their own devices at the cleared dining table. A nurse's aide, Valeria had met him at the Russian nursing home where she still worked. He was a genuinely caring man who had patiently won Valeria's reluctant heart over the years.

Duscha slid short glass cups of clear tea onto the timber tabletop, where her mother was smoothing out a large square of faded royal-blue velvet. Valeria sat back down, picked up the Russian gypsy oracle cards and began a fast shuffle, her gold bracelets jangling.

Duscha said, "Delicious *piroshki*, Ma. Thank you for taking the trouble."

"Ah, Duschka, you're the best excuse to make them. You like the potato ones, eh?"

"Dumplings slathered in butter, bacon, and onions—gets me every time. Plus plenty of leftovers for you both." Duscha leaned across and bent to peck a beaming cheek. Studying her preoccupied mother, she sipped piping hot tea. She noticed a few grey hairs scattered amongst Valeria's jet-black mane, and crow's feet deepening at the corners of those merry eyes. Unbidden, it struck her that if she ever needed to draw on quintessential beauty for inspiration, she need only look in her mother's dark brown eyes reminding her too much of Noelle's. Instantly, a deathly sadness drained her. She took a deep breath, exhaling jaggedly.

Valeria held out the thin deck of black-backed square cards. "Are you okay *malysh*? It's your turn, baby. Let's ask about the circumstances around that house. Is it good for you is what we want to know. Just close your eyes, shuffle, and think of the address. You know the way."

Duscha sat back and shuffled the cards, still sharp-cornered despite countless situation analyses, prognostications, predictions, and counselling sessions arcing back in time to her early childhood. The same group of ethnically diverse women would come to their house to consult the cards, drink endless cups of tea, and fritter away a Saturday afternoon obsessing about their husbands, children, dreams, and passions. Always, it was Valeria, front and centre, offering her all to solve every problem. The women loved the drama, loved the eye-popping possibilities in the cards and loved Valeria for her compassion and uncanny knowing.

With the house address at the forefront of her mind, Duscha cut the deck, turned the pile face down and stacked it on the velvet square. Valeria laid out the cards, five to a row. When a cryptic picture matched an adjoining card, she would turn them to align perfectly and continue on. With the whole deck laid out, Duscha knew better than to speak.

"I see your grief, my child. It flutters close by like a raven."

Duscha leaned elbows on the table, her chin in one palm. "I love ravens. Especially their glossy black feathers that show all the colours of the rainbow when the sun strikes them. They're fascinating…gorgeous. You know I used to see them around the university. They're smart, too."

"Oh, my bird-girl. I had forgotten your love for feathered friends. You have to let grief fly away one day."

"I'm working on it."

Valeria straightened two cards. "Best get a wriggle on. There's a woman here. In fact, there are another two…four… five women here. One known from the past. Not sure who's alive." When Duscha made a strangled sound, Valeria reached out and clasped her wrist. "So sorry, I didn't mean Noelle. I know her energy and she's not here. The known one is critical to you while the others have influence of some kind. All interwoven and intricately enmeshed."

Duscha nodded. "Women couldn't be further from my mind. What about the house? What are you getting?"

"Money is an issue. Lump sums and arguments." Valeria leaned over the cards, flicking their edges. "The foundation of this whole arrangement, this house, seems to be vulnerable somehow. But in time, all will be made good. Does that fit?"

"You read Cliff's letter. You know as much as I do. Should I just get rid of the damned thing or not?"

Valeria turned in her chair to face her daughter, square on. They stared at each other intently, safe within a mutual appreciation of the other's worth. At last Valeria said, "I'm going to be seeing you plenty because you're going to get very, very tired too often. And on the other side of tired is something very, very good for you. I feel your father relished his bequest—the house comes to you with the best of intentions. This gift and his letter reveal his deep love for you. And I am well pleased. Keep it, my Duschka. Live in it, enjoy it. I love having you home!"

Sprawled in the single bed that was a relic of her adolescence, Duscha tried to slow her zigzagging thoughts sufficiently for sleep. She had the three-hour drive back to Wagga in the morning, and being well-rested would be helpful, but her mother's insights played on her mind. Who were all those women, and what were they to her? At the ripe old age of thirty-eight, she might consider another relationship one day, but not right now. Noelle's death still weighed heavily. Releasing it to allow someone new in was a big call, not to mention frightening.

At the same time, she knew Noelle would expect her to move on. She'd said as much before she passed away.

Don't waste your life weeping for me. The price of love is loss. That's the deal. One of us had to lose the other eventually. It happens to be me going first, sooner than expected. I have to go and you have to live. Don't forget me, but let go when I'm gone. Please let me go. And then find love again.

Duscha let out a heavy sigh, eyelids scratchy with fatigue. "Easier said than done, my love. I can but attempt it."

CHAPTER FOUR

The next morning, having taken a quick detour off the main highway out of Canberra, Duscha stood on a footpath in Hargraves Crescent in Ainslie. She eyed off a massive gum tree near the southern-most paling fence of her new old house. Was it a *Eucalyptus blakelyi*? She estimated from its size that the gnarly red gum had been there the best part of a century. Two people might hold hands around its trunk, at a stretch. It certainly dwarfed the modest weatherboard and terracotta tile-roofed house, just visible from the road through overgrown foliage. A red Canberra-brick driveway led past the house and on toward a single garage further in the property.

She unlocked the front door, stepped into the lounge room and stood stock-still to get her bearings. The place smelled faintly musty. A rumbling hum underfoot gave her pause until she realised it came from rush-hour traffic on Limestone Avenue, only a street away. The carpeted room was empty except for a vintage wooden wall cabinet and a scruffy bentwood armchair.

She wandered through a narrow dining area into an adequate kitchen, and then down a central hall to a bathroom, laundry, and two empty bedrooms. The aging Regency-style cream and maroon-striped wallpaper in the lounge room, hall, and bedrooms was coming loose.

In one bedroom that was appreciably bigger than the other, the wallpaper was particularly dilapidated, especially on a wall that butted up to the back of the chimney. An octagonal art deco-style mirror hung on the same wall, looking lonely. To the north, a large window added a pleasant light through dappled shade. She would make this her bedroom. But the first job would be removing the ghastly wallpaper—it had to go, pronto.

At the end of the hall, the rear door resisted opening, its edge binding against the frame. She gave it a firm shove and found herself on a narrow deck beneath a shaded pergola.

Duscha glanced up. "Whoa. You're a monster, whatever you are." She stepped off the deck into deep shade and approached a soaring tree that stretched out thick horizontal limbs with broad lime-green leaves and dangling black blobs. She reached up and picked one of them, popped it in her mouth and licked purplish-red fingertips. "Oh Lord, you're a black mulberry. Woo-hoo! Lucky me!"

She ate the very last of the mulberries as she peered through the undergrowth. There was a metal garden shed in there somewhere, plus a few stone-fruit and apple trees, a sprawling lemon, a leggy fig, a couple of enormous camellias, some azaleas and roses and a good many unidentified shrubs. Down the north side of the house, she found a wall-mounted washing line and a tiny paved courtyard for garbage and recycling bins. And behind that, a veggie patch full of rampant knee-high couch grass. Despite the neglect it was obvious that, once upon a time, someone had designed, planted, and loved this garden.

Sitting on the edge of the hardwood deck, she went over last night's phone conversation with Michele, who she hadn't yet had time to visit.

A librarian employed by the National Library of Australia, the usually softly-spoken Michele had positively squealed, "You should have come home months and months ago. Now you have every reason to. Why are you still thinking about it? It's a no-brainer."

"But I've just started a new job in Wagga."

"So? And?"

"What do I say to the planning people? They've spent plenty on finding the right candidate, helping me move there, patiently waiting while I get my act together."

Michele was momentarily silenced. Then she said, "Don't you think your father's death and your inheritance are good enough reasons? Surely they'll understand. And they'll appoint whoever was their second choice, plain and simple. It's easier for them that you haven't actually started yet. They'll move on, as should you."

Duscha chewed a lip. "I know it's weird, but I feel like I'm betraying Noelle. She never wanted to stay in Canberra. Hated the place." Michele sighed, and Duscha could almost hear the cogs turning in her friend's eminently logical brain.

"Much as I respected Noelle, you gave up a hell of a lot to go with her and be wherever she wanted to live. Unless I've misunderstood, that was her preference, not yours. I appreciate that you loved her dearly, but *I* love you dearly. And I lost you to wherever the hell you were. Anywhere but here!"

Duscha's throat contracted. "I know. I do know, Mischa. I've missed you."

"Look. Wherever Noelle is, I don't think she'll mind you coming back. Don't you realise that this couldn't have happened at a better time, give or take a few months? Still, it's your decision, girlfriend. My feeling is you have been gifted an opportunity by your absent father. They say don't look a gift horse in the mouth. At least none too carefully."

They had chatted only a few minutes more before Duscha promised to keep her posted.

She swatted away a lazy fly and tucked a stray curl behind an ear. Last night Michele's advice had made perfect sense and she'd been persuaded. Now she wasn't so sure. The house was small and well-worn, which she could tolerate while renovating. At the same time, it seemed to her that there was something uplifting about its energy, despite its current state. A joyous lightness and warmth seemed to exude from its ageing framework. Once upon a time, it had obviously been appreciated. It could be again.

Her father's letter popped into her head, especially the part about Aunt Charlotte and "Sylvia, a close friend." Just a friend or lesbi-friend? No way of knowing, but that genetic trait had to come from one or the other side of the family. It might as well be Cliff's.

Her thoughts turned to the wilderness surrounding the house. It was a mammoth job, too daunting for her to take on alone. With that, she stood up, dusted imaginary debris off her jeans and stepped back into the house. To tackle that garden, she would need a whole lot of help from friends, and likely the odd professional.

CHAPTER FIVE

Six thirty a.m. and Honor Boyce was running late. She fielded an almost-burnt slice as it shot out of the toaster, slapped it on the cutting board and slathered it with soft butter.

Vegemite or peanut butter? Whatever was nearest would do. She opened the pantry door, spotting the crunchie first. She sunk her teeth in, chewed fast, took a big gulp of tea and looked at her watch. No time to dawdle. She carried the mug to the bedroom door and chugged down the last mouthful. The lumpy form under the bedclothes was motionless.

Honor crouched down to smooth back the straight chestnut hair. "Merrin…love? I'm off now, be home for lunch. The slow cooker is on with a chicken tagine for dinner. Let me know if you need anything, okay?"

Her partner stirred, briefly opening a grey eye. "Hm, hm."

Honor pecked the pale forehead and strode back to the kitchen. She shoved her cup in the dishwasher and wiped down the bench, making a mental note to get to bed earlier.

She backed the vivid blue Holden GTS utility out of the garage and sped down the street. It was imperative for her to be on site before everyone else arrived for work. On Belconnen Way, the morning traffic was building up. The climbing sun made her squint. She was accustomed to suffering the equally dazzling setting sun when she drove home to Higgins every evening.

At a set of traffic lights she tapped anxious fingers on the steering wheel. She was under pressure. The physically hard yakka of the current contract was taking its toll on her and her staff. Her landscape gardening business, Landladies, worked for private households across Canberra, sometimes refurbishing gardens, but more usually routine maintenance such as planting, mulching, pruning, weeding, and spraying. It had been that way for years. That was until recently when Honor's ambition got the better of her, and she won a minor local government contract. The task was to remodel a fernery and improve runoff management near The Lobby restaurant in the National Rose Gardens' precinct. Now she and her four hard-working female staff were under the pump to have it completed on time. Heavy autumn rains hadn't helped.

Once she'd fought her way through the rush-hour traffic down Northbourne Avenue and over the lake via Commonwealth Bridge, it took only three minutes to the Parliamentary Triangle. She pulled up at the usual kerbside spot on King George Terrace where she parked the ute. No sign of the others. Honor jumped out, appraised their work so far and made a rough estimate of how long it would take to finish the job. It looked like going home for lunch would be a no-no. And it could be nigh on dusk before they finished.

The Lobby restaurant, popular as a wedding venue, nestled beneath its own canopy of large conifers and deciduous trees. Their leaves were happily yellowing with the shortening days and cooler nights, but still magnificent. Honor's breath formed momentary clouds in the sharp morning light. Local knowledge told her the frosts would hit soon. April's Anzac Day, when the overnight temperatures first became icy, was a mere fortnight away and signalled mid-autumn. She sat back against the bonnet, making a mental note to text Merrin that she wouldn't come home at midday. Not that her partner would be too fussed. She seemed to care less these days.

Thoughts drifting where she rather they didn't, Honor crossed her booted ankles and examined her palms, calloused in spite of the constant protection of gloves. From a back pocket, she pulled a worn soft-brimmed denim hat and slipped it on, careful not to dislodge her long black plait, the end of which was anchored to the back of her head so as not to get in the way while she worked.

Her partner Merrin had once been her definitely straight employee who had unexpectedly morphed into her definitely bent partner. Soon after they got together, Merrin had fallen ill with a long list of debilitating yet vague symptoms, finally diagnosed six years ago as chronic fatigue syndrome. Despite that, Merrin managed to help Honor by fielding phone enquiries, making appointments and mastering control of the Landladies' finances on a computerised accounting system. In quick time, Honor gave her carte blanche with the accounts, she did so well. But the intimate side of their relationship had petered out within that first horrendously difficult year. For a moment, she tried to remember what love making felt like but then chose not to dwell on it. No point in torturing oneself.

A horn started Honor to attention. Another ute cruised past and came to a halt. Her team had turned up. It was time to get cracking.

At close of day, Honor left her grotty work boots by the back door. Still in her damp socks, she padded through the kitchen. Merrin was stirring a bubbling pan of pasta.

"Is everything cooked, love?" Honor pecked her cheek.

"Just doing some spirals to go with the tagine," said Merrin. "I knew you'd be late and I had some energy, so—phew, you pong to high heaven."

"Chook poo and tan bark. I've been shovelling all arvo. On my way to the shower. Won't be long."

Merrin pushed the bridge of her rimless glasses back up her thin nose. "Before I forget, Lance is taking me through the latest software update over a few nights at the end of the month. I'll have dinner with him and his wife because I'll get home too late to eat with you."

An image of their accountant, Lance Roach, flashed through Honor's mind. An insipid bloke bearing an unfortunate facial resemblance to a potato, Lance was a meticulous bean counter who had gone through high school with Merrin, who seemed fond of him. When Honor gave her the business finances to manage, Merrin had been keen to employ his services. Honor had readily agreed, knowing she would have little to do with him. She nodded and turned on her heel.

Merrin called after her, "Check your messages by the phone. One needs a ring back tonight."

In the hall, Honor hovered near the phone table, unbuttoning her maroon flannel shirt as she scanned three yellow sticky notes. Two messages were from landscape suppliers. A third one gave her pause. About to undo the belt holding up her twill work trousers, her fingers slowed to a stop. Frozen-still, she held her breath and then read the name again, whispering it aloud. The surname meant nothing, but the first conjured up a gently mocking smile. And a knowing look from a pair of almond-shaped blue-green eyes that had once held a teenaged Honor spellbound. Long, long ago. It couldn't be, could it?

"Hey, hurry up! Dinner's nearly on the table."

"Sorry. On my way."

CHAPTER SIX

On a bright and brisk Saturday morning in her father's old house, Duscha leaned across the kitchen bench to switch the kettle on for a brew. There was something so lonely and pathetic about unpacking a kitchen by one's self. She hated it. And hated doing it all over again, so soon after moving to Wagga. But it was completed, and she'd slept in the house for a week now, having taken her time with the onerous task. Her mother and Michele had helped with the lounge, bedrooms, and bathroom, but she'd done the kitchen alone, perhaps because it conjured poignant memories of all those dinners shared with Noelle. They had enjoyed cooking together. Many of the gadgets, including the electric wok, were Noelle's. Much to Duscha's bemusement, the unwieldy thing had slid into an under-bench cupboard perfectly.

Clasping an oversized mug of strong, milky tea, she stood staring out the kitchen window at the backyard wilderness. Sipping, she considered her plans for the coming week. The landline had been connected, which meant she could arrange for the Internet service provider's tech-head to supply a modem and set up her computer with Wi-Fi. She could access job-seeking sites and see what might be available locally. Earlier in the week, she had rung Jim Fielding about her cash inheritance. He'd apologised, saying he would investigate why it wasn't yet in her account.

Given that winter was on its way, she figured now was the best time to get the garden under control, or at least the worst of it cut back and taken away. Michele had supplied the name and number of a gardener. Having received a call back, Duscha had her doubts. In spite of the woman's barely coherent input, Duscha had chosen to trust Michele's advice and made an appointment for a quote this morning. If this particular gardener wasn't suitable, Duscha could always find another. Yet she hoped it wasn't a complete waste of time because there was too much else to do. She needed somebody capable, hard-working and worth their pay.

Fitted into the front door was a vintage mechanical doorbell that required a brisk twirl to get it to work. Duscha registered its metallic whir and put her half-drunk mug of tea in the microwave for later.

When she opened the door, the woman looked up, tawny eyes wide, and asked, "Should I go down the side and meet you around the back?" She backed away and hesitated, feet shuffling.

Duscha glanced up and down the street, noting the handsome blue ute. "Um, okay. There's a galvanized gate—"

The woman waved over one shoulder as she quick-marched away to the gate near the side fence. Duscha blinked, shut the door and walked back through the house. When she stepped off the back deck, the woman strode from around the back of the house and came to a sudden halt at a good distance from Duscha.

"Honor Boyce from Landladies, at your service."

With a polite smile, Duscha tilted her head. "Hello, I'm Duscha. Have we…met before?"

Honor shrugged. "Canberra's a small place. I was born here. What about you?"

"The same." Duscha stared in puzzlement at the brusque gardener. "Right, then. Let me show you around and you can tell me what you think."

Twenty minutes later, they had agreed on what needed immediate attention, requiring an estimated six days labour spread over the next three weeks. They discussed the hourly rate. Honor had mumbled a promise of a rough quote emailed by Sunday night.

When the gardener had gone, Duscha reheated her cold tea, wandered down to the main bedroom and sank into her aging, much-loved wicker chair in one corner near the bed.

Low to the ground, the chair was incredibly comfortable. It allowed her to stretch out her legs and rest her head against a propped cushion. Through narrowed eyes, she sipped tea and admired the small and simple, yet charismatic art-deco mirror on the wall facing the bed. She hadn't the heart to take it down. Its octagonal, bevelled edges exemplified the quirky taste of a bygone era. Was it a 1920's original or a 1950's pseudo-deco remake? She didn't know, but it was pleasing. On the other side of the same wall was the adjoining lounge-room fireplace that would disperse its heat, helping to keep the bedroom warm in winter. But the tatty wallpaper would be first to go. She would hire a stripping machine and do it herself—a vigorously sweaty job best suited to the current cooler weather.

Duscha's thoughts strayed to the barely grunting gardener who seemed knowledgeable enough about plants, and according to her business card, held qualifications to that effect. At least time wouldn't be wasted in idle chitchat. What about the amazing, long black plait tied at the back of the head? It reminded her of someone. She took a mouthful of tea, closed her eyes and drifted...drifted.

Metal-mouth girl. She swallowed sharply as her eyelids shot open. And Duscha recalled a moment in time, years ago, when she was at university and had worked part-time in a local supermarket.

* * *

Under the grey-haired woman's sour regard, a nineteen-year-old Duscha struggled with the meat-slicing machine's temperamental performance, a wedge of cured meat slipping treacherously against her gloved fingers. Why did prosciutto have to be wafer thin? She stopped to push back the jaunty white cap mandatory as part of her uniform at the delicatessen counter at Queanbeyan's Woolworths supermarket. Hairclips loosely secured the pointless shape to her rebellious hair.

The customer said, "Emily? Excuse me, Emily? That will be sufficient. Could you hurry up?"

Duscha glanced sideways, and then remembered she was wearing Em's name badge. As a temporary casual, Duscha hadn't a badge of her own. Each shift, she borrowed whomever's—any one of a number of badges left at the staff entrance where they clocked on.

"Just a moment." Determinedly she wrapped, weighed, and labelled the package and placed it on the eye-level countertop. Her cap tumbled to the floor, and she bent to pick it up. Upright again, she realised her customer had disappeared and, in her place, stood a small-framed schoolgirl in a green Karabar High School uniform. The girl wore two shiny black plaits, each pinned behind an ear. With lively eyes a close match for the patina on a Thai gold amulet, the girl smiled the sweetest, dimpled smile and ran a self-conscious tongue tip over steel braces. She caught Duscha's look, staring a little too long.

"Pen! For heaven's sake, we're out of time!"

Duscha watched the girl race away until she caught up with the woman, just as they disappeared down an aisle. How old was she? Probably sixteen, give or take. And had they met before and Duscha since forgotten? The girl was memorable, if not merely for being decently good-looking, definitely for the dorky plait thing. With a shrug, Duscha scoped out the next customer, hoping she wouldn't have too many other impatient, harassed souls to deal with before shift's end.

Over the next two weeks, Duscha saw the girl twice more. Once, she sauntered past the delicatessen with two school friends who looked across at Duscha, and then giggled, nudged and elbowed each other. The girl rolled her eyes, grinning sheepishly as they all stumbled out of sight. The next time, the girl approached the counter while her two friends pretended not to watch from a discreet distance.

"Excuse me. May I get a bag of those cooked chicken wings...Janelle?" She was peering at the random name badge pinned on Duscha's chest.

Duscha reached into the heated cabinet with a pair of tongs. "How many?"

"Janelle. Isn't your name Emily?"

Duscha held open a heatproof bag and, unable to control her lips twitching with amusement, met the girl's nervous stare. "It's neither. How many, young lady?"

The girl dropped her gaze as colour flushed her cheeks. "Um...six, please. For me and my friends."

Duscha sealed the bag and slapped on a price sticker. She dangled the bag off the counter while deadpanning, "Duscha is the name, don't wear it out." Then she gave the slightest wink.

The girl's eyes widened. As if memorising, she mouthed Duscha's name. A glad smile lit up her solemn face.

"C'mon, Pencil!" called out one of the girlfriends.

She snatched the bag and jogged off to join her friends. Duscha laced her fingers on top of the counter as she watched the girls go. She couldn't help but savour the pleasing mischief of some sweet young thing unexpectedly flirting with her. She shook her head and grinned. Who knew peddling cooked chook could be this entertaining?

"A hundred grams of prosciutto, as thin as you can."

Duscha looked past the older woman's glower, only to catch a worried smile from Pen, the metal-mouth girl. The slicing machine behaved itself. Duscha wrapped up the prosciutto in record time. She dropped it on the countertop, just as the girl gave a quick wave. Duscha looked away, not before she noticed a hard stare from the woman who pursed her lips and threw the package into her trolley without a word.

On her way over to the next customer, Duscha muttered under her breath, "Not my circus, not my monkeys."

Exactly seven minutes later, the woman reappeared in front of her.

"Just so you know. My family and I will never shop here again." She leaned in with such naked malevolence in her eyes that Duscha inhaled sharply and flinched. "Especially not my daughter. Do you understand?"

Duscha opened her mouth, but no sound came out. Lips curled in disgust, the woman's searing gaze flickered over Duscha's rigid form. Abruptly, she turned and stalked away, leaving Duscha with a shaking hand edging to her throat. Nauseous, shock spread through her insides. What on earth had just happened? What could she possibly have done to deserve the woman's barefaced contempt?

Lying sleeplessly that night, she could only reason that if the woman couldn't control what came naturally to her daughter, she could at least punish those who happened to draw her daughter's interest—that is, those who might be of a similar persuasion. Duscha decided she had been subjected to a verbal assault based on nothing other than purely vengeful spite. There was no other logical explanation.

Weeks went by before Duscha heard Janelle had been sacked for disrespecting a customer, allegedly. Too late for her to do anything about it, she felt terribly guilty and sick to the stomach when she realised what had happened. And pretty metal-mouth girl, the one called Pen...Pencil? Duscha never saw her again.

* * *

Until today. Duscha stomped out to the kitchen where she put her mug down too hard in the kitchen sink. Full mouth set in a grim line, she snatched up the gardener's business card. Somehow, Honor Boyce was "Pen," she was sure of it. Even freakier was the name "Boyce." It was unusually well-known around Canberra, courtesy of Sir Denholm Boyce who had once resided with his family at Government House in Yarralumla, back when he was the Queen's representative: Australia's Governor General. Was the gardener related to His former Excellency in any way? It was an unlikely occupation for one so well-connected. Highly unlikely. Perhaps the gardener hadn't recognised Duscha, either. If it were not for the bad taste the whole sorry episode had left in her mouth, none of it would matter nearly twenty years later.

Duscha slid the glossy card next to the phone. She would wait for the quote and decide on its basis alone. And from then on, should she employ the baffling Ms. Boyce, she resolved to keep her mouth shut, and any interaction entirely businesslike.

CHAPTER SEVEN

Honor peered through the kitchen window, using her hands as blinkers the better to see inside. She had tweaked the front doorbell and then knocked politely on the back door to no avail, probably because Pink was singing unintelligibly in the background. It was just after seven thirty a.m. She was ready to get started yet couldn't gain Duscha's attention.

But she could see her standing in the lounge room, back toward Honor, holding a flat, hosed apparatus that belched steam against the wall. Her other hand steered a wide stainless-steel scraper that slid up and skived off the soggy wallpaper in long ribbons. She was wearing a grey racerback sports bra, cut-off denim shorts, and bunched-up white socks in a pair of mustard suede steel-caps. Honor grinned to herself, suddenly in no hurry. Rivulets of water mixed with sweat ran down Duscha's arms. Defined muscles worked sinuously over the full length of a long back topped by square shoulders. She crouched down and sprang up with such ease that Honor all but lost her train of thought. Except the one that noted she hadn't seen a near-naked woman, other than Merrin, for quite some time—certainly not one who looked as remotely enthralling as Duscha Penhaligon.

Under her breath, she muttered, "In your dreams, Honor. Get real."

She sucked in a breath and rapped loudly on the glass. Duscha turned and bent to switch off the machine. Then she reached for a faded blue shirt, slipping it on as she headed for the back door where Honor waited.

"You're late."

Honor half-smiled, looking Duscha in the eye. "Not really. It took a while to get you to open a door."

"Right, then. Know what you're doing?"

"Positive." The coolness surprised Honor, but she wasn't about to show it. She turned on a heel and headed down the garden path, pushing a wheelbarrow cluttered with tools.

The back fence was obscured by a Mexican firethorn that hadn't seen a pair of secateurs for donkey's years. Several metres high and equally wide, it was covered in long thorns. It was by far the nastiest job ahead.

Being Honor's nature to do the hardest task first to make the rest seem easier, she set to work with long-handled loppers, avoiding the vicious thorns as best she could. Lean and strong, she soon fell into a rhythm of cutting and pulling branches aside, enjoying the scent of undergrowth and earth—enjoying the solitude. She could have called on one of her part-timers to speed up completion, but she'd chosen to work alone and take her time. Any excuse for lingering in the vicinity of the owner.

Duscha's animated figure popped into her skull. Honor dismissed the distracting image with a self-deprecating nod. She had more pressing things to think about, specifically her father's seventieth birthday dinner party on Friday evening, at which she was expected alone, as usual.

When she and Merrin first got together seven years ago, Honor had taken her along to family gatherings. It soon became obvious that Merrin was genuinely uncomfortable with the Boyces' wealth and cultured manners, while Honor's parents and two much older brothers and their spouses struggled for common ground, let alone conversation, with Merrin. After a plethora of Merrin's excuses as to why she couldn't attend, Honor knew to stop asking her.

When they'd last spoken by phone, her father had said he wanted to discuss some investments he'd made on her behalf. Her decision to study horticulture and start the Landladies business had met with raised eyebrows from the family, purely because she would never have to work a day in her life, if she so chose. It was her father who had encouraged her to start out on her own for valuable life experience and to gain a personal sense of achievement.

Despite her protests, he had insisted on creating term investments for her, insisted that Merrin should not know about it. They had argued at length, but he had been adamant. He did not trust Merrin, he had said. Not as far as he could throw her, he had said. Honor had to concede it was his money he was investing for his only daughter, under specific conditions, like it or not. Honest to a fault, she didn't like it one bit. But he was her father: much older, wiser, and deserving of respect. The whole of Australia had thought so when he was governor general for five years, back in the noughties. Now well into retirement, he continued to command that respect, and retained long arms of influence across the military, the diplomatic corps, and the judiciary. Her dad, Sir Denholm Boyce, was a valuable friend and preferably avoided enemy.

Honor traipsed back across the property, dragging branches behind her, and out to the box trailer hitched to her ute for the first of many trips to the tip. There was no sign of Duscha, except for a waft of distant music. Honor roped down the load and contemplated the instantly recognisable woman, so well were Duscha's features etched into her sixteen-year-old self's memory.

It was love at first sight. Her first-ever romantic crush. Her friends had teased her mercilessly, and she had taken it gracefully, made invincible by undying love. Or so it seemed. When her mother began to shop at a supermarket further away, supposedly for better produce and prices, she protested.

Mother then said they wouldn't shop at Duscha's store again. What's more, Honor wasn't allowed anywhere near the place. No matter how many times Honor asked, "But Mum—" her mother was mute. True to her word, they never returned.

Yet besotted Honor couldn't stay away. As the indulged daughter, she owned every toy and gadget her father could think of, including a digital camera with a telephoto lens. Over four late afternoons, Honor loitered under trees at a safe distance from the Woolworth's staff entrance, capturing rapid-fire shots of Duscha as she left work. Most were blurred profiles, but finally she scored a couple face-on, as if Duscha had turned and was deliberately looking at her. Instinctively she had ducked, heart pounding while jubilation soared through her chest. Spooked, she left and never went back.

Two photos were near-perfect. She had them made into prints and kept digital copies on a thumb drive. Late at night, she would look at the photos and dream of Duscha's eyes, her mouth, and enveloping arms. And then she withdrew into herself, took cold comfort from friends who soon ceased their good-natured teasing. They left her alone to get over it. In the small hours, she wrote too many effusive, explanatory love letters that never saw the light of day, never were posted.

Does a broken heart mend, or merely learn to live in pieces?

In time, she burnt the incriminating letters and looked less often at the photos, until she could at last admit to herself that her own marginally unhinged, obsessive behaviour had made even her uneasy.

That was until two years later when she met Rose, a talented artist in the fantasy genre. Mesmerised by her new friend's gift with gouache and coloured pens, Honor asked an intrigued Rose to get creative with Duscha's image. The result was a luminous acrylic painting of a female centaur emerging from a dewy-green lake, its shores of lush vegetation ascending steep slopes to snow-capped mountains. Wearing a low cut and provocatively tight tan leather vest, the statuesque centaur held a bow and arrow at the ready. Beneath wavy flaxen hair that cascaded past her shoulders, the bold stare from Duscha's intense, topaz-blue eyes never failed to make Honor's breath catch.

The picture had adorned Honor's bedroom wall for years, wherever she happened to be living. Until the day came when Merrin said she hated it, and could it go somewhere else? Now it hung on the study wall, out of Merrin's line of sight. Having never explained its significance, Honor had to give Merrin points for feminine intuition.

Honor stilled the secateurs and squeezed together her sweaty eyebrows. So far, Duscha had started out civilly enough and then fast turned into cool, bordering on curt. Perhaps she just didn't care for Honor or was simply not very nice. Honor conceded the problem with putting people on a pedestal when one was very young was that they had further to fall, and a commensurately harder landing. What had she expected? Maybe just a friendly conversation, even though she knew she had been terribly tongue-tied when she had turned up to give Duscha the quote. Unsure as to what she had subsequently expected, Honor shrugged away her disappointment. She would come back tomorrow alone, but maybe bring two of the team next week to get the job finished fast. Their one-sided fantasy romance was over half her lifetime ago. What was the point in dredging up feelings best forgotten? She tensioned the secateurs and plunged back into the protesting firethorn.

That evening, Honor sat on the bathroom stool after her shower, dabbing antiseptic into the many scratches on her arms, plus a few on her thighs from thorns that had pierced her work pants. In that moment, she twigged that Duscha knew full well who Honor was. Also, from her abrupt manner, she had to be pissed off about something. Honor squeezed a black thorn tip out of her right knee, wondering what she'd said to incite that annoyance. She had enough experience with her complicated mother to know that anger stemmed from hurt, a sense of lack of control, a feeling of "what about me, eh?" Yes, Duscha was definitely pissed off. Armed with an inkling of insight, Honor looked forward to a good night's sleep and the morrow.

CHAPTER EIGHT

Under a screaming hot shower, Duscha mulled over the morning's brief exchange with the gardener. Too many hours of wallpaper stripping had left her fatigued yet delighted with the resulting bare walls that would look terrific with fresh paint. She'd done the worst of it—only the hall and her bedroom to go.

She was patting herself dry when it first crossed her mind that, logically, Honor could well be unaware of her mother's vitriolic tantrum, which gave an entirely different perspective to how Duscha might feel toward her. Perched on the end of the bed, she towelled her hair, ran a brush through damp tendrils skimming her throat and resolved to at least give the gardener the benefit of the doubt.

Early the next morning, Duscha's attention followed the gardener's petite form as it effortlessly pushed a wheelbarrow full of tools toward the back of the property. She tracked from room to room, until she spotted Honor attacking the yellow jasmine with hedge shears. The woman cut precisely and methodically, shaping the overgrown copse into something resembling restraint. A too-small, well-worn khaki T-shirt strained across ropey back muscles, biceps, and chest. When Honor stooped to scoop broken vegetation into the barrow, the shirt rode up at the back, revealing sun-shy flesh.

In the shadow of the bedroom curtain, Duscha hovered and folded her arms, eyes clearly focused. It had been a while since she had stared surreptitiously at a woman, and Honor's physique deserved to be made the exception. Her figure barely perceptible beneath the shapeless work clothes, she was well proportioned, if top-heavy. And her features, devoid of makeup, had matured into a fine-boned prettiness that was arresting. And so it was that four minutes dawdled by until Duscha drew a thumb across well-moistened lips, and stalked off to the kitchen to take the cake out of the oven.

Half an hour later, she soundlessly strolled up to a glowing Honor collapsed back in the emptied wheelbarrow, legs and arms dangling.

"Lying down on the job, then?"

Honor started, climbed out and returned Duscha's amused look. "Just congratulating myself on conquering the jasmine. What's up?"

"Tea and *keks* on the deck. Care to join me?"

Lagging behind, Honor skipped to catch up with Duscha who pulled out two aluminium chairs around a timber-topped outdoor table. On it stood a white porcelain teapot that featured a galloping red horse with a golden tail, its pattern repeated on the elegant milk jug and sugar pot, serving plates, cups and saucers. Honor shuffled her feet and said, "May I wash my hands?"

"Sure. The laundry is just inside the door. There's soap and a towel. Do you take tea with milk and sugar?"

With her hands in the old concrete laundry trough, Honor called out, "Just a little milk thanks."

Duscha poured cups of tea and slid them next to the plate of cake slices, hearing Honor struggling to shut the stubborn door.

Honor reappeared. "You really should get that looked at. Could be dry rot."

"It's on the list, along with umpteen other to-dos."

Honor dropped into a chair and looked up. "I feel a tad underdressed."

Smiling, Duscha said, "Don't worry. We Russians like to use our crockery. It's not just for collecting dust in china cabinets." She offered the plate. "Try the *keks*, otherwise known as cranberry and apricot loaf. Its secret ingredient is yogurt."

Honor took a bite of the creamy cake. "Yum, very good." She waved the slice at Duscha who sat down. "I know an excellent carpenter, Stuart Sermon, if you want a recommendation. He's very festive."

"Festive?" Duscha noticed Honor's beginning grin. "Ah, I see. I could do with some gay and convivial company. Do leave me his number."

Between bites, Honor asked, "What kind of Russian name is Penhaligon?"

"Not even remotely Russian." Duscha met Honor's enquiring look. "It's a bit of a story. All right, my mother was not married when she became pregnant with me. To assuage her parents' embarrassment and protect the Verstak family name, she dredged the Canberra phone book, and chose the most British sounding surname she could find. And then she legally changed hers to Penhaligon. Before I was born."

"Well, that's...conscientious. And protective, I suppose." Honor took another mouthful.

"Speaking of mothers, how's yours?"

Honor's jaw stilled. She took a sideways look at Duscha, resumed chewing and then swallowed with difficulty. "So you do remember me."

"It took a while, but yes." Duscha smiled gently, gaze lingering on the wary eyes.

"I'm amazed." Honor felt her colour rise and she ducked her head. "I was very young."

"We both were." Duscha studied the younger woman's averted face. "Hey, it was last century. Don't worry about it. How come your mother called you Pen that time in the supermarket?"

Honor relaxed a little and gulped tea, the dainty cup emptied in next to no time. "My much older brother's sense of humour. When I was a kid, Miles called me HB, which turned into Pencil. You know, small and thin, HB pencil, ha, ha. Which turned into Pen. It kind of stuck." She peered into the cup. "That hardly touched the sides."

Duscha stretched across with the teapot and refilled the cup. Honor added a splash of milk and sipped quietly. A long silence was broken by the scratchy sound of claws on the gutter above the two women. Both looked up to where a large glossy black-winged bird fixed on them with an unblinking white eye.

"A *corvid*. Australian raven," said Duscha. "I think she has a nest way up in the mulberry. It's unusual for them to breed in suburbia. I am honoured."

"Honoured?"

Duscha turned and caught the teasing smile, complete with deepening dimples that lit up the gardener's face, the first to be genuine since way back when they first met in the supermarket. Duscha couldn't help but grin. She felt herself examined by the lively eyes, caught her startled heart doing a little tap-dance and had to look away. She said, "Indeed, by her presence, and yours. Am I the only one that you honour?"

With a clatter, the gleaming raven took flight, disappearing into the sky beyond the neighbour's towering conifers. Honor swallowed the last of her tea and clambered to her feet. Quietly she said, "I have a partner, if that's what you mean. I'd better get on. Thanks for…this. I don't expect it."

Duscha quelled a distinct sense of disappointment at Honor's admission. She stood to gather crockery. "Rest assured it'll cost you. I plan to pick your brains about what to do with the garden."

Glancing around at the overgrowth, Honor said, "How about a goat? Just joking. Maybe some chooks."

"Chooks? Way too domestically settled for me."

"Oh. You're not planning on staying?"

With the tea things tucked safely on a tray, Duscha met Honor's uncertain glance. "I think I will, but owning a place is really weird. We moved around a lot, me and my partner. It's just me now. And I have to get my head around all sorts of new tricks."

Honor lifted her chin high. "For the record, my mother's in care. She has been for almost four years. Early-onset Alzheimer's."

"Oh, Lord. I'm sorry. That's awful."

Honor gave a wan grin and turned away, tossing a wave over one shoulder.

Duscha frowned at Honor's disappearing figure, calling after her, "Thanks for all your hard work!"

She picked up the tray, saying to no one in particular, "Me and my big mouth. Damn." Just as she was carrying the tray indoors, the phone rang.

Jim Fielding's voice held an uncharacteristic tremor. "I'm sorry, Duscha. Your half-sister is contesting the cash settlement in your father's will. We can't get it out of the trust account, not until a magistrate considers it. This could take months."

"I don't understand. Why would she do that?"

"Any one of a number of reasons. Resentment. Jealousy. Greed. She's entitled, you're not. Just because she can. Certain people can justify anything when they feel hard done by."

Duscha's mind raced, a gnawing beginning in her belly. "What about the house?"

"The title is already registered in your name. Reversing that process wouldn't be easy."

"But she could try."

Jim snorted. "She's got Buckley's chance. It's unlikely, Duscha. Please don't worry. I wager she won't get far about the cash either. But I can't rule it out completely."

"Thanks for letting me know. Talk to you soon."

At dusk after Honor had left for the day, Duscha went outside to see where the gardener had been. The back fence was now easily discernible through the heavily cropped firethorn hedge.

Standing next to it and looking back to the house, she could see Honor had made good progress. She was impressed. That she was somewhat more than merely *impressed* with Honor Boyce was made even more disconcerting by the news that Honor was not single. Yet that fact made any developments far simpler. Honor was not free for the having.

Hands on hips, she peered up into the mulberry, knowing that any self-respecting raven with young would have already retired for the evening. Out loud she said, "So it is, Mistress Raven, I live to fight another day on my own. As to the gardener, intriguing as she is, I must leave well alone."

In the cosy gloom at the top of the mulberry, two raven chicks fought for position under Raxa's wings, chirping indignantly as she fluffed up her plumage with its blue-green sheen and wrapped them in close. Idly, she pitied the peculiar plight of the land-dwellers and the horror of being featherless. A curious chick's head popped out. Raxa tucked it back in with her fearsome beak, uttering a low murmur that meant, 'Sleep now."

CHAPTER NINE

Alone in the kitchen at her father's sprawling ranch-style home in the up-market estate of Greenleigh, not far from Queanbeyan, Honor finished stacking the dishwasher. After a lighthearted evening celebrating their father's seventieth, her older brothers, Owen and Miles, had just left with their respective spouses and children. With the kitchen benches wiped down and leftovers stowed in the fridge, she took a final look around to make sure her father need do nothing in the morning, dried her hands on a kitchen towel and went looking for him. She found him in his ensuite dressing room, studying his profile in a full-length mirror.

"That particular shade of purple really suits you, Dad."

A slim, once dark-haired man of less than average height, her father did a mini pirouette. 'You like? It's not too tight is it?" He stood side on to the mirror and pulled in his older-man's small paunch, smoothing the fabric down, front and back.

Honor leaned on the doorjamb, hands in pockets, and tilted her head. "I don't think so. You look pretty good for a fella in a frock."

Wagging a finger, Denholm turned dancing eyes on her. "Naughty girl. I want to wear it tomorrow night for the Seahorse Society's soirée. All of us ladies will be dressed to the nines."

"Are the others friendly?"

"God, yes—very helpful and supportive, despite me being a late bloomer. I'm intrigued by how many of us dressed up when we were very young, as if the feminine part of our psyche demanded to be acknowledged. We *all* acted out. And then got the need either shamed or knocked out of us, of course."

"I guess Mum would struggle with you expressing yourself this way. Things have changed, haven't they?"

He cocked an eyebrow. "Somewhat, but not enough by a long shot. But everyone in the Society is very accepting. For me, it's a joyous 'coming home,' of sorts—a part of me fulfilled. You wouldn't believe how exciting it is to put outfits together, to talk about hair and makeup with the others—pure fun. Wait. I'll slip on the shoes and you can tell me what you think." He wriggled stockinged feet into a pair of size eight black court shoes and tugged the brown bobbed wig into a snug position over his ears. "What say you?"

"Love the new wig. You look as pretty as a picture." She stepped in close to kiss his cheek. "Dad, I'm so proud of you for embracing this side of you—it takes courage. Now are we going to talk finances or not? I've got the usual half hour drive home and I'm knackered."

"Of course. It won't take too long." He slung the wig on a polystyrene stand, shrugged his way out of the dress and slipped his arms into the tartan dressing gown she held open for him. "Thank you, my girl. Have you time for a nightcap in the study?"

"I'm driving, remember."

"Chamomile tea for you plus a whiskey and water for me please." He leaned down and kissed her forehead. "See you in the study."

"As you wish, Your Excellency. Yes sir, three bags full sir." She strode out of the room.

Denholm muttered, "Cheeky beggar."

Five minutes later, she found him in his favourite leather chair, smoking a tipped, aromatic cigarillo. She put the crystal liquor glass on a low wooden table between their chairs, pushing aside papers to find a space. "Why are you still puffing on those nasty things?"

"Because I like 'em," he grumbled, holding out a document. "It's my party and I'll do what I want to. Have a look at this spreadsheet."

Fanning away smoke, she scanned the columns and read numerical totals with too many commas. "What am I looking at?"

"Term deposits with five different banks. As you know, I like to spread risk. The final total is the sum of the deposits and all the interest they have earned in the last seven years. What I want to do is set up a family trust with a self-managed superannuation fund in your name, for when you eventually retire. And to move three-quarters of these monies into it."

"Why only three-quarters?"

He balanced the cigarillo on an ashtray and clasped the whiskey glass. "Once money is in a super fund, it's legally tied up and not easy to access until you retire. And I want you to always be liquid, to have relatively easy access to cash, should you need it." He coughed and put down his glass. "There are legal hoops that I need you to jump through to put all this in place. Just a matter of signing a few documents for my accountant. Confidentially."

Honor shook her head and stared at him. "Seriously Dad? I hate all this subterfuge. Merrin doesn't deserve this. She is my partner and, by rights, owns half of everything I have under the de facto laws. Besides, I haven't had to sign anything before. Why now?"

Denholm took another slug of whiskey and met her stare. "Because up until now, the term investments have been in your mother's name for tax reasons. And Merrin wouldn't have been able to touch them when your relationship falls over. To set up a super fund, it has to be in your name, all legal and above board. Therefore, you must make sure she has no inkling."

Temper rising, Honor reached back and tugged her plait across her chest. "Please stop it. Our relationship is not going to 'fall over,' as you put it. Enough with the negativity. I appreciate that you want to do what you think is best for me, but the Landladies business is ticking over just fine. I've worked hard at building a reputation and we're doing okay—"

"Face facts. It's physically hard work, you could be injured and you won't be young forever. Expect the best and plan for the worst is good business practice. Be sensible."

"And hide stuff from Merrin? Just because you neither like nor trust her." Honor tossed the spreadsheet on the table and stood up. "It makes me feel as guilty as hell, knowing we care for and support each other. Regardless of what you think, our relationship is rock solid and I'm sick of hearing the same-old, same-old arguments. Keep your guilt money. Do what you like with it."

As she turned to leave, he scoffed, "Love and trust her, do you? Going to marry her? Now that you can."

She pulled the study door firmly shut behind her.

By the time she'd driven as far as Parkes Way, a four-lane highway that skirted the lake through the centre of Canberra, Honor had ceased seething. She berated herself for the "guilt money" remark. What was that about? It must have been meant to sting her father who, because of his career, had been absent through much of her pre-teens. She had seen him Christmas and birthdays, if she were lucky, alternating hating him for being away with worshipping him when he was home. He felt guilty, and she'd rubbed his nose in it.

But what disturbed her far more was his jab about marriage, which had slid like a lance through her armour and buried itself in her furious heart. Merrin and she had discussed marriage years ago, as an intellectual exercise, holding no hope of it ever becoming an actuality in their lifetimes. With same-sex marriage only recently passed into Australian law following a heated, divisive national postal survey, Honor had been frantically busy with work, and they had barely spoken of its significance. If anyone had asked Honor a month ago, she would have said it was on the couple's agenda for when Merrin felt up to par again. Now she might reply differently. What had changed?

Honor steered the gleaming blue machine with its low throaty exhaust into the underpass beneath Acton Peninsula. Reluctantly, she acknowledged that she knew full well what had changed. Or more to the point, who.

CHAPTER TEN

After she'd cleaned up the mess made by the final round of wallpaper stripping, Duscha had rehung the octagonal art deco mirror, which had looked rather stark without its striped background. The bedroom was painted light green, complemented by a faded mauve in the lounge room. Throughout the house, the woodwork was white, and the walls either the same green or mauve that had grown drab with time. She quite liked the combination and planned to repaint with updated versions of the original colours.

Fresh from a shower and wearing her cornflower-blue towelling dressing gown, Duscha strolled back to the bedroom, occasionally running a hand over the newly naked plasterboard walls as she went by. Alarmed, she spotted the mirror on the carpet, face up and wedged against the skirting board.

She knelt down, anxiously checking to see if it was broken. It didn't seem to be, but she lifted it carefully and examined the back where an old metal chain was strung between two hooks in the oak backing timbers, still intact. She picked it up, laid it on the bed and had a closer look at the wall where it had been hanging. A long, lightly rusted slot-head screw was fixed into a dowel in the brick. She tugged on the screw gently. It was firmly in place. No amount of staring at it made it looser, despite several more tugs. Like it or not, there was no obvious reason why the mirror had been on the floor. Frowning deeply, she rehung the mirror, and then stood back to study the whole scenario.

Below the mirror and immediately above the skirting board, a ripple in the plaster caught Duscha's attention. Stooping, she ran a hand over a brick-sized area that was slightly proud of the rest of the wall. She hadn't noticed it when she was stripping the wallpaper. When she crouched down to see better, it looked like a piece of thin paper had been glued over a join. She picked at one edge and lifted it enough to get a grip. With deft fingernails, she tore back the paper until an oblong of plywood emerged. It had been wedged in the wall with one edge butting up to the chimney, perhaps to mend it.

Duscha cocked her head and studied the shape, concluding it was too symmetrical to be random damage. Curiosity piqued, she rummaged through her lowest bedside cabinet drawer where she kept a spare torch and stray tools until she found a beaten-up Swiss Army knife. She pried around the plywood until she gained some leverage. The piece popped out of the wall, and with a soft thud, hit the bedroom carpet.

She peered into the cavity, spotting what looked like a metal brick. The pocketknife helped to pry it out far enough for her long fingers to get a hold and pull out a lidded tin imprinted with three pictures of Australian native birds. She shut the knife with its characteristic loud click, turned over the tin and read a label proclaiming that it contained "1½lbs. of Nestlé's High Class Milk & Dark Chocolate Assortment (All Foiled)."

The lightly rusted lid resisted, and then slid free to reveal no chocolates, high class or otherwise. Instead, a pale green ribbon bound a bundle of envelopes, the top one addressed in blue-black fountain pen ink to Miss Charlotte Coxall, 21 Hargraves Crescent, Ainslie, and post-marked Goulburn, 1960.

Duscha left the opened tin on the bedside table. She headed for the bathroom to brush her teeth, thoughts about the tin's contents tumbling over each other. Why was it so thoroughly hidden? Was she intruding on her aunt's privacy if she read what seemed to be personal letters? Intrigued though she was, the fact remained: late Aunt Charlotte deserved every respect.

Once comfortably propped up in bed by two pillows, Duscha carefully lifted out the bundle of envelopes. Squished up at one end of the tin, she found a tatty metal badge with purple, white and green stripes, and a gold-coloured brooch wrapped in tissue paper. Mounted on top of a two-inch strip of gold, the brooch had three round stones: green, clear, and purple. She put the two objects to one side and picked out six stalks of crumbling lavender that must have been intended to deter any bugs. Beneath them was a mass of folded tissue paper with something soft inside. Delicately, she unwrapped a sash made of three fabric strips in green, white, and purple, hand-stitched together. The central white strip was embroidered with black thread to form the words: VOTES FOR WOMEN. She wrapped it up again, careful to replicate the original folds and put it with the brooch and badge.

She picked open the tightly knotted green ribbon, and studied the postmarks on the top few letters, deciding to start with the earliest. Its single sheet of notepaper still smelled faintly of lavender. A woman's handwriting strung a lively cursive, despite some words jumbled up and scratched out.

My darling Lottie, I'm terrified of losing you forever. It's been three weeks since we last spoke. It's driving me spare not to hear your voice, not to know how you're coping. Please, please write to me at my Aunt Beryl's address at the end of this letter. She's the only one who will help me. Everyone else is being ghastly, if they speak to me at all. You are so very blessed that your parents are more understanding, but I won't push our luck by writing again until I hear from you.

That rotten sod, my little brother Billy. He followed me to the phone box that day I last rang you. Listened in. And then ran home and told Mother. God, how I hate that mummy's boy. Always telling on me, always getting me into trouble. Now he's wrecked the only happiness I've ever known. You and I, dearest Lottie. I cannot bear us to end this way. I've been forbidden to have anything more to do with you. Well, damn them. Damn them to Hell and back! And may God strike me down if I don't mean it! I fear we shan't speak ever again, but I beg you to at least write.

In spite of everything, I'm continuing my duties in the general ward at Goulburn Base Hospital. Are you settling well at Canberra Hospital, and are the other nurses still nice to you? It's only been five months, but us training together already seems a lifetime ago. Dearest, I know I'm not supposed to contact you. And doubtless, you can't easily reach me, even though we're only a slow hour's drive apart. But writing is better than nothing.

I'm dreadfully sorry because it's all my fault. If you can forgive my carelessness for not spotting my snooping bratty brother; if you can forgive my parents for castigating your parents for raising you, then write to me. My heart beats for you, only you. Your Sylvia.

Eyes growing gritty with fatigue, Duscha barely absorbed what she'd read. She folded the page, pushed it back in the envelope, and dumped the tin and its contents on the bedside table. She needed a decent night's sleep for the interview in the morning with the ACT Planning Authority for a town planner's position.

Even though she held some confidence about the outcome because she knew someone on the interview panel, she would have to be sharp to impress. And early the following afternoon, she was expecting Honor's carpenter mate, Stuart, to turn up and quote on replacing the back door and its frame. Honor had sent an email that she would not be back to finish the garden until the following week. Duscha had shrugged off a twinge of unsettling disappointment that she preferred not to dwell on.

Light off, she hunkered down under the bedclothes, reflecting that if she'd had any doubt about Aunt Charlotte's persuasion, Sylvia's letter had completely cleared that up. As recent nursing graduates, they both must have been in their mid twenties at a time when being queer was a very bad idea. She did not envy them their lot one iota. And she wondered how long they had been separated by family and distance. Obviously they did reunite, but she could only imagine how difficult it must have been to be so near and yet so far. For both of them, it must have been terribly isolating and lonely, especially not knowing if they would ever be together again. A dreadful uncertainty.

In that fluid place between wakefulness and sleep, Duscha relaxed and allowed herself to miss Noelle. She yearned for their closeness: that feeling of being touched, being held, the sensation of warm, tender skin on skin, bracketed with whispers of abiding affection, of care and of comfort. Although she missed being loved, she missed loving far more. A huge part of being with Noelle was that Duscha got to love her, got to share herself, joyously and bountifully. It had been a gift that had given her infinite pleasure in as many ways.

Just for a moment, despite now accustomed to living by herself, she acknowledged her underlying loneliness before drifting into sleep.

* * *

Duscha thought she heard a car door close. She left her half-eaten cheese and lettuce-filled brioche bun on the cutting board and went to open the front door. A dark-haired fortyish man sporting designer stubble and a baseball cap stuck out his hand.

"Hi, I'm Stuart. You're Honor's friend?"

"I'm Duscha. Just her client. Come in, come in." She was momentarily dazzled by his catwalk looks, not to mention the tight denim short-shorts, and the best pair of long bronzed legs she'd ever seen on a bloke. He stalked in wearing pull-on Redback safety boots, casually hefting a toughened fabric tool bag in one hand.

Luscious lips parted to reveal very white teeth. Stuart said, "Where's your problem?"

She led him through the house to the back door. "If you would give me an approximate costing, that would be good. You'll find me in the kitchen." And she left him to it.

After scarcely five minutes of light hammering, plus the ominous crack of shattering timber, Stuart reappeared. "You'll have to see this for yourself."

Still chewing the last of her lunch, she trailed him down the hall to the open back door. He picked up a torch and shone it into the gaping doorjamb. She peered in, wondering why it seemed to be alive with tiny teeming pale things.

"Termites," said Stuart. "Also known as white ants. That's why the door was binding on the jamb. It's swollen with termites going about their business. Eating your house."

Morbidly fascinated, she said, "How bad is it?"

"You'll have to get a pest controller to check the whole house. By law, you have to have a pest inspection when you buy a property. It should have been picked up then."

She exhaled sharply and blurted, "I inherited it from my father."

Stuart grunted sympathetically. "I'm sorry it wasn't better maintained through regular inspections. And I can't tell you how bad it is. The door lock will hold for now, but it needs fixing sooner rather than later. I can help you with that. Hate to say it, but you must have the place inspected and damage assessed, as soon as you can. It could cost hundreds, more likely thousands. These little buggers are bad news any time of day."

Straightening up, she shook her head at him. "I had no idea. I'll get back to you after I get an inspection."

At the front door, she waved him off as he sped away in a highly polished red Toyota RAV4 that somehow suited him perfectly. Fighting an overwhelming sense of dismay, she trawled the net for a pest inspector, and booked an appointment in two days' time.

At least that morning's job interview had gone well. She'd ended up chatting amicably with the panel, discussing who knew who in the various planning departments in the region. But she wasn't counting on being appointed, and the much-needed cash from her father's estate could be a long time coming. Not one to catastrophise, she plumped for an early night with some light reading.

Charlotte, my heart, my love, my rock, my life! I was delighted to get your letter, to know we can at least write. I understand your embarrassment over your parents having to find out about us this way. It's awful, isn't it? I know everybody wants us to feel ashamed. But sod it, Lottie, I refuse point blank. Never in a month of Sundays will I ever feel ashamed of loving you. It was horrid that your parents got told off by mine. As if it was their fault. It's nobody's fault, because there is no fault. Who shall I thank first for having you in my heart? Your parents or mine? I'm joking, of course. And they wouldn't get it anyway. Pearls before swine. Sorry, I shouldn't be nasty, but it infuriates me. All this "who shall we blame" bulls-wool.

Do you think we might be able to see each other, if we can coordinate shifts? The Sydney coach comes through on Fridays and Mondays, on its way to Canberra. I can get away and stay at the YWCA for two nights. We could see a film or have a meal. I know it sounds stupid, but lovely Lottie, I miss you so much, it physically hurts! Sometimes I can't breathe for thinking of us together again. So easily can I feel your hands at my waist, your dear breath at my throat, the scent of you that lingers. Sweetheart, please let's meet! Tenderly, I kiss your wrists, your eyes, your unforgettable mouth. Your Sylvia.

Duscha slipped the letter back in the envelope, and into its original place in the pile. Sipping a milky chai tea, she savoured its vanilla notes, and guessed that there were around twenty similarly sized envelopes. Except for a shorter one she hadn't noticed before, right in the middle. She thumbed through the pile and pulled it out. A mature hand had addressed the sealed envelope in scratchy black ballpoint, "To Whom it May Concern." She smiled at its quaintness as she opened it. The letter's first few words made her eyebrows arch and her mouth fell open.

Dear Duscha. I know you'll read this. It came to me as a recurring dream. A vision of this letter in your dexterous hands. I'm gone, of course, long gone. Dear Duscha, we never met, much to my regret. But I saw your baby photo and one of you at eighteen, the spitting image of your father and not unlike myself. You have found precious correspondence from my beloved Sylvia (my wife in all but name) from when she lived with her parents up until we set up home together, here in this house. I have treasured Sylvia's letters, could not bear to dispose of them, even after she died in 1994. Of course, I wrote back to her. She tried to keep my letters hidden, but her mother always somehow found and destroyed them. Thusly it seems a very one-sided story, but I assure you it was not. In reading them, you will discover her family wanted to lock her up and throw away the key. But my aunt, Irene Coxall, who was far from well and then aged 82, stepped in to give Sylvia sanctuary until her parents gave up looking for her, gave up trying to control her very life. Aunty died of pneumonia in September 1960, unexpectedly leaving me the house. Sylvia and I were able to move in together. She never went home again, not ever.

What becomes of the letters now, I shall never know, and you may never read this but I have faith that you will. You see, this house has a sentience, a mind of its own (indulge an old lady, will you please?). And will conspire both to enlighten you, and bring you to more happiness than you can possibly imagine.

It's blessed, you see, by the local Ngunnawal people who used to congregate across the road at Corroboree Park, long ago. The aboriginal presence in this area goes back tens of thousands of years. Today the park is the spiritual heart and soul of the heritage precinct (Sylvia and I used to play tennis there). The house was built in 1927, bought new by Aunt Irene. I don't know much about her, other than she came from a very wealthy Sydney family, and was a prominent women's suffrage activist at the turn of the century. She moved to Canberra with her secretary, Ruby Milborne. The jewellery belonged to them, including the three-stoned bar brooch in with these letters. Aunty gave it to me when I turned twenty-one. She was adamant that it never be sold and that it be passed down to direct descendants, where possible. All the other pieces are for you to do with as you will. The silk sash was made by Aunty and worn by her at all her suffrage outings, as was the little badge. Both are keepsakes I hereby pass on to you.

My brother Cliff, your father, who you will have had no chance to get to know as other than an unfaithful rogue, deserves you to know better. He and I were brought up by our avant-garde liberal-minded parents, who themselves had homosexual siblings like Aunty, which was considered merely Bohemian in Sydney, from whence they came to Canberra. Solely for Sylvia's safety, Cliff, having just turned twenty-two, willingly married her in December 1960 at our parents' bidding—a registry office affair annulled three years later. It was a generous and noble thing to do. Thereafter, she was known as Sylvia Coxall, could continue her career in nursing and live with me in peace, albeit ostensibly as sisters. We owe your father a great debt, possibly Sylvia's life—her sanity at the very least!

I have bequeathed the house to your father, presuming I pass before him. Cliff has assured me that you are named as its inheritor in his will. This house is a unique treasure. May it bless you as completely as it has blessed your ancestors. Sincerely, your aunt, Charlotte Coxall, R.N.

Duscha let her hand holding the letter fall into her lap, her thoughts scampering about like spring lambs on speed. How exactly did Charlotte end up living with Sylvia? Why did Irene move to Canberra with her secretary? Jewellery…what jewellery? She'd found only the aforementioned brooch and badge. And the house had "a mind of its own." Huh? Charlotte's veiled explanation was doing her head in. And she was absolutely dumbfounded that a youthful Cliff had married Sylvia. No wonder her parents couldn't find her! Even if they had, she would have been Cliff's wife, therefore virtually his property and beyond their clutches.

To the deco mirror on the wall facing where she sat in bed, she said, "Aunty, you do realise that all that raises more questions than it answers, but I appreciate the thought. And thank you for the house. I'm astonished by what could be construed as overconfidence, based on a single, solitary photo of a pimply and clueless eighteen-year-old girl. But I don't know what you were told about me. And Dad? Turns out he was a lifesaver. Well, there's a complete surprise if there ever was one." She returned the letters to the tin and switched off the light.

CHAPTER ELEVEN

It was late afternoon in a backyard in the Canberra suburb of Chifley. Honor and Karen, one of her employees, were clearing out an old garden as part of a renovation for its new owners. An ex-rental, it had been neglected for years. Typical of Canberra investment properties, a few miserable shrubs still struggled in the parched garden bordered by recycled ironbark railway sleepers that were cheap and fashionable in the 1980s. A few remaining sleepers were destined for a large skip bin on the nature strip, already half-full with debris.

The earth still slippery from recent rain, the women each held one end of the extremely heavy two-metre-long length of timber, only one of many they had already carried around to the front of the house and heaved into the bin. Karen was a head taller than Honor, fit and well-built. But at the corner of the house, a skidding boot threatened to slide her into the splits. She dropped her end of the sleeper. When it hit the ground and bounced, the vibration jerked the other end out of Honor's gloved hands. It thudded down with its full weight across the arch of her left foot, precisely where it was unprotected by the steel-capped boot. Honor squealed, dragged her foot from under the sleeper and crumpled into a writhing heap. Swearing freely, a stricken Karen leaped to her side, bending to help her up.

"No, no, wait!" Tears of agony running through the grime on her cheeks, Honor tried to flex her foot. "It may be broken. Get your car. We have to go to accident and emergency. No choice."

Gentle Karen as good as carried Honor into Royal Canberra Hospital's emergency room.

Honor sat at the kitchen table. She was home alone and going rapidly stir-crazy. Merrin was out, reluctantly shopping. An X-ray had shown a hairline crack—no breaks. But the flesh had swollen quickly. The duty doctor had strapped the foot, giving instructions to re-strap it once the swelling came down. The flesh had turned black and blue, the foot still too sore to bear weight. She had been told to keep off it completely and use crutches for a fortnight, followed by a moon boot for another three to four weeks.

For days, she had played phone tag with clients, apologising and rescheduling where she could. Her staff could work without her sometimes, but often not. For the moment, she was unable to drive, which meant she couldn't give quotes. Just when the business was running like clockwork, this had to happen—an accident that was no one's fault. Karen was abjectly contrite, despite there being a confluence of factors: wet conditions, an awkward, heavy weight and the women's mutual fatigue. Honor recalled her father's prescient remark about debilitating injuries. She had to admit he was right. She wouldn't always be young and fit, her present situation being a salutary lesson in preparing for the unexpected.

She lurched to her feet, wedging a crutch in each armpit. With much jigging and shuffling, she made her way down the hallway and into the office. Perhaps she could help with the paperwork by checking for unpaid invoices or make phone calls to hurry up tardy clients. She swung herself into the rotating office chair and turned on the computer. Not having looked at the accounts for a while, it took her a few minutes to locate the right files. When she tried to open the current financial year's spreadsheet, a pop-up asked for a password. Eyebrows arched, all she could do was stare. Since when had the files become password protected? She tried to open the previous financial year's spreadsheet, with the same frustrating result. Merrin hadn't mentioned the need for a password.

How long was it since she'd accessed these files? Landladies had been consistently busy since before last Christmas, more than four months ago. Honor pursed her lips. So much for good intentions. She closed down the computer, swung around in the chair and stopped to stare at the bookcase that held no books. It was jam-packed with Merrin's burgeoning collection of jigsaw puzzles.

Back when Merrin first became ill, she'd been stuck at home for weeks that turned into months, then years. At first, she just lay on the sofa and dozed, watching daytime television when she was awake. Feeling better, yet with little strength to do anything, she revisited a childhood passion for jigsaws. A large coffee table, permanently parked in front of the TV and protected by a sheet of felt, had become a feature in the lounge room. There was always a puzzle in progress, fresh ones in boxes on the floor and completed ones stacked on shelves close by. Merrin mostly bought them on eBay, a new one delivered every few weeks.

Honor started counting the boxes on the bookcase and stopped when she got to a hundred and twenty. She had never understood the attraction and wasn't about to start now. With eyes squeezed shut, while she did her best to conceal it, she felt terribly sorry for Merrin. And Merrin knew it. Doing a few accounts, jigsaw puzzles, and watching the idiot-box all day was no kind of life. Typically, Honor did as much as she could, including most of the cooking, grocery shopping, vacuuming, and cleaning house, mowing lawns and gardening. Sometimes Merrin would prune the roses and trim a few plants, but the effort was often more than she could handle. Today Merrin had struggled to the shops and Honor knew nothing but guilt. Fretfully, she swung the chair again, this time Duscha's bold stare from the painting catching her eye.

Honor considered the pictured woman's unmistakable challenge, one unchanged by the intervening years. She'd seen it again in Duscha's eyes, the day they had talked over tea. And she'd avoided thinking about that interlude...about Duscha. With her foot injury, she couldn't see Duscha now if she tried, which made her wonder how much the accident was fate versus how much was avoidance. Her father had always contended that every cloud held a silver lining. One just had to wait and expect to see. Right now, Honor was struggling to find any silver lining in her situation.

She felt herself disappearing into Duscha's eyes, and for an instant allowed herself to do so, her breath slowing and heart quickening above a primal response low in her belly. Not that she wanted to feel that intense sensation of being drawn into Duscha's arms, elated by her soaring energy, deliriously conjoined for eternity. No, not much. Honor closed her eyes and indulged herself in feelings, long repressed. Feelings that slammed awake her shocked senses, scaring her silly with their strength. Her eyes flew open in dismay. A fiery obsessive beast had smashed its way out of an icy cell, once locked away in the remote recesses of her heart. What was she doing? What the hell was she thinking?

Honor covered her face with both hands and rocked herself. Getting crazy about Duscha, all over again, was a very bad idea. Just like all those years ago when it was a one-sided fantasy that went nowhere, it would undoubtedly end in heartache. Now she had a successful business that she loved, plus a decent and stable, if predictable, relationship with Merrin. She had everything she could possibly ever want.

The front door closed. Honor scrambled for the crutches, hurrying out of the office. Barrelling down the hall, she muttered to herself, "Don't go there. Stay away from her. Never in a million years. Just don't."

CHAPTER TWELVE

Duscha shut the front door. She slung keys and mobile phone onto the kitchen bench, and it occurred to her that she felt better about life than she had in years. Definitely since Noelle died. So far, coming back to Canberra was turning out rather well.

She'd met her mother in Civic at Gus's café for a light lunch, which had been such a pleasure. And one of the many reasons she was coming to appreciate her hometown again. It really was a beautiful self-contained city with its carefully planned streets and town centres, and great swathes of treed corridors between suburbs earning its nationwide reputation as "the bush capital." Each town centre had offices and plentiful shops, usually in undercover malls with well-patronised restaurants and sidewalk cafés. Civic was the oldest centre, typically packed out and buzzing with a cheerfully multicultural populace at lunchtime. And for Duscha, it was a brisk ten-minute walk from her house.

She hung her black woollen ankle-length coat back in the free-standing double wardrobe and wandered back out to the kitchen to check her mobile. The pest inspector had sent her a message that she'd received in the café and only partly read. Before he left yesterday, he promised her a detailed diagram of where he thought the damage was, plus a quote. His message said the old red gum growing on the boundary likely housed the termite nest. It would have to be poisoned to kill them, endangering the tree only slightly because it would have a huge root system. He'd said since termites needed water, she should check for plumbing leaks and have any fixed.

She scrolled to the house diagram where it seemed the only damage was next to the chimney in her bedroom, along the floor plate around the edge of the room and through to the back door. Duscha forwarded the message to Stuart the carpenter, along with a request for a quote for repairs, hoping that it wasn't tens of thousands of dollars.

With the kettle on, she headed for the lounge room. Across the coffee table she had scattered paint charts and colour swatches. She had yet to decide on the perfect green and the equally perfect mauve paint. Her mobile rang.

"Hi Stuart, that was quick."

"Yeah, nah. Hi. I've had a client postpone on me, which means I can give you a few days this week. How about I have a look at your place tomorrow morning? I can pick up a doorframe and door from the hardware store. If you look at doors online, message me what you want and I'll grab it. Just make sure it's the right size, solid core, and weatherproof. You can reimburse me. That way I can get started and you'll be safe and secure by lunchtime."

"Wow, that's service. What time?"

"Seven okay?"

Duscha chuckled. "I should be vertical by then. See you in the morning. And thanks, Stuart, you're awesome."

* * *

Duscha had run through the shower at six thirty a.m. and dressed warmly, the chilly Canberra morning quickening her senses. The electric radiator was on full blast taking the chill off the kitchen. Out the back, Stuart was noisily dismantling the doorframe with a crowbar.

"Stuart? May I talk to you for a minute?"

Looking snappy in his short-shorts and boots, he'd strapped on black rubber knee protectors so he could kneel without abrading his skin. He nodded, put down the crowbar and followed her through the house.

She handed him a printout of the pest inspector's diagram. "Could we go through what needs to be done besides the back door?" Shoulder to shoulder with him, she inhaled his aftershave, and said, "You smell nice. What is it?"

From beneath dense black eyebrows he peered at her. "Sauvage by Dior. You're not chatting me up are you? Honor said you were family."

Smirking, she shoved him with a shoulder. "Yes I am. Don't worry."

"Phew. That's all right then." He grinned down at her, improbably white teeth flashing. "To business. See here, it looks like the termites have come up near the base of the chimney, eaten their way across the floor plate in your bedroom, into the laundry, chewed out the back door and were heading for your deck. But it's hardwood and they don't like it. Blunts their little teeth. Let's go look in your bedroom."

On hands and knees, he tapped along the skirting around the chimney and along to where the bedroom met the laundry wall.

Duscha said, "Have you seen her recently?"

"Who, Honor? I dropped in yesterday. She's got cabin fever. Hates not being able to work. Unlike her so-called partner who wouldn't know hard work if it leaped up and bit her on the bum." He clambered to his feet and looked at her. "You must have met Princess Merrin."

"Um…can't say I have."

"Oops. Thought you knew them. Pretend I said diddly-squat." He picked at the bedroom doorframe with a screwdriver. It sounded like crumbling papier-mâché. "Honor's foot is just about good enough for her to be able to drive again. That'll make her happy." He tapped the lintel with the screwdriver's handle. "The buggers have been up here too, just one side of the frame, possibly heading for the roof. I'd better climb up through the manhole and check it out later. But for now, most of this skirting has had it. I'll have to replace it."

Duscha folded her arms and scowled at him. "Is it really bad?"

"God no, it could be heaps worse. I'll write you out a swag before I go. Just let me get the door finished and we can talk, okay?" He backed out of the room.

"A swag?"

He stuck his head around the doorjamb and grinned. "A scientific wild arse guess."

Shaking her head, Duscha took a moment to absorb his words. Things were never simple…never what they first seemed.

"What are you up to?"

Duscha looked up from the colour swatches. "Trying to decide a colour scheme for the whole house. It's a lot harder than it looks."

"You should ask Honor's advice. She's good at design, layout, and colours. All that sort of thing." Stuart had his phone out and was scrolling through messages, a baggie of sandwiches in his other hand. "I'm stopping for a bite. It's been a long time since breakfast at quarter past six."

Duscha made her way toward the kitchen. "Would you like a hot drink?"

"Could murder a decent coffee. Shall I call her to come over?" He put his baggie down and held up his phone.

With a start, she said, "What? Er…if you like. I could pick her brains about the garden. Do you think she'd mind?"

Head down and dialling, he said, "Nah, she'll be desperate to get out of there."

Whatever he said to Honor was drowned out by the coffee machine. As she put out cups, she half watched him pacing and talking. It was then she noticed the hairy arms and fingers were not matched by his glamorous smooth legs. When he hung up, she said, "How do you take your coffee?"

"Long black, one sugar. She's ten minutes away and closing, as we speak."

She stirred the cup for a few seconds before handing it to him. "You shave your legs."

He looked down at himself. "Well spotted. I cycle long distance most weekends. If you come off, gravel rash on hairy legs takes much longer to heal. The voice of experience, trust me." His phone rang, and he put down his coffee. "Have to take this. Hi, pumpkin." He walked off to the lounge room, grunting more than speaking.

Duscha made herself a milky, strong coffee and sat on the sofa next to him, waiting until he hung up.

"My daughter. Take my advice and don't ever have teenagers."

"You have a daughter?"

"And a son. My wife and I are divorced. Very amicably I might add. We married young." He took a big bite of a wholegrain sandwich full of what looked like ham, cheese, and salad. Mayonnaise slid down a finger, and he slurped it off. "I have my own place. We share the kids, week about."

"Good on you." She was briefly silent. "How did that happen?"

He grinned as he chewed, twinkling eyes on her. "I didn't know any better. To be brief, I loved my wife and still do. I trained as a Baptist pastor, got married, had kids and was very happy. I even had my own parish until five years ago when I worked out what was wrong with that picture. I 'fessed up, lost my job and was thrown out of the church. But I'm blessed by having a true friend, my ex-wife. She's been very understanding, very supportive."

Lost in thought, she didn't hear the polite knocking. Stuart took another mouthful and pointed at the front door. Gathering herself, she stood up and let in a barely recognisable Honor on crutches. The work garb had been replaced by a grey puffer jacket over a scoop-necked long-sleeve tee in a blue and green marbled pattern, and a pair of skinny jeans. One foot wore a charcoal suede ankle boot, the other a moon boot. Honor's intensely dark hair was neatly brushed and tied back into a freely swinging ponytail that fell far enough to skim her hips.

Trying not to stare, Duscha said, "How are you doing?"

"Stumbling about but getting there. I'm training myself to walk around on just the moon boot. At least I can drive. Hey Stu." Honor bent to peck his rough cheek. "Is this a party or what?"

"Just inhaled some tucker and java juice." He rose and touched her shoulder affectionately, giving her the once-over. "You scrub up well. Looking peachy. Sorry, but the back door won't wait. Leave you two to talk."

Duscha hovered near Honor. "I'll take your coat. Make yourself comfortable." Honor shrugged off the jacket, did a one-legged squat and slipped onto the sofa, moon boot sticking out past the coffee table. Duscha sat back down as they both glanced sideways, waiting for the other to speak.

Duscha lurched forward and snatched up two swatches. "Stuart tells me you know about putting colours together. I want to freshen up the interior with brighter versions of the original paint. Would you have a look for me?"

Honor blinked to focus on Duscha's hands and frowned at the swatches. "Are they the original colours?"

"I've no idea what they were originally. And I can only get close by holding up brochures against the paintwork. I've found two that are almost the same." She passed the swatches to Honor who studied them.

"When was the house first built?"

"I've been told it was 1927."

"Any idea of the original owner?"

"My great-aunt, Irene Coxall."

Honor's brooding eyes stretched open, and she studied the floor. "Irene Coxall. That name rings a whopping bell. The Womanhood Suffrage League based in Sydney. Rose Scott was the League's secretary and a prominent campaigner. They would have known each other, would Irene and Rose. I learned all about them in first year women's studies at the ANU, before I switched courses." She raised a finger to wave at Duscha. "Your great-aunt was a blue-stocking. A suffragist. Very outspoken and influential back in the day." She lined up the swatches. "And these here, combined with white, are suffrage colours. Green, white, and violet. GWV, purportedly standing for 'give women votes.' You're living in Irene Coxall's house. And I didn't know she'd ever lived in Canberra."

Duscha swivelled to fully face Honor. "That fits with something my Aunt Charlotte told me. She also said she was well-to-do. I might see what else I can find out about her. In the meantime, what do you think of those two brighter colours? Would they work?"

"It's personal taste. Can't see why not. You could think about a darker violet or green to use very selectively as an accent. Or home ware items like vases, frames and cushions."

Duscha listened and nodded, fighting to keep her focus well above Honor's taut neckline. It got easier when she stared at Honor's blood-red heart-shaped ear studs that she hadn't seen before and asked, "What are they made of? Your earrings, I mean. They're very pretty."

Honor stroked an earlobe. "I'm think they're banded carnelian, courtesy of my Scottish grandmother. And who knows who before her. I believe they date back to the turn of last century. Victorian rose-gold mounts." She stared back at Duscha, her expression unreadable.

The stretching silence was broken by Stuart's boots echoing down the hall. He appeared and said, "The frame's in, the door's next. I forgot to buy hinges this morning. I'll be back in twenty minutes, no worries."

They sat mute while he closed the front door behind him. Honor's gaze flickered over Duscha with something like anguish, ill-concealed. Duscha reached over and touched Honor's wrist. "Are you okay? Not in pain, are you?"

Honor almost flinched, then crossed her arms and focused on the door. "I'm fine. Have to go."

"So soon? How about a coffee? I was going to ask you about the garden. The mulberry's leaves are turning gold. When might you have healed completely?"

"Another week, max. I should be back late next week. No coffee thanks, but I'll let you know." Honor flashed a tight smile that didn't extend to her eyes and hauled herself up from the sofa. Duscha passed over the jacket.

At the open door Duscha said, "Good to see you. Are you off home?"

"Nope. Greenleigh. To see my father."

"Is he who I think he is?"

Honor wobbled along the path, calling out over her shoulder, "Probably."

Duscha lingered until the ute sped off down the road. Back inside, she strode from room to room, hands on hips, a worrying thought gathering strength within her. Coming to a halt in the bedroom, she addressed her grim reflection in the wise old mirror. "What on earth do you think you're playing at by touching her? Keep your hands to yourself or you'll end up with more trouble than you can poke a stick at. Take a hint."

CHAPTER THIRTEEN

Honor took the back road past the airport and out toward Queanbeyan. The ute was an automatic. She could drive with the moon booted left foot held immobile while her right foot did the work. Yet her focus strayed from the traffic ahead, and she snuck glimpses at her wrist. The last few days had been disturbing enough, but today Duscha Penhaligon had touched her. Physically touched her for the first time ever. She'd been in love with that magnetic bloody woman for more than half her bloody life and, wonder of wonders, Duscha was flesh and blood. She rubbed the hallowed skin, a self-mocking grin stealing across her face.

Should she shower ever again? Might she draw a marker-pen heart around it with an "X marks the spot" in the middle and take a selfie? Have a couple of fingerprints tattooed right there? She snorted out loud and fell to giggling to herself. More soberly, she realised that she had nearly freaked out when Stuart left the house. That could only mean it was getting harder for her to stay in control—progressively harder to conceal her feelings. And she had to keep them concealed because there was far too much at stake.

Only three nights ago, she'd had an awkward conversation with Merrin about the Landladies files. Mid-evening, she had finally remembered to ask her why the business accounts were password-locked.

Immersed in an episode of *Home and Away* on the TV and an intricate landscape jigsaw, a stony-faced Merrin looked up at Honor. She pressed the mute button on the remote and proceeded to manoeuvre three jigsaw pieces around the felt tablecloth.

"Lance said we should password-lock confidential business files. If we have a break-in, and thieves steal all the hardware, they can't access our information. The bank passwords are in a master file, also locked on the hard drive. You don't have to worry about these things, sweet. Lance and I have it covered. Honestly."

Honor nodded, instinctively wary when anyone used the word "honestly." If they were honest only now, what were they the rest of the time? She asked, "What if you get hit by a bus tomorrow, heaven forbid? How would I access the Landladies data?"

"That's easy. Lance has them. He's been helping me with the Tax Office's new quarterly statement rules. And in case of an emergency."

"Really? Good to know." Honor followed Merrin's wandering attention that drifted to the actors on screen. "But I'd like to check some figures for myself now. What are the passwords?"

Merrin glanced at her and pressed the mute button again. The TV characters resumed their chatty melodrama. "Gosh, I can't remember just like that. They're really long and complicated with letters, numbers, and symbols. Tomorrow, okay?"

Somehow it had slipped Merrin's mind and, three days later, Honor was none the wiser. With time aplenty to think, she had sat in the garden with her foot up, lost in contemplation of the recent subtle and not-so-subtle changes in her household. Over the past few months, every time Merrin had obstructed or obfuscated, she had unwittingly hammered a nail into an invisible coffin. The one representing the death of their relationship. Honor had so hoped not to get where they were, with Merrin hammering in increasingly bigger and bolder nails, as if Honor were as thick as two short planks. Had she imagined things, perhaps made mountains out of molehills? As Stuart would say, "yeah, nah."

Honor pulled into her father's driveway bordered by row upon row of lovingly tended red roses, her mother's favourite. She parked the ute, admiring her childhood home with its magnificent pergola covered in kiwifruit vines busily dropping their leaves. The property was a choice block facing northeast, its expanse of lawn interrupted only by stands of silver birches beneath which multiple bulbs would flower into a riot of colour in spring.

The place held many memories. Some good, some not so good. But it was her home once. A place where she belonged once. She had tried to create her own home in Higgins with Merrin by putting in long hours landscaping and developing their suburban block into a cool oasis in summer and a cosy place to hang out in the winter sun.

A home was a place of affection and friendship, both of which she had thought she had with Merrin. Now she wondered if either truly remained between them. Just mulling it over made her leaden.

Yet she still held hope they could pull things together. She would give Merrin a few more days to come up with the passwords before she asked again and made an issue of not being able to access her own business records. In the meantime, just as a precaution, she would sign the superannuation documents for her father. That way, everyone would stay happy, the status quo preserved, everything under control. Theoretically.

Her father stood at the front door, watching and waiting. She waved and clambered out, thankful the moon boot would be gone before week's end. Then she could get back to work.

CHAPTER FOURTEEN

It was after eight a.m. at Hargraves Crescent. Honor had been in the back garden for less than half an hour. Duscha hadn't been home when she'd arrived, but Stuart was hard at it somewhere inside. She came in to look for him, stopping to admire the new back door and its merbau timber frame. The nail holes had been filled with wood filler, ready for sanding. She stepped into the hallway and called out, "Stu? Where are you?"

She followed a muffled reply and found him kneeling head down, bum up, on the main bedroom floor. He had jimmied off the skirting boards and pulled back the carpet and underlay. With a claw hammer and gloved hands, he tugged out pieces of the tongue-and-groove floorboards that he'd cut free with a circular saw.

She hadn't been in Duscha's sparsely furnished bedroom before. Tentatively she sat on the very edge of the queen-sized bed. "How's it going?"

Stuart leaned back on his haunches and tossed a board into the wheelbarrow next to him. "Better than I thought but making it up as I go along. It's not easy to see the damage until I run into it."

"Any idea when Duscha might be back?"

"She's gone to the doctor. You know what they're like. You might wait five minutes or fifty."

"Is she sick or something?"

He shook his head and looked up at her. "She's having a DNA test. A paternity test, she told me. Something to do with her inheritance. She's got a half-sister who's querying her right to the house. Bloody-minded, by the sound of it."

"Bit of a worry." She frowned at her watch and stood up. "I can't do much without discussing what she wants done out back. And I wanted to run something past you about Merrin, if you can spare a few minutes."

He got to his feet, holstering the hammer to swing from a hip. "Let's put the kettle on. She said it was okay to make ourselves at home. C'mon."

They leaned like siblings against the laminated kitchen bench, his arm around her shoulders. He said, "What's up with her highness?"

She rocked her head back and forth, rubbing her neck. "She's password-locked me out of the accounting system for the business and keeps forgetting to tell me the passwords, despite me asking. It's been nearly a week."

Scratching his dark stubble, he stared at the kettle as it reached a crescendo, belched steam and turned itself off. "Just replacing my carpenter's hat with my pastor's hat, everyone deserves the benefit of the doubt. You mustn't jump to conclusions, Pen. Ask again and give her enough rope, even if it's sufficient to hang herself. She must know you need access. You're the boss." He turned to search her expression. "Maybe it's a power play. It happens all the time in relationships. People who feel lesser have to throw their weight around. And she must feel powerless much of the time."

She retrieved two ornate mugs from the sink drainer, lining them up on the bench. "Too true. I feel sorry for her because managing the financial side of the business is all she's got."

"Correction. She's got you as well." He leaned in and nuzzled her cheek "And you, my dear Pen, are pure platinum. The real deal. Even she knows that. You pay for everything, do most everything and look after her. She'd be barking mad to jeopardise all that, eh?"

"Do shut up." She grinned sheepishly and patted his furry forearm.

The front door closed. Honor spotted a dressed-for-success Duscha approaching and felt her knees give, as if she'd just inhaled God. She clutched at the bench and shied away from Stuart's startled glance. Searching in a cupboard for teabags helped her regain some semblance of normalcy.

Duscha slid keys and phone onto the bench. "Morning all. Looks like I'm just in time. Or have I missed something? Teabags are in the canister in the overhead cupboard. Love one, thanks." She turned away and walked off toward the bathroom.

Honor found yet another mug and flung in a teabag. Stuart's lips twitched almost imperceptibly as he reached in front of her to pour. "Anything you care to share?"

Eyes squeezed shut, she said, "Not at this precise moment."

"It seems to me you're having trouble enough breathing let alone speaking." His smile held as much concern as mirth.

"Stuart. Please don't say another word. I mean it."

"Sure thing, honeybunch. I'll leave you two alone." With mug in hand, he retreated.

She took slow deep breaths and stared sightlessly at the steaming tea. With a conscious effort, she grabbed a teaspoon and decanted the teabags, found a carton of full-cream milk in the fridge and topped up the mugs. She simply must not make a further fool of herself. It was not an option.

"Good to see you on your own two feet again."

She glanced up at Duscha and pointed at a mug. "For you. Have you time to discuss the veggie patch?"

"Certainly. Lead on, Macduff."

Outdoors, they traipsed east across the yard to a paved area under the washing line bordering what had once been a vegetable garden, now knee-deep in couch and thistles. They stood side by side, cool hands wrapped around warm mugs.

"There are a number of options depending on how much of a hurry you are in to get plants in the ground."

Duscha grunted. "Does anything grow through winter in Canberra?"

"Surprisingly, yes. Brassicas. And leafy greens like spinach, kale, and collards. Provided you get them in immediately. The problem is the couch because it has deep runners. I could pull out as much as possible and dig it over for you, but it would take many hours and I'm not fit enough for heavy digging or lifting yet."

"Isn't there an easier way? A spray or something?"

Honor sipped tea, savouring its tang and heat. "There is a certain lunatic fringe that advocates spraying with glyphosate, waiting for everything to die and then planting veggies straight into the denuded soil. That stuff is supposed to be non-residual, but I wouldn't risk my health if I were you. Another method is solarisation. I could lay out sheets of black plastic or tarpaulins, hold them down with bricks and let the sun's heat work its magic. The thing about Canberra's winter is that although the nights are cold, the days are brilliantly sunny. It would do the job in about a month, if it doesn't rain. Which it probably won't. Then you could get some broad beans in for spring harvest."

"I don't think I like broad beans."

"Then you haven't had the home-grown variety. Young and tender and fresh out of your own backyard, they're the best."

Duscha finished her tea, flicked out the residue and tucked the mug under her folded arms. "What about a bit of both? Could you solarise most of it, but prepare a small section so I can get greens in. I love spinach."

"Do you?" Honor looked into Duscha's limpid eyes and cracked a smile, dimples deepening. "Tell you what. I could do you a no-dig garden big enough to keep you in spinach. I use cardboard, which will keep the couch subdued for the duration.

Just need hay, lucerne and manure. It would take me only a few hours, easy-peasy."

Silent, Duscha's pupils dilated. Honor dropped her eyes and shuffled her feet.

"It's a done deal," said Duscha, and she turned to walk toward the house. Midstride, she pulled up suddenly. "How long before you're fully fit for heavy work?"

"Best guess, another three weeks. But I have other clients waiting."

Duscha nodded, one hand on a hip. "Are you any good with a paintbrush?"

"Passable. Why?"

"I'd pay you to help me repaint the interior during that time, if you can manage a ladder. I start a job with ACT Planning's Urban Renewal Division in three weeks. Would that suit you in the interim?"

Honor looked beyond Duscha to the towering mulberry preparing for winter, steadily dropping its yellowing leaves. Bereft of thought, she instinctively turned and took a blind step into the unknown. "I enjoy painting. It's instantly rewarding. Yes, definitely."

Duscha tossed a brilliant smile, turned on her heel and strode back to the house. Honor paused to slow her galloping heart, left with no choice but to follow her teenage dream.

CHAPTER FIFTEEN

Sitting up in bed with Aunt Charlotte's box of letters, Duscha was starting to feel like a voyeur. Sylvia's missives were so tender. She wondered what the woman had looked like. Was she homely, a plain Jane, or a surprising stunner? Her words were affectionate and feisty, her intention consistently determined to be with Charlotte, come what may. To what extent was that an asset or a liability in 1960?

Her thoughts drifted to her new job. A phone call had offered her the maternity-leave position. It would be for a minimum of a year and a proverbial foot in the door. While not ideal because it wasn't permanent, she had accepted the position and would see what opportunities might arise thereafter. It was a weight off her shoulders and had boosted her morale, not to mention shoring up the bank balance. Stuart's quote for house repairs had come in at just under five thousand dollars, with the understanding that he would advise her should it threaten to blow out.

She missed Noelle in many ways, not the least of which was her mental, emotional, and financial support. She reflected that to have been young, financially insecure, and lowly paid nurses like Charlotte and Sylvia must have been a constant worry, and very much limited their options in life. Back then, even if women had amassed a moderate amount of money, they couldn't borrow to buy property without a male relative going guarantor. They were on their own, their love for each other their only strength in the face of persistent opposition.

Duscha had read all the letters, bar one. In previous notes Sylvia had discussed nursing duties, interesting cases, friends' families and outings. The most recent letter commiserated with Charlotte about Aunt Irene having developed "a woman's problem"—lay person's code for any one of the possible reproductive cancers. Now she opened the last letter, its contents markedly tear-stained.

Dearest Charlotte, it is with utter dismay that I tell you they are coming for me. I can't begin to describe how scared I am. Mother keeps finding and burning your letters that I hide so carefully in my room. I have no privacy, no succour, and no option other than to do as my parents dictate. I am to cease any contact with you and particularly to desist in writing to you. Yesterday they forced me to consult the doctor, presenting him with a litany of complaints about my behaviour, my abnormal affection for you. He agreed that I am sufficiently certifiable to be incarcerated in Kenmore Asylum. Yes, that hellhole here in Goulburn. Many go through those monstrous doors and far fewer leave upright.

Kenmore, my darling? You know what that means. Shock therapy and barbiturates, at best. Mother and Father are completely convinced, stoked to the Heavens with righteousness that Kenmore is the only hope, the only cure for my "extremely sick and chronic perversion."

I have no arguments left, Dear Heart. I've tried every possible persuasion and they will not listen. Even if I agree to their conditions, I have a horrible feeling they're going to commit me anyway. For my own good, no doubt. I'm a goner, darling. I'm fighting the horror of its inevitability, moment by moment. My Lady Lottie, please let go the dream of us and get on with your life. Find another to love and be happy, in spite of this ignorant, hate-filled Godforsaken world.

Please remember this: whatever they do to me, I will always love you, shall dwell beneath your heart for all eternity. Always, my darling. Your Sylvia.

Duscha swept trickling tears off her lips and found a tissue to blow her nose. She had heard about the reputedly haunted Kenmore Psychiatric Hospital. It had closed in 2003 amidst allegations of malpractice. Even though Charlotte's note said Sylvia had been spirited away before being subjected to that nightmare, poor Sylvia couldn't have known and must have been numb with fear. How on earth would anyone reconcile themselves to such a fate? And how on earth did Aunty Irene pull off such a stunt? She turned off the bedside light and sank like a stone into sleep plagued by nonsensical dreams.

CHAPTER SIXTEEN

August 1960

At twilight, Irene Coxall slowed her pale-green 1955 Austin A30 to a stop on the gravel verge opposite a vintage brick house on Mundy Street in Goulburn.

From the passenger seat, young Charlotte whispered, "This is it. Sylvia's Aunt Beryl's place. Shall I just march straight in?"

"No need to whisper, girl," said Irene. "And she's expecting you. Now gird your loins and go get her. We're running out of light. You need to be quick about it. It gets pitch black around Lake George after dark, and I'd rather not be there then. Get a move on."

The door slammed, and the little car shook in protest. Wearing green tartan slacks and a tan cardigan over a gingham blouse, Charlotte scampered across the road, her short blond curls threatening to escape a matching tan Alice band. She tapped on the front door and disappeared from sight.

Irene turned on the ignition, checked the petrol gauge and peered at her wristwatch reading four forty-five p.m. It was going to be a long, cold night. They'd had some rain on the road from Canberra and by the look of it, would run into more on the way back.

The passenger door opened abruptly, and the vinyl-covered front passenger seat was tilted forward. A young woman in sneakers and cuffed jeans scrunched herself up, climbed in the back and sat heavily. She tugged her lustrous dark hair into a ponytail and slipped on an elastic band, saying, "Hi again Irene, it's only me. I'm very sorry to get you involved in my troubles."

Charlotte peered in, a cream school case in hand. "Aunty, would you open the boot?"

"It's not locked. Just twist the handle. Hello Sylvia. Everything is going to be fine. Don't you worry."

Moments later, Charlotte clambered in and joined Sylvia in the back. Irene pushed the passenger seat back into place and pulled the door shut. Ignition on, she started the reluctant 800cc Austin engine, shoved the gearstick into first and scooted smoothly out of the gravel. She steered the curvy two-door vehicle through the back streets of Goulburn and out onto the highway toward Canberra. In her rearview mirror, she caught glimpses of the two young women talking, and heard snatches of conversation over the engine noise.

"Oh, dear God. I'm so scared they'll catch me. Lottie, they'll do their worst. Really they will. Father came knocking at Aunty Beryl's last night and I hid in the chook shed. Sister or not, he might kill her if he ever finds out she lied through her teeth. Or damn her to hell for eternity."

"Hush, darling. You know your Aunty doesn't believe in all that hellfire and damnation nonsense—she's not a runaway Catholic for nothing." Charlotte had an arm around Sylvia's huddled shoulders, her other hand holding Sylvia's. She raised chilled knuckles to her lips. "It's not going to happen. You're twenty-five and a voting adult. They have no right. Besides, they'll never find you. Aunty Irene will make sure of that." She paused to say louder, "Isn't that right, Aunty?"

"What's that, dear?"

"That they'll never find her."

"My very word, don't you worry about that. You're perfectly safe with me, I promise." Irene accelerated to sixty-three miles per hour, which was close to top speed for her chariot of choice. Night closed in. Streetlights disappeared rapidly behind them. Irene concentrated hard because her night vision wasn't what it used to be, but her gnarled hands steered with their familiar steely determination. By the dim light of the central instrument panel, she could detect the two silhouettes in the back seat. There was a lot of hugging, weeping, whispering and kissing going on. She grinned to herself. *Oh to be that young again, like fifty-odd years ago when she and her beloved Ruby first met.* She needed Ruby right now to ride shotgun. But Ruby had died on Christmas Day in 1950. They'd overindulged in roast hogget for lunch and taken an afternoon nap. Lying next to her, Irene's last memory of her dear sweet girl was Ruby's death rattle as her heart stopped. Ten years later, she still grieved.

Rain on the windscreen was smeared by the wipers, and Irene eased off the speed. She turned on the heater, pleased she had decided to have the expensive optional extra installed for Canberra's icy winters. The warmth cleared the damp inside the screen and thawed her toes. They were close to Lake George where the road narrowed to a sharp drop to the lake on the left side and a sheer wall of rock and undergrowth on the right. Visibility was not good.

The rockslide caught Irene by surprise. It wasn't much, but enough to litter her side of the road with a scattering of football size lumps that caused her to swerve, brake and swerve again. The car came to a lopsided halt, half on the bitumen and half on the gravel roadside. All three women straightened themselves and looked out the windows.

"I think we've blown a tyre." Irene pulled up the hood of her woollen car coat and scrabbled about with both hands in the open parcel tray. "There's a torch here somewhere."

Charlotte piped up, "Can I help?"

"Only if you can stay dry long enough." Irene flicked on a small metal torch and got out of the car. She walked all around it, stopping at the left back tyre that was perfectly square at the bottom. Two figures flanked her. Irene said, "No point us all getting wet. Lottie, find a scarf for your head. Sylvia, get back inside. No time to argue, please."

While Irene jimmied off the hub cap, Charlotte hauled the spare out of the boot. They positioned the jack under the best anchor point, jumped up and down on the wheel brace to loosen the nuts, jacked up the car and swapped the wheels. Charlotte threw the blown one into the boot, tossed in the jack and slammed the lid down, by which time they were both wet through.

Back in the car, Irene started the engine and moved forward cautiously, eyes peeled for further debris, but they had an uneventful trip all the way to her house. As she pulled into the Hargraves Crescent driveway, she became painfully aware that she was shivering. Truth be known, at eighty-two years young she was getting too old for this game. She knew she wasn't well. It was about time she took her own mortality seriously.

CHAPTER SEVENTEEN

Duscha was floating on a barge in a river of sleep when a loud thud rocked the boat and woke her. She opened one eye to peer at the bedside clock reading six ten a.m. There was a faint light beyond the curtains, dawn only just breaking. A distant magpie warbled with little enthusiasm for the chilly morning. She rubbed her eyes, folded back the bedclothes and swung feet to the floor, finding sheepskin slippers. Had she dreamed that noise? Possums, maybe? Only if they wore concrete footy boots.

She drew back the curtains illuminating the mess. Stuart had cut out all the damaged floorboards but had yet to source replacement material because of its pre-decimal sizing. In the meantime, he'd nailed plywood over the yawning holes so she couldn't fall through. Stub her toe, yes—fall through, no. The bad news was he'd said he had another job commitment and wouldn't be back to finish hers for another fortnight. The carpet was rolled back around the bed, a hazard she had to remember to step over or risk twisting an ankle. Dressing gown on, she walked past the bed and stopped. The art-deco mirror was facedown on the plywood. Her heart sank. It had to be smashed, surely?

She flicked on the light and knelt next to the mirror, studying both its anchoring screw in the chimney wall and the chain on its back, perfectly intact. Frowning, she lifted one side and propped the mirror against the wall. The glass was unblemished. She stood up and glared down at the misbehaving antique. Glancing around the room, she growled out loud, "That's ridiculous! You can stay there for now. Enough."

Under the shower, she decided she would have to ask her mother what to do about the leaping mirror when she had a chance. And she was expecting Honor to turn up around eight a.m. to put in the no-dig vegetable garden. They would be on their own for the day.

Warmly dressed in much-loved loose clothes more suited to manual work than anything else, she sat on the edge of the bed and absorbed the hum of morning traffic, the chatter of crimson rosellas and the ringing single high note of the exquisite king parrot. She had to think about Honor. More to the point, what she had intended by inviting the gardener to help her paint the house. The proposition had been entirely spontaneous, taking them both by surprise.

She saw Honor in her mind's eye and an ache started between her breasts. It was a telltale ache that she hadn't felt for a very long time and didn't want to analyse any time soon. It didn't bode an easy road ahead. The only thing that was certain was that she had to be very careful. Honor was in a long-term committed relationship and that was not to be interfered with, despite Stuart's scornful remark about Merrin. One's friends could not all like one's partner—she knew all about that. Noelle had polarised a few—personality clashes were simply inevitable. But what she sensed was that Honor wasn't happy.

Duscha combed fingers through her hair, fluffing it up and letting it fall softly on the nape of her neck. It was none of her business how happy or otherwise Honor might be. No relationship was perfect. And while the younger woman had once had a flattering schoolgirl crush on her, that was then and this was now. Much as she enjoyed Honor's company, it was incumbent upon her to keep a professional distance. She went looking for breakfast.

"Oh no! Don't you bloody dare!" Duscha heaved a bale of lucerne hay into the builder's wheelbarrow, intimating at Honor not to help. "I need you perfectly fit because there's heaps to do. Go make yourself useful with that line trimmer. Is it battery-powered?"

"Uh-huh. It'll take down the couch in no time." Honor pulled out the trimmer from amongst the hay bales and bags of manure in the back of her ute. She headed for the side gate, and Duscha followed with the wheelbarrow. Ten minutes later, Duscha had emptied the ute's cargo into the backyard, and Honor was whizzing through the veggie patch weeds. Duscha waved her to a halt.

"I'll be inside sanding and prepping the old woodwork for a fresh coat of white. Yell if you need anything. Or a cuppa when you want a break. Please don't overdo it."

Honor bobbed her head, squeezed the trimmer's trigger and sliced low into the grass.

From the kitchen window, Duscha watched the gardener working with an effortless rhythm, a long-sleeved maroon flannel shirt flapping loosely over her T-shirt. Yet, from the way she shifted her weight, she was still favouring that healing left foot.

In the living room, Duscha turned on radio station Triple J for background music, threw down drop sheets and attacked the main window frame with sandpaper. The woodwork had been repainted any number of times making it thick around hinges and catches. But she sanded only lightly, wary of the original paint that was probably lead-based—best left undisturbed. She was three-quarters of the way around the window when her mobile chimed.

Jim Fielding said, "Roxanne is contesting your father's will. She wants to see you in court."

"But what about the paternity test? It was positive. We're half-sisters, no mistake." Duscha slumped against a wall, shoved the cork sanding block into a back pocket and brushed white dust off her hand onto a thigh.

"Even so, she is contesting your entitlement to the cash inheritance."

"I don't understand, Jim. I know you'd rather not say, but she must have received the greater part of our father's estate, surely?"

"Confirmed. I'm telling you now because it will come out in court. She was given another house and a valuable commercial property. Plus twice as much cash. Since her mother and brother are deceased, it was only the two of you in the will."

"I see. Does she have a husband and kids? Is she after my house too?"

"The house is yours, Duscha. She can't touch it. And yes, she has a family."

Mouth a thin line, she said, "I have a family too. It just doesn't mirror her version. Let's get on with it then. Do what you have to do. Thanks, Jim."

She put down the phone and stared sightlessly, arms akimbo, toward the living room window. "*Blyat!* This can't be happening. *Blyat!*" She pulled the sanding block out of her pocket and chucked it hard at the front door where it made a satisfying thunk before falling to the floor.

From behind her, Honor said, "Have I caught you at a bad moment?"

Still glowering, Duscha turned and exhaled heavily. "Yeah, sort of. But I need a break anyway. A cup of tea and a shortbread will help. What about you?"

"I've cut the grass and put down the plastic. If you would give me a hand with opening bales, that would make life easier." Honor looked on as Duscha filled the kettle and put out mugs. "It must be handy to swear in a foreign language so no-one knows what you're saying."

Duscha chuckled, glancing across. "It wasn't that bad. Something like 'no…way' is a fair approximation."

"Can I help? I mean with whatever set you to sounding off in the first place."

"Maybe, but I'm sure you have problems of your own. How are you with people? When they get hostile, I struggle to understand what it is they really want."

"They usually want to be in the right." Honor shrugged. "I run a business and manage four female staff. Try me."

With a mug in each hand, Duscha said, "You'll find a packet of Scottish shortbreads in that cupboard. Come and sit down. Take a load off."

They sat at opposite ends of the sofa where Duscha briefly related what had happened with Roxanne so far, answering Honor's succinct questions until they fell into a companionable silence. Outside, a geriatric hippie on a Harley Davidson throttled past the house, and the windows rattled in protest.

Honor said, "Since you haven't met her, how about mediation? If the two of you had a conversation with a mediator present, perhaps you can work things out without setting foot in a courtroom. Because she's patently in the wrong by any legal measure and will lose in the end. A neutral party may help her see that."

Duscha counted slivers of grass embedded in Honor's navy twill pants, just below the knees. The gardener had taken off her work boots at the back door, leaving on thick grey socks with their own grassy adornment, and a hole in need of darning at the tip of one big toe. Holes in socks irritated Duscha. She thought, *darn 'em or chuck 'em!*

"Noelle—my partner—used to darn my socks. Who does yours?"

Honor peered at the hole and raised an eyebrow. "I do my own. Didn't know that one was there. What happened between you and her?"

"Breast cancer. She passed over."

Honor gaped, eyes widening. She shut her mouth with an audible clunk and swallowed hard. "Oh dear, Duscha, I'm so sorry."

"You weren't to know. It's a few years ago now." Duscha was inexplicably pinned to the sofa and didn't dare look up, unexpected welling tears getting the better of her.

"Whenever it was, I'm sorry for your loss. I'd best get on with the cardboard." Honor stood and backed away, apparently ready to dash down the hall. "Give me a hand when you feel like it."

Duscha nodded imperceptibly, not risking a reply. She started when Honor leaned over the back of the sofa and put both arms around her shoulders, across her collarbone, squeezed firmly and left a kiss in her tousled curls. She reached up, brushing a fleeting, capable hand as it left. She took to breathing deeply. It had been a while since anyone had comforted her, the last time likely being Noelle's funeral. This touch left her sensitive and vulnerable, yet grateful for the closeness. And an uncommon soul's willingness to listen with heart, and grant the selfless gift of compassion.

After Honor had left for the day, Duscha phoned Jim Fielding and asked him to negotiate a mediated meeting with her half-sister, as soon as could be arranged. If she and Roxanne could have a cordial conversation, that might be half the battle. Admittedly, she was curious about Roxanne's motives for starting a fight she was unlikely to win. Either Roxanne had had misleading legal advice or was being malicious. Since their father's will was written with zero ambiguity about his wishes, what could Roxanne possibly hope to achieve? Talking to her was a long shot, but worth a try.

At twilight, she made her way down to the veggie patch to where she and Honor had worked together putting down cardboard, spreading pats of lucerne hay and then bags of blended cow manure and mushroom compost topped with broken straw. Duscha had avoided conversation and eye contact, aware Honor watched her surreptitiously. When they had finished, Honor promised to come back with seedlings in two days' time because she was busy the next day with appointments for quotes. Apart from lunch with Michele at the National Library, Duscha would spend the day alone. She thought it was probably a good thing.

The plant-ready veggie patch looked promising. Honor had said that half a dozen perpetual spinach plants would see her with adequate greens through winter. All she had to do was water them once a week. And there was space for another crop, if she wanted to put in something else later. Tomorrow she would finish painting the new back door and its frame. At least the house would be safe and secure for winter. Since she was fatigued and emotionally washed out, an early night was in order. After the day's too-early start, she looked forward to a decent rest.

CHAPTER EIGHTEEN

Sitting at the computer, Honor's mood was buoyant. Merrin had volunteered the missing passwords and gone through how to access last year's and the current year's financial records, showing her everything that was in process, including what was outstanding and their credit-debit balances. Relieved, she was still going through it all when Merrin left for Lance's place for dinner and IT training. Logged off, Honor spun freely in the office chair and lapsed into reverie.

It had been the first time she'd touched Duscha of her own volition. It was an impulsive yet empathetic gesture that she would have done for anyone in similar circumstances. Even so, she'd savoured the realisation that her teenage fantasy lover was very real: a human animal nursing a deep grief and vulnerable because of it. This was another side to Duscha—the armed-and-dangerous centaur—who obviously had an inner life to which Honor had been largely oblivious. That vulnerability brought Duscha down from her pedestal and into Honor's world, making her more approachable. Something had shifted in that moment that brought them shoulder to shoulder and onto a more equal footing.

And Merrin had done as she was asked. It was heartening. Honor remained merely relieved that her suspicion was groundless, rather than feeling closer to Merrin, but their relationship was back on an even keel.

Was the act of her putting her arms around Duscha, albeit briefly, a step too far? She was undeniably gravitating toward Duscha who was like an irresistible force, but a definite threat to her security—her whole lifestyle and future. For Duscha to be even remotely interested in Honor was both fantastic and terrifying. And unlikely. Duscha still grieved, that much was blindingly obvious. Was it possible to carry that kind of grief and harbour thoughts of loving another in the one heart? Honor seriously doubted it in a way that was somehow reassuring.

CHAPTER NINETEEN

Duscha met her old friend from school Michele in the National Library's sprawling foyer dominated by artist Leonard French's stained glass windows over the entrance. They shared a hug and a kiss on both cheeks and headed for Bookplate, the library's café. Seated at a window overlooking Canberra's central lake, they both ordered vegetable fritters and coffee.

"Good of you to fit me in, Mischa."

"I've got plenty of time-in-lieu to use up. How is the house coming along?" Michele pushed glossy red-framed glasses back up her nose, her inquisitive grey eyes sizing up Duscha's hands. "I can see what you've been doing."

Duscha rubbed her fingers. "Paint is annoyingly difficult to get out from under the nails. And there's much more to do yet. I've hired the gardener to help me, starting tomorrow."

"I didn't think she did that sort of handywoman thing."

"It's only because she's not yet a hundred percent fit. And I can definitely use the help." A smiling waitress put generous plates in front of them. "And we work well as a team."

"A team, huh?" Michele peered at her. "Look out, sweetie. She's just your type."

"Do I have one? She's nothing like Noelle in either looks or personality. Besides, she's spoken for and has been for years."

Michele took a mouthful and rummaged in her handbag. "Hearts have a mind of their own. Be careful what you assume. Now about your great-aunt Irene. I went through the turn-of-last-century microfiche and found a couple of write-ups in the Sydney papers, plus a few society page photos and a marriage record. Have a look at this lot." She passed over a flimsy sheet protector jammed with folded photocopies.

Duscha pulled out a sheet and laid it next to her plate, reading as she ate. "This seems to be about her giving a suffrage speech in Martin Place in Sydney. Are they all like that?"

Michele smoothed down her neat mid-brown bob, sat back and considered her dear friend. "I'm realising that research is not your thing, sweetie. Would you like a précis of what's there? Then you can peruse it at your leisure."

Duscha grinned. "You're an angel."

"All right already. The work is done. No need to suck up. Let me finish my meal first." In contented silence, they ate steadily until coffee was served.

Scooping foam from the edges of the broad coffee cup, Michele said, "Irene was born in Sydney in 1878, the only surviving daughter of a wealthy businessman who imported a plethora of goods into The Rocks. She was active in the women's suffrage movement around 1900, given to making speeches and lobbying for women's right to vote. For her twenty-first birthday in 1899, her father commissioned a gold suffragette-style bar brooch set with amethysts, emeralds, and diamonds from a Sydney jeweller named Angus Armfield. There's a photo of her—an attractive blonde—coming out in society in which she wears said brooch. You can see for yourself—"

Duscha blurted, "That must be the one Aunt Charlotte put in the chocolate tin with Sylvia's letters. It's very sweet. And quite pretty. Sorry, do go on."

Michele said, "Angus must have courted Irene for a few years. Women won the vote in 1902. They married in 1903 in a documented society wedding. Over time, he owned and ran three lucrative Armfield's jewellery shops across Sydney. I couldn't find any children's birth records for them. Over in Britain, the fight for women's voting rights was ongoing. There's a newspaper article about her travelling around England in 1910 as a guest speaker under her maiden name. For the English, she was living proof that real change could happen. And then the Great War started which halted the cause for British women. Angus enlisted in 1917 and was killed the same year. Widowed Irene successfully ran Armfield's until the late 1920s when they were bought out by another jewellery company. The trail vanishes until she turns up here in Canberra in 1927, under her maiden name again."

Duscha said, "You wonder how she managed on her own. She must have been exceptionally capable for the times."

Michele finished her lukewarm coffee. "I admit I was impressed. But you have to remember she inherited wealth and position, thanks to the men in her life. Without them, it would have been a very different story."

"Did women have any choice back then? The only way to own anything was by inheritance. Or so I understand."

"Indeed. We have many more options now. Not to mention freedom. How quickly we forget how far we've come, eh? Let's just be thankful we're not living the way women had to a hundred years ago. Anyway, if there's anything else you want me to research let me know, but that's about all I can find about your great-aunt."

"Hold on, I've just remembered she wasn't alone." Duscha slid her cup onto its saucer. "Aunt Charlotte mentioned that Irene had a secretary named Ruby something. Milborne I think, who is supposed to have lived with her. Would you have a quick look? Just on the off chance."

"Okay, will do. And it's just occurred to me that, if your great-aunt sold off a chain of jewellery shops, then she must have had considerable wealth when she came to what would have been sleepy Canberra in the late twenties. Without children of her own, did she leave it all to your Aunt Charlotte?"

Duscha shook her head. "I don't think so. Aunt Charlotte had a career as a nurse, which she probably wouldn't have pursued if she'd had money. And Aunt Charlotte would have willed whatever she had to her brother, my father, like as not. There is no way of knowing for sure. But I might ask my mother to look into it, just to see what she can pick up."

With a shrug and a smile, Michele said, "Why not consult the lovely Valeria? And I'll see what I can find out about Ruby Milborne, either way."

Duscha drove home on automatic pilot, her thoughts occupied with what Michele had told her. Once indoors, she checked her morning's handiwork on the back door, the semigloss white paint having since become touch dry. She would give it a fine sanding in the morning and a final coat. It looked good and she was well pleased with the result. Tomorrow she would ask Honor what she thought of the final colour choices of mauve and light green.

After her evening meal, she settled on the sofa with Michele's research documents to read the articles about Irene's exploits, both in Australia and particularly in England. Her great-aunt must have been passionate about women's suffrage to go all that way by ship. In those days, the journey was an uncomfortable six-week voyage that ended literally on the other side of the world.

CHAPTER TWENTY

London, July 1910

Inside a noisy greasy spoon in east London's Canning Town, Irene sat with four other women who were fellow campaigners for British women's suffrage. A fry up, much like a full English breakfast, had been served on tin plates alongside thick white cups of steaming hot tea. Every table was occupied, with a constant stream of nattering East End locals either coming in or leaving to go about their business.

Irene leaned forward to ask, "What's this spicy black meat? It's marvellous with the fried bread."

Across from her, Ruby Milborne fixed her with an amused glance from soulful deep blue eyes. Her lustrous black hair was pinned high on her head where a peaked cap was fixed in place with a hatpin. At her throat, a lacy Peter-Pan-collared cream blouse sported a floppy purple tie that disappeared beneath her coachman's black box coat. A pair of long-cuffed leather driving gloves lay next to her plate.

"Black pudding. Pig's blood sausage to those who don't know. Try it dipped in the egg."

Irene paused to look at the stuff on her fork and with a shrug, shoved it in her mouth. "I've eaten stranger things. This tastes better than most. Goodness, there's enough on my plate to feed a starving navvy."

"Folk work hard around here. Since it's going to be another tiring day on our feet, make the most of it, especially the Spitalfields pork sausage. It's made just around the corner."

Nursing her tea, Irene sat back and soaked up the bustling atmosphere so unlike what she was used to in Sydney. The women at her table were dressed in various muted colours of blouse and ankle-length skirt, topped with a long jacket and finished with black-buttoned boots. Much like the other ladies named Annie, Susan, and May, Irene also had her hair piled up and topped by a wide-brimmed hat. It was covered in fake flowers, feathers, and bows, and firmly skewered into place with tipped hatpins.

"May I sit up front with you today?"

Ruby looked up in alarm. "Miss Coxall you'll get quite grubby. But I do have a spare pair of goggles, if you insist."

"Please stop calling me that. I'm Irene, thank you. In truth, I'm Mrs. Angus Armfield, but I won't thank you to call me that either!" She picked up her knife to saw at a sausage. "The inside of your van is frightfully stuffy and uncomfortable. If you don't mind."

"As you wish, Irene." Ruby's gaze fell on the plain gold band on Irene's left ring finger and then lingered on the gold bar brooch pinned to her green blouse. The brooch was set with a central clear stone, flanked by a pair of stones: one green and one purple. "If I may say your brooch is most becoming."

"It was a twenty-first birthday gift from my father, to do with my suffragist campaigning in Australia. I wear it always. Do we have a long way to go today?"

Ruby said, "The plan is for two stops not far from here, where we are expected to rouse the crowd and rally them to the cause. But we'll not be too late because tomorrow is the march through Hyde Park. That will be a monster. Banners and buntings and a very long walk!"

Five ladies traipsed out to Ruby's blue Albion van. With the others safely seated on chairs in the back of the van alongside their equipment, Irene stepped up off the running board and into the driver's cramped cab. From outside the driver's window, Ruby reached in, flicked a black switch and pulled out a knob on the dashboard that was labelled "choke." Standing at the front of the van, she leaned down, took a firm hold of the crank handle and swung it vigorously. The engine burst into life and set to chugging contentedly. Ruby leaped into the cab, pumped the accelerator and found first gear first time. Sticking out an indicating arm, she steered away from the buildings into the motley stream of passing cars, vans, two-and four-wheeled horse-drawn carts and the occasional omnibus.

The noise was considerable, causing Irene to keep her thoughts to herself. Instead of the goggles, she wrapped a long scarf over her hat to cross most of her face, one hand holding it in position, the other hanging on to the side door for dear life. After ten minutes of driving around slower vehicles and weaving in and out of traffic, Ruby pulled in to park outside a town hall.

Irene risked a question. "Where are we?"

"Bow. Down the road is Sylvia Pankhurst's East London Federation of Suffragettes establishment. Time for the banner."

Let loose, the three ladies bundled out the back of the van. Red-haired Susan helped the others to each put on a purple, white, and green sash reading "Votes for Women." Irene had her own hand-made version that she shrugged on over her coat. Then came a tall banner bearing the same slogan they unfurled between them. Irene ended up holding one of the supporting posts, while the three ladies walked arm in arm with her. As the strongest, Ruby carried the other post alone. They set off down the road and must have walked at least a mile, stopping frequently to banter with locals who glared or smiled or shouted or laughed or clapped or waved. And sometimes asked questions. The morning all but gone, they found themselves outside a one-time baker's shop emblazoned in gold with "Votes for Women." They rolled up the banner and went inside. While the others talked with the women running the place, Irene bought a small round tin-plate pin with purple, white and green stripes as a keepsake.

Once again outside, they resurrected the banner and walked all the way back to the van, noticeably slower. Ruby fired up the Albion that carried them to Stepney. They walked a circuit of the Stepney Green Gardens, dawdling back to the van, footsore and too weary to hold up the banner. To everyone's relief, Ruby drove them up to Bethnal Green Road where they sought out a tea shop for refreshments.

All the worse for wear, the women flopped indecorously onto straight-backed chairs. Blowing across the top of her cup to cool her brew, Irene asked anyone who might answer, "Where are we staying tonight?"

With a face as long as a lighthouse, May said, "There's a women-only doss house two streets away from here. It's clean and comfortable enough at only one-and-six for the night. May have to share a bed if they're busy. But you can sluice yourself down and fill up on bread and jam for breakfast. It's in the price."

"That's not at all expie for around here," said Ruby.

All Irene wanted to do was unbutton her ankle boots, if she could find a place to lie down, but it was obvious that wasn't going to happen. The ladies were far too content to take tea and natter over slabs of fruity loaf. But she didn't mind too much because her work here was nearly done. In two days' time, she would sail home to Sydney. Tomorrow, a rousing round of speeches in Hyde Park would be her last contribution to the cause. She had enjoyed much of the trip, plus the good-natured, if terribly earnest women alongside her. But then her country had given women the vote already and, once upon a time, she had been equally fervent.

Her thoughts came to their very capable driver, Ruby Milborne. Where had the woman acquired such manly skills? She would have to ask before they parted ways. Sitting quietly in that cosy tea house, Irene sensed a looming melancholy that drained her far more than the occasion merited. Was she homesick? That must be it.

The doss house was packed. Like it or not, it was two to a narrow bed, with ten beds to each long room. Around each bed ran a head-height orange curtain that afforded some physical privacy. Almost a corridor away was a water closet for the night soil.

"Thank the Lord for small mercies," muttered Irene. "At least there's plumbing."

The other three had been quick to choose where they wanted to bed down, which left Irene stranded with Ruby—she of the very broad shoulders—not her first choice for comfort's sake. Next to each bed stood a rickety wooden table with a lit candlestick and spare matches. At the end of the bed was a dresser with a porcelain washbowl holding a jug full of water.

Ruby eyed off the amenities. "Would you mind stepping out while I wash?"

Irene slipped through the drawn curtain, following the murmur of gossip that drew her to the queue outside the water closet. Later, she strolled back deliberately slowly, crossing paths with Ruby who was wearing a long nightgown, her hair freshly brushed and plaited. Concealed by the curtain, Irene could strip off her clobber down to her chemise and wash, a welcome ritual. But she would have given her eyeteeth for a proper bath. She slipped into the bed, sat upright and tied back her abundant wavy blond hair with a green cotton ribbon. Idly, she rubbed her left shoulder that had started to ache more than was bearable.

Ruby shut the curtain behind her and climbed into the bed. Around them was the pleasant murmur of women talking, the occasional laugh or fit of giggles, derisive snort or teasing profanity. Someone guffawed and bellowed, "What a load of footle! Your cousin Mabel? She's off her bleeding onion, not a word of a lie. And don't you go getting the hump with me for tumbling to it. Bleeding toe rag."

Irene squirmed on the hard mattress. "I hope there aren't any bugs for us to fight over. I'm afraid it's going to be a long night."

"Rest assured, Mrs. Angus Armfield. We'll have to make the best of it." Ruby snuffed out the candle and shuffled down the bed, her back to Irene. Others still had their candles alight—it wasn't completely dark until they were all snuffed. Conversation dwindled, finally petering out.

Once horizontal, Irene noticed there was a window only a few feet above the bed that was bright with a near-full moon. Her eyes adjusted until she could see passably well in the gloom. Careful not to back into Ruby, she perched her head on the slab-like pillow they were sharing, trusting exhaustion would ensure some kip. With her eyes squeezed shut to simulate sleep, the left side of her body she lay on had other ideas. Pain began to radiate from under the shoulder blade, up into her neck and across to her arm. She stuck the errant arm out into the void beyond the bed, clinging on to the horsehair mattress with her right hand to maintain position.

"I stand corrected. It appears I'm sharing with Miss Fidget, not Mrs. Armfield. Give it a rest, won't you?"

Pain and fatigue got the better of Irene. She blurted hotly, "Sorry. I can't help it."

Ruby sat up, whispering, "What's wrong?"

"My left shoulder is giving me gyp. I think it's from carrying the banner pole. It's played up before." She dragged herself to a sitting position and leaned back against the wall, wedged up against Ruby. Moonlight cast a ghostly glow over their tiny curtained haven.

"Shush. Keep it down." They sat in silence for a moment and then continued in whispers. "I might be able to help. Turn and put your legs over the side of the bed. Sit still."

Irene couldn't read Ruby's expression, but she did as she was told. Ruby wriggled across and slung her legs either side of Irene's hips, her hands landing lightly on Irene's sore shoulder. Fingertips pressed and moved, pressed and moved until Irene winced. There, Ruby lingered, slowly increasing pressure when she found a sensitive spot, and then moving on to the next, concentrating on the upper spine and neck.

Irene whispered, "How do you know what you're doing?"

Voice soft and low, Ruby replied, "My mother was a laundress. She worked with a China woman called Lee who would use her fingers like this on the other women who broke down. She showed me what to do. You push just hard enough to make the muscle let go, wherever it hurts."

"Is this why you grew up strong?"

"Nothing to do with it. I started helping my mother when I was seven years old. I would turn the mangle for her while she fed it clothes. All day doing washing for the toffs. Shirts and collars, blouses and underclothes, sheets and towels, all boiled in a massive copper, washed with soda and rinsed, ready for the mangle. It was sweaty, hard graft. And never-ending."

"She must have depended on you."

Ruby's hands slid over to Irene's chest and stopped. "What's this?"

"My brooch. I've pinned it to my chemise to keep it safe. I'd hate for it to stray."

Ruby's fingers pressed into the shoulder socket where Irene's arm began. Irene let out a low, lingering moan. "That hurts so badly, it's good." Tittering started among the surrounding bedmates.

"For pity's sake, shush! You'll have us thrown out."

"Whatever for?"

Ruby seemed to choke. "I've done all I can. The problem is, however, that the only way we're going to get any sleep is by spooning. If I lie on my right side with you in front of me, back toward me, you can protect your shoulder. If you can tuck your left hand into your chest, that would be even better. Let's try it. Move over to this side and I'll get in behind you."

Irene slid back across the bed, as she was bidden. Ruby climbed in behind her, slid her right arm under Irene's neck and lay still. Relatively pain free, Irene sighed with relief, her breathing slowing to the pattern of someone on the edge of sleep. In a place deep inside, she noted a foreign sensation of complete peace and utter safety, entirely attributable to the encircling arm. Maybe she imagined the brush of warm lips at the nape of her neck? As it was, she was too tired to care.

In the broad light of day, a score of women all in white marched into Hyde Park. With a drum and fife band fallen in behind them, they carried a banner held high. Being their honoured guest speaker, Irene was front and centre. Ruby was discreetly off to one side, dressed in her usual driver's coat and clutching one of the banner's posts. At one point on the path, they were halted by a man carrying a camera on a tripod. He dashed out in front of them, proclaiming that he was from the Daily Mirror. Keen for any and all publicity, they stood proudly while he fiddled with the apparatus. When he'd finished they made their way through the thousand-fold throng, dispersing to any one of the four speakers' platforms strategically placed around the park.

Irene climbed up high to a platform to where a group of unsmiling women were seated on bentwood chairs, waiting for her to take her turn. Below was a sea of floral hats and gentlemen's boaters, plus a handful of uniformed bobbies keeping the crowd in order.

"Good day to you all," Irene boomed out, waiting for heads to turn. Many had no chance of hearing her, but she spoke as loudly as she thought she could maintain to say her piece. "I come from Australia where women won their enfranchisement, their right to vote, over eight years ago."

A smattering of clapping and two wolf whistles made her smile fleetingly.

"Thank you. Australia is the better for it, as will be Great Britain when she follows suit. Your womenfolk who fight for the vote are fighting to be free and equal because they are not now. When a British woman does the same job as a man, she is paid less. Many working women earn barely a quid a week. Some a mere few shillings with which they pay rent, support children, the old and the poorly. A twelve-year-old girl can be legally married off. Who thinks she's fit to bear children and take the brunt of running a household?"

Protesting grunts and boos rippled through the crowd.

"As a wife, she could work every day of her life for her family and, in the end, her husband can take every penny she earned to do with whatever he fancies. And if he really wants to get rid of her, he can say she was unfaithful. Never mind that he could be a serial philanderer, because the law wouldn't blink an eye. The law says he can take her children and throw her out, make her homeless and penniless. Where's the fairness in that?"

A gruff voice called out, "Bet the tart deserved it!" Ripples of laughter rose and fell away.

"You could be right," said Irene, targeting the crowd where the voice came from. "Maybe she did. But the law should treat the husband and wife as equals. Chances are he was a tart long before her!"

Hooting, more feminine laughter burst out and faded.

"Truth is, the husband decides every blind thing about the children. How they're raised, where they go to school, even what religion they take up. The wife has no say whatsoever *under the law*. For centuries women have trusted men to make the law, to legislate fairly and in the best interests of all concerned. Look where that has got British women today. Inequality is entrenched in the law. Why is this so?"

"Oh, or'right. Tell us!" Another wave of chuckles.

Irene bellowed, "Because legislators have no time for the disenfranchised! There have been no political consequences for ignoring the plight of British women. But there are now because we are not going away, we will not stop fighting until we get the vote."

Waving a finger, she paced back and forth across the platform, leaning out over the crowd.

"Don't make the mistake of thinking that women want the vote for a lark. Women want the vote to change laws, to bring better conditions for their families, communities and themselves so that they are genuinely the equal of men. Morally, industrially, socially and politically. Give women the vote!"

She threw her hands in the air, waved briefly and clambered down from the platform, the sound of clapping and whistling following her exit.

With a satisfied smile, Irene picked her way through the crowd in the direction of the next platform, at which she would give much the same speech, depending on the crowd's reaction. She enjoyed stirring it up and bantering with the hecklers, knowing that many did listen. And if she could get through to them with simple facts, it might make them think differently. Perhaps they would in turn influence others to re-think their attitudes. Only three more opportunities to incite change remained. She would do her level best to make them count.

Midafternoon, Ruby fell into step beside Irene who was strolling, on the lookout for a spot to wait for the others. The crowd was dispersing. Bunting was being taken down and packed away. Platforms stood empty, ready for dismantling.

"Good afternoon, Irene." Ruby's considering look flickered appreciatively over Irene's somewhat dishevelled form. "It's been a long day for you. I've been charged with taking whomever I can back to the East End. Do you need a lift to a particular destination?"

Irene looked up and spoke softly, her voice a little the worse for wear. "My belongings are in your van. If I may accompany you for a last look at London from up front, I would be obliged. Thank you, Ruby."

They caught up with four women waiting at one of the exits who bundled themselves into the back of the van parked nearby. As Ruby drove through the still-busy streets, Irene savoured the sights and smells, including the unavoidable horse droppings and exhaust fumes. In the heart of the city, they passed train stations, new hotels, Selfridges and other glamorous shops where the footpaths were scattered with people shopping, paying visits, en route to elsewhere or just leisurely promenading.

Toward the East End, the shops dwindled to manufacturing sites that multiplied the closer they drove to the Thames River docklands. Ruby went out of her way to deliver each woman to her chosen destination, while Irene absorbed everything into memory. In Poplar, Susan was the last drop off. She briefly waved to them before disappearing into a corner public house.

With the Albion's engine idling, Ruby asked, "Where can I take you?"

"Well, my idea is to take the train to Portsmouth in the morning. Do you know of a comfortable hotel where I can stay the night? Preferably near a station."

Ruby slowly shook her head. "There's nothing much that's decent in the East End. Unless you mean something like the Great Eastern in Shoreditch. It's the newest, but rather expie."

"Ruby, I'm not short of a quid. And I want somewhere with a good bed, its own water closet and a bath. My hair needs washing before I step onboard a cramped ship, with its barest amenities, for the next forty-odd days."

With a patient nod, Ruby accelerated the van down the street, twisting and turning through narrower lanes and along wider carriageways, skilfully avoiding slower vehicles and congestion. She pulled into a curving street that wound along the forecourt of a magnificent six-storey red brick building and parked near the entrance.

Irene made no move to step down from the van, a sense of urgency piquing until she felt vaguely bereft, as if cut adrift from some critical destination. It dawned on her that she was not willing to see the last of her enigmatic companion. Not yet.

"I have a favour to ask. Share a room with me, Ruby. My shout."

"I beg your pardon? Why would you shout?"

"I mean I'll pay for everything. A spacious room for two, a meal, a bottle of fizz. Whatever takes your fancy. Please do me the honour…grant me the pleasure of your company for my last night in London. It would mean a good deal to me."

Ruby looked at her, solemnly wide-eyed, and Irene knew she was losing her audience. Eyes downcast, she took a risk without knowing precisely what she was risking. "In truth, I want to get to know you as a friend. As much as you are prepared to tell because I find you…very interesting." Then she returned Ruby's steady gaze.

For a moment the driver looked away, staring out beyond the van's bonnet. Irene held her breath until Ruby smiled almost imperceptibly, graciously inclining her head.

"If that is your heart's desire. The Great Eastern has a top-hole reputation. In truth, it will be an experience I'm not likely to repeat. I would be delighted to join you on this opportune occasion."

* * *

In the hotel's foyer, the concierge gave a discreetly waiting porter the key to a room on the second floor. The uniformed young man gathered up Irene's suitcase, taking the marble staircase ahead. Ruby admired the elaborate mosaic floors before climbing the stairs with Irene. The room featured floral wallpaper, pinstriped carpets, and voluminous drapes, all dominated by a large brass bed. The porter left the suitcase and door key, bowing his way out.

Ruby hovered, unsure as to what was expected of her. Irene opened what turned out to be a connecting door into a bathroom with a porcelain lavatory, hand basin, and cast-iron bath. Ruby could see half a dozen monogrammed towels with bars of Pears soap piled up on top.

At the bathroom door, Irene said, "Would you mind lighting the fire? I know it's not cold, but it is a little damp. I've ordered a pot of tea from room service, plus two freshly laundered nightgowns, one for each of us if you would like to use it. I'm going to run a bath and wash my hair. And there should be a menu from the kitchen included. Perhaps you might read it out to me when it arrives? Thank you." With a tentative smile, she disappeared inside. The harsh sound of splashing water filling the bath echoed through the suite.

Looking around, Ruby found a box of matches on the mantelpiece. She crouched to light the coal fire that drew slowly at first. Then she sat back in one of the two wing chairs while the fire took hold enough to throw comforting warmth.

The room was nothing like the kind of place in which she usually slept. If not bedding down on a narrow bunk in her mother's cramped few rooms in Poplar, she would camp at any one of a number of boarding houses around London. Here amongst the finery, she was out of her depth, yet determined to make the most of every precious moment with the remarkable Irene Coxall.

Her head was more than a little turned by not only Irene's comely face and figure, but also by her friendly manner that was extraordinary from someone definitely so well-to-do. Perhaps Australians were like that? Devoid of previous experience of Antipodeans, Ruby had no idea. Part of her was cautiously suspicious of Irene's motives, but she couldn't think, for the life of her, what possible ulterior motive might lie behind the invitation. It wasn't like she had anything worth stealing! Well, nothing except her peaked hat, driving gloves, and greatcoat. And what likely use would Irene have for them? She dismissed the thought with a wave of the hand.

More importantly, she had Cyril's van overnight. Her deliveryman friend lent it to her in exchange for mechanical maintenance, an arrangement that suited them both admirably. Still, when she returned it tomorrow—a day late—he might have something to say. From where she was sitting right now, it was a hundred times worth a smutty mouthful from Cyril.

She closed her eyes, struck by the memory of Irene's lily-white throat, so warm and soft beneath her stealthy lips. The woman couldn't be interested in her that way, could she? Under her breath, she said to herself, "Leave it out, Ruby-girl…what a load of footle!"

Ruby jumped up to place the fireguard in place, just as a uniformed chambermaid entered carrying a silver tray set with a Royal Albert patterned tea service, a menu tucked in one corner. She placed two nightgowns on the buffet table and slipped out of the room. Ruby poured herself a tea that she took with the menu back to the wing chair where she studied its offerings. From the distant pouring sounds, Irene was in the midst of washing her hair.

Ruby cleared her throat. "Do you want me to read this to you now?"

"If you would, please."

To save shouting, Ruby rose and stood by the bathroom door. "Fried eel. Fried oysters. Lobster patties. Sorrel soup. Pommes frites. French beans."

"What would you like?"

"Fried oysters, pommes frites and French beans."

"I'd like to try the fried eel as well. And a bottle of *premiere cuvee* fizz. Would you order that from the concierge? I'll be out in a minute." Judging from the sound of water rushing noisily down the exposed pipes, the plug had been pulled. "I'll refill the bath for you while you're out. If the maid left the nightgowns, would you bring me one please?"

"Are you covered?"

"As good as."

Taking two steps into the bathroom, Ruby draped the pale gown over the handbasin near where Irene stood with a towel wrapped around her middle. With legs as white as milk bottles, she was using a second towel to blot her hair dry. The fresh scent of Pears soap and the loveliness of her companion threatened to disarm Ruby completely. She backed out saying, "Won't be long."

* * *

Irene beamed, eyes bright. "This has to be the best picnic I've had for years." The two freshly bathed and gowned women sat either side of a small parquetry table cluttered with cloche-covered dishes, their dinner plates and two shallow champagne glasses. "I think I prefer the oysters to the eel."

"Both go well with the buttered beans. The chopped hazelnuts were surprisingly good." Ruby took a sip and contemplated the glowing coals. "I think I've had ample sufficiency."

"You are frightfully well-spoken for an East End girl, you know that don't you?"

Ruby looked over her glass. "Is that what you find 'very interesting' about me?"

"It's true that I'm intrigued about your background. I'm asking, if you're of a mind to tell me."

They both sipped in silence. As if her thoughts had fallen back into unpleasant memories, Ruby said, "My father was the youngest son of a large Welsh family. Well-educated landed gentry. In his early twenties, he fell out with his parents and came to London to find his own fortune. A failed venture or two later, he found work helping to build the new horseless carriages. Then he got the chuck, but he earned a living repairing any and every kind of automobile because he was good with his hands…good mechanically. As a child I would watch him work, hand him tools and try to help. Anything to get away from the mangle!" She chuckled, casting an amused glance at Irene who smiled back, watching intently.

"He taught me the basics of engines, of how and why they work. And what can go wrong. It's been useful, but it's dirty work. Not what I prefer. Or want to do for long."

Irene sat up straighter. "Do you have any idea what that might be?"

"Since you ask. He also taught me letters and numbers, which is a sight more than most of the other nippers in Canning Town ever learned. After this summer's holidays, I go back to commercial college where I'm learning to type, to take Pitman's shorthand and hope to gain a diploma in bookkeeping. That's where the jobs for single women are growing into the foreseeable future. In businesses and offices." Ruby rested her thoughtful gaze on the wedding band on Irene's hand draped around her champagne glass. "I'm not the marriage and motherhood kind. It behooves me to support myself in all things, as best I can."

Irene harrumphed. "You keep your cards close to your chest. I would never have suspected. I'm impressed by both your foresight and initiative. And can't help but think that you'll do well."

"As well as any woman of my class can in a world of male privilege. That's why I chose to be a suffragist, albeit only a driver."

"It all helps the cause. We don't have such a rigid class system in Australia. Those who are enterprising and willing to work hard can go far. The country was built on the 'backs of sheep' and British convicts who made the most of every opportunity. It's a pity English attitudes curtail your own enterprising folk, such as yourself."

"But what of you, Mrs. Armfield?"

Irene met Ruby's inquisitive look and rose abruptly from the table. "Would you please press the bell for room service to have the remains of our meal cleared away? And order a noggin of whiskey for me, plus one for yourself if you fancy a nightcap. I'm just going to freshen up." She made haste to the bathroom where she rinsed her mouth with salt water, washed her hands and sat on the edge of the bath. She could still see herself in the mirror as she vigorously brushed her wild blond mane into some semblance of neatness, now that it was almost dry. Green cotton ribbon in hand, she tied it back and paused to reflect on Ruby.

How much did she believe the driver's stories? In London town that teemed with conmen and opportunists, could she trust her own instincts...her own judgment of Ruby's character? To the casual eye, Ruby seemed to be a model of integrity. Yet how likely was that, given her background? Her class. Irene had to raise her eyebrows and ask herself, *look who's being class conscious now?*

She shivered at her reflection. Had this city, with its culture of competitive suspicion, got the better of her? Stranger to London she certainly was, but babe in the woods she wasn't. She knew a good deal about business, and she knew people. That sense of warmth, safety, and comfort she'd noticed every time she came close to Ruby was not imaginary. It deserved some credence. So be it. She put away the hairbrush and opened the door.

Ruby had turned off all lights, except for a standard lamp near the brass bed. She stood in front of the dying fire, dark hair plaited behind her back. "The maid promised a decanter and two glasses, any minute now. I can only apologise if my inquiry made you uncomfortable. That was not my intention. Your business is your own."

Irene was about to reply when a maid knocked and entered with a tray that she placed nearby on the buffet table. She glanced at both women, backing out with a quick bob of the head. Irene poured a modest noggin into each whiskey tumbler. "With water?" When Ruby shrugged, Irene added a splash. "No apology necessary. I didn't think you were interested enough to ask. You took me by surprise. Perhaps you were being polite."

"Not a bit of it," said Ruby. "I would like to know more about you."

"Let's take this to bed, shall we?" Irene held out a glass.

They sat up in the brass bed, their backs supported by too many European and standard pillows. Irene offered up her tumbler saying, "To women's suffrage. And us who fight on."

Ruby clinked her tumbler, took a small mouthful, and put it on the bedside table. "Do you have children?"

After a quick sip and a hasty cough, Irene said, "None that carried full term. Then the doctor advised that we not try again, or it could finish me off. We've been married seven years now. Angus was heartbroken for at least a year. His sadness was overcome by long hours of sheer hard work. My husband is a jeweller. A designer, manufacturer, and retailer of very fine commercial and custom-made jewellery. He owns shops across Sydney that he stocks and manages, in part with my help. He has excellent business sense and knows what people like to buy. We specialise in suffrage ornaments and jewels, preferably with an Australian theme. Such pieces are inordinately popular. He designed and made the brooch my father gave me."

"A beautiful thing. You've not pinned it to your gown."

Studying Ruby, Irene put her tumbler to one side. "I trust it won't stray tonight."

Ruby guffawed and poked Irene's arm. "You cheeky Australian blighter! What do you take me for?"

"It wasn't you I was worried about in that doss house," Irene protested. "I nearly went to bed fully dressed thinking they would have thieved anything and everything, even my clothes, given half a chance!"

"What tosh. You were perfectly safe with me."

Irene searched out and found one of Ruby's hands, held it firmly. "Was I? That kiss on my neck. What do you call that?"

Ruby seemed mildly contrite and took her time before replying. She stared up at the dimly lit ornate ceiling. "I call it appreciation and perhaps a kind of reverence. For in the moonlight, your translucent throat filled me with awe. A magical vision of loveliness. Some might say affection. Others might call it temptation." She glanced down at their hands entwined. "It was just a kiss. What can I say?"

"Just a kiss. What are you, Ruby?"

Ruby turned her head, chin held high. "I know more what I'm not than what I am. For instance, I know I'm not the marrying kind. Take from that what you will."

They sat in a silence that hung between them.

Matter-of-factly, Irene said, "My shoulder is in need of attention."

Lips barely twitching, Ruby's eyes darkened. "Then we should attend to it. Swing your legs over the side." And she shuffled over to slip a thigh either side of Irene's hips, thumbs quick to probe shoulder and neck, seeking the sharp intake of breath that flagged a sore spot. She pressed and adjusted, pressed and shifted her thumbs and fingertips, then rubbed both shoulders from the spine outward.

Irene relaxed back into Ruby's chest, allowed arms to encircle her waist and lips to explore her neck. "Would you hold me like you did last night?"

Obligingly, Ruby scooted backward, and Irene followed her, backing into waiting arms that cradled firmly. Irene snuggled in as close as she feasibly could. "It's beyond my understanding, but I feel utterly safe with you like I never have with another. I would trust you with my very life, which frightens me. Do you find that as peculiar as I do?" And she swivelled to look at Ruby, breath fast against her throat.

"Downright queer." Ruby found Irene's mouth that leapt backward at first touch, like a startled kitten. And then sought her out tentatively…eagerly. They kissed into the complicit night.

In the early morning gloom, Ruby said, "What do you call this?" Irene's drowsy head was languishing on her shoulder, one arm and a leg slung across her torso.

"This?" Irene's eyes fluttered open. "I call this unutterable fondness. At home. At ease. Closeness." She glanced up. "A particular understanding."

"Ah, we have an understanding. And you go home today."

Irene moved and propped herself up on an elbow. "Needs must. I have a husband who relies on me for certain business matters. He is a good man. Kind, considerate, and generous. And attentive, although he longer troubles me with manly needs of the flesh." Then she sat up, putting a pillow behind her back, against the brass uprights. "Ruby, whatever this is between us now, I had no inkling when I made a promise before God when I married him. He has done nothing to warrant my breaking that promise."

"I can appreciate that...respect you for it."

"And you have a future mapped out for yourself here. An exciting future because you are so very capable and determined. With ten thousand miles between our very different lives, you and I are worlds apart."

"All too true." Ruby sat up and flopped a pillow behind her. She took Irene's hand between both of her own. "If I may ask, what is your age?"

"Goodness, what an odd question! I'll be thirty-two later this year. And you?"

"Just turned twenty-eight. It's only that I want to remember every detail." She lifted Irene's hand to press her lips to its inner wrist. "Because I know I won't ever find another to compare."

"Oh, Ruby. My dear sweet girl. I shan't ever forget you. Or this extraordinary time we've had together. It's been a revelation, unlike anything I've ever dreamed of or could have imagined if I'd tried. Let's keep in touch. And I'm not just saying that. I mean it with all my heart. Writing may be too painful or too difficult. It's up to you. Tell you what. How about a postcard every Christmas, letting me know where you are, come hell or high water? Promise me, please?"

"A postcard once a year." Ruby pinched her eyebrows. "I can do that. It's a promise."

"I've something for you." Irene climbed out of bed and rummaged through her clothing to find her hat. Fiddling with it, she sat on the bed. "It's in here somewhere...this is it." She pulled out a long hatpin with a flowery clump at the blunt end. "Eighteen-carat gold and all the gems are real. It's been my fallback, should I lose my belongings by hook or by crook. I want you to have it in case you run short. Here, take it."

Ruby held the six-inch-long spike gingerly. "I can't accept this."

"My very word you can. And if you have to flog it, don't accept a penny less than twenty guineas!"

CHAPTER TWENTY-ONE

It was a bitterly cold morning, with ice crusting the back deck at Hargraves Crescent. Honor was in the veggie patch, planting out spinach seedlings. Through the kitchen window, Duscha could just see her kneeling figure moving about as she worked.

In the much warmer lounge room, Duscha set up the aluminium platform to paint the cornices and ceiling. She had both a large aluminium and small stepladder handy. Canvas drop sheets were scattered over every inch of the floor. She poured paint into a wide roller tray and screwed a roller handle onto a pole, ready for use. But first she would have to cut in the cornices with a broad brush, ahead of the rolling.

The back door closed, and Honor padded down the hall. "The spinach is in. Plus some pansies to keep them company."

"One can never have too many pansies. Are you ready to sand the skirtings?"

"Sure, but I'm afraid I may not be able to do a full day's work. My foot is none too flash."

Duscha met Honor's anxious look as she handed her a sanding block. "Understood. Please protect your knees as well. Kneel on something soft because crawling around the hard floor is tiring. I'm about to start painting in the far corner. You might follow from the other side of the room. If you find any dents or gouges, there's a tub of wood filler for you to use as you go." With a reassuring smile, she adjusted her favourite paint-spattered baseball cap. "Do as much as you comfortably can. It all helps."

To the sound of intermittent sanding, Duscha climbed onto the platform and brushed paint onto the ornate plaster cornice. Every metre or so, she rolled a square on the ceiling, slowly working her way around the room. When she caught up with Honor, she moved into the centre, rolling and overlapping paint as she went. They said very little to each other, but Duscha was fully aware of Honor working away, and couldn't help but notice her own peace and contentment in that inherently companionable silence. Close to an hour later, she had finished the ceiling.

"I'm stopping for coffee. Would you like one?"

On the floor, Honor was head down, meticulously pushing filler into the skirting with a putty knife. "If you're giving it away."

"Chance is a fine thing." Duscha headed into the kitchen, vigorously washed her hands and powered up the coffee machine. While it was a pleasure to have company while she worked, Honor's presence was so soothing as to be positively addictive. It was a long time since she'd been so sensitive and easily attuned to another woman. Vaguely disturbed, she tugged off the baseball cap and tossed it on the bench. While waiting for the coffee machine to prime, she combed back her rebellious hair with comforting fingers. There was something in the way Honor's energy filled the space between them that was both uplifting and disquieting. She put cups under the machine's spout and pushed a button.

"You seem to know what you're doing. Painting-wise, I mean."

Caught unawares by the very subject of her reverie, Duscha shot a startled glance at Honor casually propping up the doorway. "I've had to, I'm afraid. I've lived in many a tired rental house. And became very good at conning the owner into paying for paint in return for me freshening up the place. It makes a huge difference, I reckon." She poured frothed milk into the cups. "Would you help me finalise the colours for the walls?"

Honor said brightly, "Love to. I thought you'd already decided."

Duscha held out a cup. "Been waiting for you, naturally. Let's have another look. I'm itching to start the walls."

They sat on the sofa and examined swatches, holding them up to the light and laying them out in different combinations. It took ten minutes, but they narrowed it down to three possible pale greens and two less-than-ideal mauves.

Honor said, "Have you thought of a strong accent colour, a darker version of any one of these? You might want it for a feature element or highlight."

"That's an idea. Somewhere here there's a swatch of 'Cleopatra's Gown' which is a deep, rich purple and just gorgeous. Here it is."

"I see what you mean. You could get half a litre and tint a few cans of white as far as you want. And one of these greens goes perfectly with it. What do you think?"

Duscha grinned. "Decision made. Well done, you. But now I have to paint another ceiling before lunch. Back to the salt mines."

Just after midday, Duscha downed tools and disappeared into the kitchen. She called out, "Did you bring your own lunch?"

"I usually do but figured I wouldn't last the distance." Honor stood up and dusted off her knees. "It's true enough. I'd better wash up and head home."

"I've made fresh rice-paper rolls, if you would like something before you go. Join me if you feel like it. There's plenty." Duscha put a plateful, plus a dipping bowl on the kitchen table while

Honor washed her hands. With a mouth full of roll, Duscha lined up the swatches, ready to go to the hardware store.

Honor sat next to her and picked up a roll. "What's in them?"

"The usual. Noodles, cucumber, carrot, garlic chives. Some are barbecued pork, some shredded duck. The dipping sauce is lime juice, soy and sweet chili sauce. Nothing fancy."

"Seems pretty fancy to me." Honor dunked the roll and took a bite.

"Not in my mother's house. This is standard fare. And she would complain that I've omitted ingredients. Tell me I'm getting lazy." She pulled out two paper napkins from a back pocket. "You'll need one of these. Do you mind if I ask if you'd studied landscape architecture at all?"

"That duck is delicious. Where did you buy it?" Honor wiped her fingers and took another roll. "Actually I started out studying landscape architecture before I realised that I enjoy building gardens myself, rather than just designing for someone else."

Duscha said, "The cold cuts are from a Chinese takeaway in Civic that roasts their own ducks. As it happens, I was wondering about you because my new ACTPA job is in urban renewal, creating urban green spaces. Does that interest you?"

"Possibly. Because of this injury, I'm rethinking the long-term plan. My father helpfully pointed out that the business is vulnerable to my incapacity." Honor smiled wanly. "He can be annoyingly spot-on sometimes. When I think about it, I could tack a diploma onto my degree, but studying again after running my own business is a hefty commitment. I have a couple of units in landscape architecture already, so I could consider it."

"What does your partner think?"

Suddenly sombre, Honor paused to meet Duscha's probing look. "That level of planning ahead bores Merrin. I think because she finds it too complicated, therefore stressful. She's far more comfortable with routine tasks. If it's business, I talk to my dad."

* * *

Taking her leave of Duscha, Honor nursed a slight limp out to the ute, grateful to rest up the protesting foot during the drive home via Lake Ginninderra. The lake was near the Belconnen town centre where she often stopped to unwind after a job. Out of the ute, she covered a short distance, finding a park seat all to herself where she could put her foot up. The lake was calm except for ducks, black swans, and moorhens going about their business. A few couples were out walking, but it was pretty quiet for the early afternoon on a weekday. She and Duscha had continued to chat for another five minutes before she left, feeling guilty because what she'd said about Merrin sounded lame. And because she'd hated to leave. Talking to someone on a similar wavelength, and with similar interests, was novel and enjoyable. It was something she'd never really had with Merrin.

Head in hands, she closed her eyes for a few minutes, in an attempt to tamp down a welling frustration versus a hopeless yearning mixed with the undeniable joy that besieged her in Duscha's presence. She had to either manage that volatile mix or stay away…make an excuse…back out…disappear…vanish.

She slapped her cool cheeks and shook herself back into the present. The fact was she was *not* of a mind to quit seeing Duscha until she'd helped finish painting that house, as promised. Not one to break her word, maybe she should never have agreed in the first place. But she wasn't about to back out now.

CHAPTER TWENTY-TWO

In the massive metal shed that was the local hardware store, Duscha stood in line at the paint counter waiting for her order to be mixed, eager to see the new colours on the walls. A young bloke in front of her was dithering, helped by an impatient sales assistant. She let her thoughts drift to Honor and the startling revelation that she didn't talk business with her partner. Duscha tried and failed to think of a time when she and Noelle hadn't discussed their plans and made decisions accordingly. What sort of one-sided partnership did Honor have? It struck her as strange, but she had only her one serious relationship to go on.

Her mobile chimed. Stuart had texted that he would drop in briefly late tomorrow to check in the roof space for termite activity and take more measurements for materials. While she didn't want to be too obviously nosy about Honor's private life, she was mystified enough to push the bounds of discretion beyond her norm. Perhaps Stuart would have a clue?

She had just lugged all the new paint cans into the laundry when her mother let herself in the front door and sought her out.

"Duschka! Where are you?"

"Hi Ma. I'm in the laundry." Duscha emerged and kissed her mother's cool cheeks. "Let me show you the mirror. It's in the bedroom."

They sat side by side at the end of the bed, Valeria holding the mirror facedown on her knees, compact hands running over the aged oak backing board, as if searching for something.

Valeria said, "I brought the cards and the pendulum, should we want specifics answered. First let's see what I can pick up freely." She was silent for a barely a minute. "It's older than you think, could be close to a hundred years. Always owned by one woman or another. It feels 'womanly' but not necessarily feminine. Women of strong character."

"What about the falling-off-the-wall thing?" Duscha lifted the mirror's near edge until they could see their torsos reflected.

"It's jumping, not falling. A risky yet controlled manoeuvre, much like those of its previous owners."

Growing impatient, Duscha said, "That's all very well, but it's too weird for words."

Valeria's eyebrows went up. "It's meant to be, don't you see? It wants your attention."

"Great. The mirror's a drama queen. Just what I need."

"How can you be so obtuse? It's trying to *tell* you something. Or draw your attention to something." Valeria glanced around the room. "You told me you found a tin of letters. There may be more to it. I'll ask the pendulum." From a blue velvet pouch she rolled out a brass bob on a short chain. Held between finger and thumb, the bob swung briefly back and forth, and then it raced into a clockwise circle. "There's an unambiguous 'yes' for you."

Duscha crossed her arms. "All right. I might leave it on the floor so it can't jump anywhere. But I have some questions about the previous owners. Let's use the dining table for the cards."

Walking out of the bedroom together, Valeria said, "There's nothing even remotely unpleasant about that mirror. But it feels anxious, like there's a need for urgent action. You need to consider that."

At the table, Valeria shuffled the gypsy pack and handed it to Duscha. "You shuffle and cut. I'll take it from there. Your questions?"

"About Great-Aunt Irene. She moved here from Sydney in the 1920s with a woman named Ruby, supposedly her secretary. Were they a couple and why did they come?" She cut the pack and left it on the table.

Valeria laid out all the cards in five rows of five, twisting them when adjoining pictures matched. "You see the hands clasped here? And the ring right alongside? They were as good as married." She paused and tapped another picture. "This is gossip…nasty gossip. And at the end of the whole sequence is the angel of peace. It would be fair to say they came to where they could live in peace."

Duscha met her mother's solemn look and nodded. "Sounds like escaping prejudice. That makes sense."

"I'm deeply grateful that we live in more enlightened times, my Duschka. Unlike many people in those days, your happiness gladdens my heart."

After her mother left, Duscha wandered back into the bedroom, sat on the bed and stared at the innocent-looking old mirror. It stared back at her, inscrutable. Although her rational mind protested vigorously, the evidence was propped against the wall. Impossibly, it had "fallen" from a solid wall anchor and landed intact. Twice.

Over the years, her otherworldly mind had absorbed from Valeria enough eyebrow-raising stories of the improbable and technically impossible to allow that there might be method in the mirror's apparent madness. The unnerving truth was that Aunt Charlotte had addressed a letter specifically to Duscha, the niece she'd never met, and had told her about the house. It fell to Duscha to accept it all in good faith, albeit with a pinch of salt. Who was she to argue with either the precognisant dead or an apparently sentient house?

She jumped up and stepped to the doorway. Looking back at the mirror, she said, "I bet you've got a cunning plan. Just don't freak me out too much, okay? We're agreed."

CHAPTER TWENTY-THREE

Halfway up the ladder, Honor was cutting in a border of mauve paint with an edging pad butted against the cornice. Duscha waited below, loaded roller in hand. They had spent a good half hour measuring and mixing syringes full of purple paint into decanted containers of plain white, until they had the shade Duscha preferred. On a whole wall, it might look too pale or too over-powering. They were about to find out. Honor ran the edger vertically down the corner, across the top of the skirting and backed out of the way with the ladder.

"Here goes nothing." Duscha rolled the paint from top to bottom, blending smoothly. Honor had moved the ladder over, clambered up to extend the cutting-in further along and did the same again just above the skirting. In ten minutes, they'd done the one wall. They stood side-by-side to evaluate the result.

Duscha glanced at a silent Honor. "Bite me if I'm fantasising, but that's magic. Love it."

"Nice. Different. Unusual."

With a wry smile, Duscha briefly squeezed Honor's shoulders. "I'm the one who has to live with it."

"I could live with it." Honor looked up, gold highlights in her eyes glinting. "Quite happily, even. Shall we finish the room?"

Duscha nodded and stepped away, silently admonishing herself to keep her hands off another woman's woman. And definitely not to gaze into Honor's eyes for too long. They finished the room within forty minutes and took a break. Duscha fetched two kitchen chairs that she plonked in the middle of the floor. Like a comedy duo, they sat with their arms crossed and admired the paintwork.

Honor said, "Have you decided which rooms will be which colour?"

"Not entirely. My bedroom is preferably mauve and the utility areas better in the light green. Not sure yet. How about we share painting the woodwork in here today? Then that's one room completed."

"You're the boss."

Each with a brush, a pot of white paint and a substantial bank of windows, they started on the frames. Guessing Honor might be interested, Duscha related what she knew about the house's previous owners—first Aunt Charlotte's story and then Great-Aunt Irene's even vaguer details. They settled into a peaceful rhythm of painting and companionable discussion, with Honor asking the occasional question and Duscha filling in as best she could.

Her wrist was beginning to complain. Ignoring it, Duscha spoke from a stream of consciousness, rather than awareness of her audience. "I think Irene and Ruby could fly under the moral police's radar more easily than Charlotte and Sylvia, simply because after the First World War there were so many unmarried women. Irene had actually lost her husband. Lesbians would often trot out that old chestnut about a fiancé who was killed in battle. But by the fifties, society was becoming worldlier, and not in a good way for homosexuals. It just goes to show that progress can regress all too easily."

Working a loaded paintbrush along a windowsill, Honor said, "Do you really think Sylvia was in danger of being locked up in the loony-bin?"

"From what I've read of her letters, that's what her parents intended. Her own mother and father. How shocking is that? She was at their mercy…or lack of it. Even though she was an adult with a career. Isn't it amazing how hard some people tried to destroy those who loved each other? It boggles my mind."

She straightened up and squeezed tight shoulder blades together. "Anyway, I think we'd better stop for the day. We can put the brushes in water and resume tomorrow."

Honor had stopped painting and was watching her, expression drawn, as if engulfed by sorrow.

Duscha said, "Are you all right? Don't let me depress you with my ramblings. Or overwork you, eh?"

Honor gave a hollow laugh. "Something like that. I'd better quit while I'm ahead." She lifted the brush out of Duscha's hand. "Let me put these in the laundry and I'll get washed up."

Duscha's line of vision followed Honor's supple form until she disappeared. She grew uneasy, her heart sinking. Following down the hallway, she carried the dreadful thought that Honor meant to quit permanently, not just for the day.

Honor was doubled over by the laundry tub. At Duscha's sharp intake of breath, she straightened, turned away and croaked, "I'll be okay in a minute, no worries."

"Sorry, not buying it. What the hell is the matter?"

With a laugh bordering on the hysterical, Honor turned and blurted, "You are. You're the matter. You've always been the matter." She waved her hands in the air. "I thought I could do this. Be around you, be cool, walk away unscathed." Duscha took two long paces, only to stop when Honor held up a hand. "Don't touch me unless you mean it. Please. Leave me some dignity."

Heart in mouth, Duscha ventured a thumb to wipe the tears from Honor's cheeks, ran trembling fingers down and around to the back of Honor's neck, and pulled her close. They stood entwined, pulses racing like newborns until Honor's tension eased. Duscha drew back and looked at her.

"Don't. Don't even think about it unless you mean—"

Duscha pressed her mouth to Honor's so gently and briefly, it was almost chaste. Then she hugged her, hands caressing the small of her back. "I do mean it. But what that means for each of us in the circumstances, I don't rightly know. On the face of it, you have a partner to consider and I have to protect myself. Both my feelings and my personal integrity. Do you see?"

Honor stepped back with a grimace. "Of course I do. I feel the same way."

"Come on, let's go and sit down. And I promise to keep my hands to myself!"

In the kitchen, they sat at opposite ends of the table in silence.

Then Duscha said, "I held you, kissed you and I shouldn't have because I know you're not free. And I meant it because I like you a good deal. I could put my feelings in stronger terms but I don't think that's helpful." She leaned forward, elbows on knees and wrung her hands. "You have a long-term partner you love and who presumably loves you. Perhaps I'm just a blast from the past and that's where I belong. In your past." Unable to look at Honor, she fidgeted. "I've never been in this situation and I don't like it one little bit. But I want you to know that it's taken me by surprise. I honestly thought I'd never care for anyone after Noelle. Like she was my one shot at happiness."

In little more than a whisper, Honor said, "Were you very happy together?"

"Blessedly so. And I can't imagine how conflicted you must feel, if you love your partner as much as I loved Noelle. I feel kind of useless because my first instinct is to help you and I can't. In fact I'm the last person."

"I know. I have to sort myself out." Honor rose awkwardly, as if her foot ached. "I'd better go."

Duscha followed her to the front door. "Does that mean I've lost my painting buddy? Thought as much."

To the rapidly closing door, Duscha said, "Take care!" But she knew it fell on deaf ears.

"Damn. Damn. And triple damn!"

* * *

Honor couldn't go straight home...couldn't face Merrin. She cruised through the inner northern suburbs until she found herself outside Tilley's women-friendly café in Lyneham. It was quiet inside except for a few late-lunch patrons. She found an empty dark-timbered booth from where she ordered a coffee. Sitting back in the comforting gloom, she allowed herself to think about the encounter with Duscha and ran into her own turmoil.

She had blown it...absolutely blown any chance of the two of them finishing the painting together. She'd been so looking forward to spending time with Duscha until it was completed, including the opportunity to put some of herself into Duscha's home with all the love she could muster. But she had not been able to mask her feelings a moment longer. In speaking up, she'd lost the excuse to be near Duscha that silence had afforded her. Yet there it was, out in the open, feelings exposed, with no one but herself to blame. And she'd broken a promise to herself to make the moments—the dream—last, no matter what. All was lost. She was bloody hopeless...what a loser.

The coffee was delicious. Lazy jazz played in the background. She closed her eyes and just breathed for a while, recalling the sensation of Duscha's superlative physique enveloping her once more. She mustered a wry smile. Maybe all the anguish was worth it for that moment. And that fleeting kiss that had left her breathless and trembling. Come what may, she would never willingly forget the taste, touch, and feel of the living and breathing, flesh and blood, dream come true, Duscha Penhaligon.

Numb, she finished her coffee and drove home.

CHAPTER TWENTY-FOUR

At Hargraves Crescent, Stuart bowled in. "G'day Big Dee. How's everything going? I can see you've been at it."

She groaned. "Big Dee? Spare me that one please."

"I'm an Aussie. Can't help myself." He grinned broadly. "Where's your manhole?"

"In the hallway. My ladder's in the lounge."

Grasping the ladder, he clanked his way into the hall, scrambled up to the manhole and pushed the cover up into the roof space. Once inside, he leaned down. "Would you hand me that torch please?"

Duscha passed up the powerful waterproof torch. He was gone for ten minutes. She could hear him bumping around up there. More clanking told her he was coming down.

"What's the verdict?"

He scratched his sandpapery cheek. "They've only eaten out the top of your bedroom doorframe, but that's as far as it goes. It's all good in the roof. I've had a decent look and I'm happy with that. I'll measure your bedroom again, if that's okay?"

Duscha followed him to sit on the edge of the bed, watching him feed out a metal tape. "Stuart, can I talk to you about Honor?"

Leaning over one thigh, he scribbled figures on a small pad with a blunt builder's pencil before glancing sideways at her. "A bit tricky. She's a close mate. It depends."

She pulled a face. "Fair enough. If I said I have feelings for her, would that make a difference?"

He measured a right-angle across the room, chewing his bottom lip. More figures appeared on the pad that was then shoved in a back pocket, and the tape measure hitched onto his belt. He sat down next to her, studying her expression. "Can't say I'm surprised. She's a bit of a babe. What do you want to know?"

The scent of aftershave and wood shavings permeated his clothing. She breathed out and said, "Strange as it may seem, about her partner. How they met and what their relationship is like. I won't do anything with such information. I'm just trying to understand Honor. And what's going on between us."

Lips pursed, he laced fingers around one knee, rocking back on the bed and taking his time before replying. "What you're asking is clearly sensitive. But what I can tell you is that Merrin was once employed by the Department of Defence as a low-level clerk at Campbell Park offices. She was made redundant and had to take whatever work she could get, which happened to be a temporary placement with Landladies. It was a wage, outside of which she has no interest in gardening." He leaned forward to lock eyes with Duscha. "Just how serious are your feelings for my friend? Because as besties go, she's second only to my ex."

Caught off-guard, she turned her eyes to the mischievous mirror, still propped against the wall. She searched for words to explain exactly how she felt. Distracting memories of Honor's easy dimpled grin and tawny eyes flashed through her head. But deeper down, in her chest and from the pit of her stomach rose a seductive ache that grew more urgent every time she and Honor were together. Now it demanded to be acknowledged.

She drew in a long breath and looked at Stuart. "Frankly, I think I'm in love with her. And I've been in love only once before. Given her situation, this is deadly serious."

He rubbed his brow, half-grinning. "I'm glad to hear it because I think you're worthy of her, which is more than I can say for Merrin. Honor doesn't say much about her feelings, but I've seen those two together. On the one hand, she is strong but a softie. She has a noble conscience and likes to be needed. On the other hand, Merrin strikes me as an opportunist who has things exactly where she wants them. Including Honor."

Duscha crossed her arms, mouth a thin line. "Doesn't sound healthy. But I can't interfere."

"Does she know how you feel?"

"Sort of. It became obvious today. We talked briefly. We've come to the conclusion that we have to stay away from each other, but it's hurtful and bewildering. One minute I'm realising how I feel about her. The next minute, I'm never going to see her again."

"Jeez. I reckon you're caught between a rock and a hard place. Well, they say that absence makes the heart grow fonder. Maybe their trip to Adelaide will bring a fresh perspective."

Duscha frowned. "What trip to Adelaide?"

He tugged his mobile out of a back pocket and scrolled through messages, until he tilted the phone so she could read: *Merrin's mother died late morning. We fly to Adelaide asap. Return date undecided.* It must have been sent after Honor got home from their morning's painting.

She slapped her forehead. "Oh, Lord, how did I get myself into this mess? I'm at the mercy of another couple's fate over which I have no control. I think it's better for everyone if I bow out gracefully."

"Not so fast." He stood up, straightened his belt and strode to the doorway where he turned. "You're deadly serious? If Honor has a thing for you and now knows you have one for her, then *she's* got to work out what she's going to do with that, if anything. In talking about it, you've already changed each other, but you don't know the outcome yet. All you can do is watch and wait. Just don't give up on her, eh? Give her a break. She's worth it. Trust me because we're close mates and I know her. She really is worth it."

Duscha didn't have the stomach to do much after Stuart left. Painting was definitely out of the question. She would have to finish it alone, which was both daunting and disappointing. Honor wasn't out of her life five minutes and already she was missing her.

She sat on the end of the bed staring at the deco mirror when it hit her. The unimaginable had happened. She had fallen in love with someone unavailable. How did that happen? When did she lose her heart? Both hands clapped to her mouth, she stilled, immobile, shocked and horrified at her treacherous feelings. Lulled into a false sense of safety by logic, she'd been helpless to resist her soulful self that had other ideas...had its sights on Honor. She'd been tripped up by her own hubris.

In the distance, her mobile rang. She bolted down the hall and snatched it off the kitchen bench.

"Hi, Mischa."

"Hi, sweetie. Just thought I'd give you a quick call with some info about Ruby Milborne. I've put you on speakerphone because I'm only just now getting to eat lunch. Please excuse the munching. How are you?"

Duscha strode to the sofa and flung herself down. "Fair to muddling. Fire away."

"It's been insanely busy here, but I found an article in the Sydney Morning Herald dated March 1949. It's about an exhibition of women's suffrage jewellery at the Art Gallery of New South Wales. Apparently Mrs. Angus Armfield of Canberra loaned a number of significant pieces to the exhibition from her private collection. And her secretary, Ruby Milborne, assisted the curator with display of said items. That's it, that's all there is."

"I guess that tells us Irene owned some notable period jewellery, and Ruby was knowledgeable enough to assist. Someone must have transported the pieces up to Sydney from Canberra. Perhaps it was Ruby?"

"Irene would have to have trusted her implicitly."

"With good reason. I'm almost positive they were a couple." Duscha added, "Half their luck."

"Oh, I seriously doubt it, sweetie. They would have to have been crazy courageous to be a couple way back then. Look, I'm going to have to go any minute now, but you sound out of sorts. Is everything okay?"

Duscha blew air noisily though her cheeks. "I've got myself into a spot of bother with the gardener."

"Aha! I warned you. Is it love or lust? And what happened?"

"Too long a story to bore you with. Far beyond mere lust, I'm afraid. But it's over before it started and it's my own fault. I knew she had a partner. I've only myself to blame."

"Hang on a minute. Her partner is her problem, not yours."

Duscha pressed the phone tighter to her ear. "What are you getting at?"

Michele had taken her off speakerphone. "It's just another perspective that Axel and I happen to subscribe to. When we signed on the dotted line ten years ago, we agreed not to own each other. There was no 'forsaking all others' clause in our marriage vows. While I love him dearly and know he adores me, his body is his own, as is mine. For the most part, he meets my needs and I meet his, but no one can be all things to someone. If we want to have sex with other people, neither of us has a problem with that."

An image of sandy-haired Axel Fogarty's teasing brown eyes popped into Duscha's mind. A systems analyst who travelled extensively overseas, she knew him to be a dreadful flirt. Smiling, she said, "Is that so, Mrs. Fogarty? And have you taken advantage of that understanding?"

"Only once, a few years ago. Axel was working in Jakarta for a month. And there was this hunky, Zimbabwean forestry student working as a casual shelver in the basement stacks. It was highly flattering, very entertaining, and lasted a fortnight."

"Why didn't I hear about this?" Duscha grinned down the phone.

"It was around the time your Noelle was sick. You were off the planet. Look, I know Axel has liaisons while he's away and

I don't care, as long as he doesn't catch anything. My point is: I want my man to be with me because he wants to be with me. Not because he feels obligated. If he falls in love with someone else, that would break my heart. It's the risk we all take when we love another. But I don't own his body like a physical possession."

"What has this to do with me and the gardener?"

"Sod it. Sorry, I've got a meeting right now. I'll email you a copy of the newspaper clipping. What I mean is, if she loved her partner and her needs were being met, would she be hankering after you? That's why I said it's her problem. And you are its undeniable, in-her-face symptom. You haven't heard the last of her. Sorry sweetie. Gotta go, bye!"

"Bye." Duscha stared at the silent phone, eyes narrowing. Just when she thought she had something sussed, she could always rely on Mischa to make her think again.

That evening she lingered over a plate of slow-cooked *osso buco*, contemplating Michele's take on managing an open relationship-cum-marriage. It seemed to her that her friend had learned to handle it, providing they kept sex and love in separate compartments. But the possibility of either of them falling in love with someone else must hang over their marriage like the sword of Damocles. Also, it seemed like Michele worried about that a whole lot more than Axel. For herself, Duscha knew she couldn't conveniently unstitch desire from heartfelt love. And neither did she want to try.

She could hazard a guess that Honor wasn't of a mind to jeopardise her partnership's metaphorical plate by adding a serving of sex on the side. As to what Merrin would do? That was a complete unknown.

CHAPTER TWENTY-FIVE

Inside a federation-style house in the Adelaide suburb of Grange, over a thousand kilometres west of Canberra, Honor and Merrin sat at a formal dining table opposite Merrin's brother Kevin and sister Deirdre. Between them on the table's highly polished timber were a small pile of papers and a sealed business envelope.

Clutching a sheet of paper tightly enough to buckle it, Deirdre said, "We figure you're not going to be too happy with Mother's decisions, Merry."

Merrin leaned forward with folded arms on the table, staring hard at her sister. Uneasily, Honor pushed back her chair and stiffened. They had flown in less than an hour ago, picked up a rental car at the airport and driven to the elegantly styled home that was jointly owned by Kevin and Deirdre. From the street, the place looked identical to their deceased mother's house, right next door.

Merrin said, "Why not? I don't mind selling her house for my share. You shouldn't either. That's her will?"

Deirdre glanced at Kevin who was busy picking his cuticles. She cleared her throat. "Mother left her house to Kevin and me. The will states her reasons being twofold. In the first place, Kevin and I have looked after her for the last five years while her health deteriorated—"

"What garbage is this?" Merrin had gone red, jaw clenching. "What have you two talked her into?"

"Nothing. We didn't have to." Deirdre smirked as she paraphrased the will's contents. "In the second place, Mother said you borrowed five thousand dollars from her over eight years ago that you didn't bother to repay. In all that time, you haven't troubled yourself to visit. Therefore, in place of a share of the house, she has generously left you ten thousand dollars in cash."

"Ten grand?" Merrin spat her words. "That's three-fifths of five-eighths of zero compared to what her house is worth. You have to be kidding me!"

"Minus the five thousand you owe. Minus interest at ten percent per annum over eight years which amounts to another four thousand. What remains is a thousand dollars. Here you go." Deirdre pushed the business envelope across the table. "It's in fifties for your convenience."

Merrin rose to her feet, glaring from one to the other. Then she threw back her head and laughed an ugly, snorting guffaw. "Ha-bloody-ha. Very funny!" She turned and stalked out of the room, empty-handed.

Honor rose awkwardly, cracked an apologetic smile at the silent siblings exchanging glances, and followed Merrin down a hall. Back in the guest room where they'd dropped their luggage, Merrin was pacing the room, swearing under her breath.

Honor said, "What's this about you owing your mother money?"

Merrin threw her hands in the air. "It was years ago! I'd lost my job, couldn't pay my rent and Mum lent me five large ones to start again. Then I got the job with you. With Landladies. And forgot all about it."

"You forgot?"

"She never asked for it."

"She shouldn't have to. Why didn't you tell me when we got together? I would have helped you pay her back. No biggie."

Hands on hips, Merrin shook her head. "I was annoyed that I had to go to her, cap in hand. Assumed she'd forget about it. I certainly did."

Honor sat on the edge of the double bed, looking up at her. "That was a very expensive memory lapse. And they have presented you with a *fait accompli*. This is a complete waste of time. Why didn't they tell you all this by phone?" Merrin ignored her. "I know we've only just got here, but I think the best thing is to turn around and go straight back home."

"No way. The funeral's on Friday. Besides."

"Besides what? If my mother effectively disinherited me as yours has, I'd take the hint that I wasn't welcome."

"They can't do this to me." Merrin was pacing again. "Mother's house is worth close to a million. I'm not going anywhere until I get my fair share. I'll contest the will." She halted in front of Honor, waving a finger. "And they'll pay to get rid of me. We're staying here until they cough up."

Honor closed her eyes for an instant. "I can't believe what I'm hearing. Unless you've got a solid case, once you start down the path of litigation you're walking into a lengthy and very expensive shit-storm."

"So what? I'm not walking away from my fair share. A good three hundred thousand dollars that is rightfully mine. No way."

Honor considered her partner's agitation. Was this the moment to reassure…to disclose that they had ample money for their every foreseeable need, thanks to her father's investments? She said calmly, "You know, it's not that much. We don't need it."

Merrin snorted. "It's *my* money. And you're not exactly rolling in it, are you, now? I know because I do the business's books. It's no gold mine. I want all I can…er…all we can get."

The moment gone, Honor was suddenly glad she'd not spoken up. She got to her feet. "You may have the stomach for this, but I don't. The vibe from those two is unfriendly, bordering on downright hostile. We're not welcome. And they won't back down in a hurry. Please, Merrin, are you sure you really want to do this?"

"Oh, they'll give in all right." Merrin's darkened eyes gleamed. "They manipulated her against me. They set this up, the pair of them. I'm not going to let them get away with it!"

Under her breath, Honor said, "This is insane."

Merrin took a step to stand over Honor. "Do you really think my brother and sister are all sweetness and light? Get a grip. Welcome to the real world where families do the dirty on each other. If I don't stand up for my rights, then more fool me!"

"I hate to mention it, but you have no right. Unless you can prove your mother's will was signed when she was incapacitated, it's extremely difficult to contest."

Vengeance dripping from every word, Merrin said evenly, "I don't care. I'll make so much trouble for those two they'll wish they'd never been born."

"You're missing the point, love. Let's not the let the facts get in the way of the argument, eh?"

Merrin crossed her arms. "I want my money."

"Ah, now we're getting to the truth." Honor stood up and bent to her wheeled suitcase. Pulling up its handle, she turned toward the door. "It's your fight and I can't, in any conscience, go along with it. I'm sorry. Won't you change your mind? It's the right thing to do. To honour your mother's wishes."

"Yeah, that'd be right. Go on. Walk out, you wimp!" Upper lip curling, Merrin turned her back. "Coward. Whatever."

Indignation constricting her throat, Honor said, "Good luck. Keep me posted."

Honor drove the white Toyota sedan back to Adelaide Airport and parked in the rental car zone. With feelings swinging wildly, rocketing between shock, disbelief, hurt, and fury, she stared into the distance, trying to breathe evenly to calm herself down. It was late afternoon, and they had not booked return flights to Canberra. She would have to find a motel to pick up a flight the next day. Eyes squeezed shut, she hugged her elbows. What was she going to do? What did she *really* want to do right now? Eyes jagged open, she realised it didn't entail sitting alone in a rented room, festering.

She got out of the car. In the rental company's office, she made arrangements to return the vehicle at Canberra Airport instead. An uncommon sense told her that a very long drive home—about fourteen hours' worth—would clear her head.

At Tailem Bend, a hundred kilometres southeast of Adelaide and close to where she had to turn off toward the eastern states, Honor stopped at a service station to top up on fuel. It was fast approaching dusk. She would be driving into the night along nearly four hundred kilometres of the Mallee Highway to Tooleybuc. The inland route was relatively remote, with only a few tiny towns along the way. At least the road was sealed, but it was a mobile black spot for the full distance. She would have to pray she did not hit a kangaroo or any other wildlife, her only company the occasional, equally insane motorist and road trains transporting goods from one side of the island continent to the other.

She had driven this way once before with her friend Julie, back when they were naive eighteen-year-olds, fresh out of school. One Christmas, they had impulsively packed themselves into Julie's cramped Honda City and driven all the way to Port Augusta where Julie's grandparents lived, even further west than Adelaide. Three days later, they drove all the way back to Canberra. Neither was popular with their parents when they returned home. But they had had great fun, and Honor relished the drive. She still loved driving, except this time she would be alone.

She used the bathroom facilities and bought a large takeaway coffee and an over-priced insulated mug to decant it into. She had to make the coffee last as long as possible while avoiding the need for a toilet stop. There was no way she was going to pull over and leap into roadside bushes. Not in the pitch black in the middle of nowhere.

Sun setting at her back, her mood both anxious and exhilarated, she took the easterly turnoff onto the Mallee. Once up to legal speed and under cruise control, she needed only to relax and steer, leaving the best part of the remaining twelve hours to mull things over.

Was Merrin justified in calling her a coward? The slight had both hurt and offended. Sure, Merrin was angry and in the mood to have a go at someone…anyone. Honor was a handy target. But should she take it personally?

In her own mind, she was anything but a coward. As a rule, she stood up for what she thought was right and took it on the chin if she was wrong. To her, contesting a parent's will for no other reason than sour grapes, unless the parent was coerced or incapacitated, was unjustified. Yet Merrin's mother's decision to punish her daughter over five thousand dollars seemed heavy-handed. The old lady must have had more than one reason to justify that action. Perhaps it was just one of many. Did Merrin have form with her family for conveniently forgetting her debts?

One thing was certain: Honor was ashamed of her partner's attitude. And that was why she'd walked away from the whole sorry mess. She muttered to the darkening sky ahead, "Oh, Merrin. I always knew you had a far thicker skin than me, but to win this one, you'll need the hide of a rhinoceros."

She narrowed her eyes, determined to keep vigilant as she drove into dusk, a time when kangaroos were especially noted for bounding across highways, wiping out vehicles and getting injured, or worse.

One of the joys of driving alone was that she could talk to herself and, if necessary, yell, scream, rant and rave. Or sing, if desperate. But she chose to rant. At Merrin.

"How could you be so dumb as to not pay back your mother? What is the matter with you? Where is your integrity?"

It was the ugly side of Merrin that she preferred not to see, but the fact remained that her partner could be mercenary. She'd noticed any number of small instances over the years and turned a blind eye, conceding that no one was perfect, least of all herself.

"For five piddling thousand dollars, you've missed out on at least sixty times that amount. What goes around comes around. Not that it matters because we have more than enough, thanks to Dad. Go ahead and have your tiff with your rels. When you get home I'll take pleasure in telling you the truth. That you needn't have bothered. The fact is I can comfortably look after us, no problem."

But would Merrin do the same for her, if their positions were reversed? Honor sighed heavily and shook her head, reluctant to answer her own question.

The road had straightened, set to traverse the monotonous Australian countryside from A to B as directly and smoothly as possible. Up ahead, she spotted red taillights. She was catching up to a road train, which suited her preference for company and safety. If she stayed behind it, any beast straying onto the road would be tossed aside by the truck's bull bars. Coming closer, she adjusted the cruise control to keep pace at sufficient distance.

She wondered about Merrin's brother and sister. On the flight over, Merrin had refreshed her memory by explaining that both of them had exited relationships that had passed their use-by date. When it came on the market Kevin had bought the house next to their mother's and renovated it with Deirdre's help. In time, it seemed only logical for Deirdre to move in, an arrangement that worked for them and their mother. But it put Merrin very definitely on the outer. It was obvious that the three siblings were not close. Exactly why, Merrin hadn't said and likely never would. The word "sorry" being routinely absent from her vocabulary, she was not one to examine her faults or recount her blunders. Short of asking Deirdre or Kevin, Honor would never know.

Merrin's only real friend was Lance, the Landladies' accountant. That bond mystified Honor. Seeing them together, Lance's leer would unblinkingly follow Merrin's every move in a way that gave Honor the creeps. And Merrin would simper at him in return. Their friendship went back many years. It was a good thing his long-suffering wife put up with him.

Honor shivered and took a sip of coffee. It was going to be a long night. Reaching Tooleybuc was reassuring in principle, except there was nothing much to the town. Definitely no services open in the middle of the night. From there, it would be another two hundred k's to Echuca, a busy transport hub on the Murray River where she would stop to refuel, refresh and briefly rest. Thereafter, another seven hours of driving lay ahead before she arrived in Canberra just before dawn. It was a plan.

Somewhere between Tooleybuc and Echuca, and on the crest of a darkened hill from which there was absolutely no sign of civilisation in any direction, she suddenly slowed and pulled the car over to the edge of the road. She killed the engine and got out. Perched on the edge of the bonnet, she listened to the engine ticking as it cooled, rotating her stiff shoulders and stretching her neck. Above her, the Milky Way was a gloriously glittering half-circle of incomparable beauty. Slowly, she leaned back until she was lying on the warm car. For a few minutes, she was the only living soul on earth, with the night sky putting on its ultimate show, just for her. Overwhelmed, she lay still until the shadowy roadside scrub grew threatening. She hastened back into the car.

Just after three a.m. and still two hours west of Canberra, in desperate need of food and coffee, Honor pulled into a busy truck stop on the outskirts of the tiny town of Gundagai. She hadn't eaten since the previous day. Sitting at a white melamine table in the café, she gulped down a well-made omelette served on chunky toast slathered with butter.

Fatigued, she now doubted her decision to leave Merrin in trouble, even if it was of her own making. What kind of partner leaves their other half in the lurch? She hated making decisions by running away from something, much preferring to gravitate toward something better. Was she running away from Merrin? If not, toward what was she gravitating?

Fork in midair, she cracked an ironic, sad smile, acknowledging she knew full well what, or rather toward whom, she was gravitating.

Half-eaten toast in one hand and takeaway coffee in the other, she hurried out into the pre-dawn cold, back to the car. At least she felt better for the sustenance and warmer on the inside. In the driver's seat, she paused to look around, contemplating the trucks and massive road trains coming and going, people going about their lives as best they could. No matter what, life went on. People constantly made choices about where to be, what to do and with whom to share their lives. All had just one life to live in the now. In a way, she had already changed direction, even if it was by default. Merrin had made a choice according to her conscience, which forced Honor to make a choice according to her own. It was not irretrievable yet bore the telltale signs.

And in all fairness to Merrin, she had to own up to being in love with Duscha. She always had been and probably always would be. As a rival for Duscha, Merrin hadn't an icicle's hope in hell.

She stuck her head out the window and looked up at the night sky, still ablaze with countless stars stretching toward infinity. At three twenty-nine a.m. she grabbed her phone and sent a text message.

CHAPTER TWENTY-SIX

A smattering of hail dashed against Duscha's bedroom window, rousing her from sleep. At least, she assumed it was hail because it had rained heavily earlier on. She emerged from under the bedclothes and focused on the alarm clock. It was five thirty-five a.m., bitterly cold and still dark. The hail had stopped, started again, stopped again. And someone was softly calling her name. She froze and listened. Confident she recognised the voice, she jerked out of bed and inched back the curtain enough to see the barest outline of a waif-like figure out there in the cloudy night.

She turned on the bedside light, found her slippers and dressing gown, and made her way to the back door, flicking on lights in passing, squinting against their blinding brightness.

"You'd better come in."

"Did you get my message?" Honor stepped inside, damp and shivering.

"Possibly." Duscha hesitated. "I always set my phone to silent when I go to bed. So I'm not disturbed. What are you doing here at this ridiculous hour? I heard you went to Adelaide."

Honor's shoulders slumped. "We did. I'm sorry. I drove all night."

"What, from Adelaide? Nutcase."

"I...just wanted to see you."

"Oh, Lord. How come you're here and not at home with your partner?"

"We had a fight. Right after she had a fight with her rels. She's still in Adelaide and I couldn't stand it. I had to leave."

Duscha tucked Honor under an arm. "You're freezing. And sleep walking. Do you need a hot drink? No? Come to bed and talk to me there."

Back in the bedroom, Duscha said, "Let's look at you. Okay, outer clothes off and here's a pyjama top. The bottoms won't go anywhere near you, I'm afraid. Hurry up." And she slipped between the sheets, leaving the bedside light on while Honor fumbled. Once the unfamiliar, lean and clammy body had snuggled into Duscha's side, head on her shoulder, she stretched out and turned off the light.

"Okay. Give me the short version of what happened."

Honor mumbled the gist of the argument with Merrin's siblings. When she described the couple's subsequent confrontation, Duscha realised Honor was crying. She squeezed her shoulders, aware she was almost delirious with fatigue.

In a faltering whisper, Honor said, "I drove all night to see—"

"Hush."

"To make love—"

"Not now. Sleep!"

Duscha had lain awake, monkey-mind chattering pointless questions and inciting inane arguments to do with her and Honor and Merrin. But she must have dozed lightly, only to awaken fully at daylight with a viper wrapped around one arm. Honor's plait. She extricated herself, donned dressing gown and slippers and peered down at the slight form tangled deep within the bedclothes, fast asleep.

"Tsk, there's nothing of you, but you're a force to be reckoned with, aren't you? My pocket-rocket."

In the kitchen, she turned on the kettle and worried. There was a lovely woman in her bed and she hadn't taken advantage of that fact. Yet she was afraid she might. Not one to act in haste and repent at leisure, she showered and dressed. With a mug of tea and a plate of vegemite toast, she went outside to where the morning sun lit up the deck. There, she started work on the dilapidated bentwood armchair.

With the sun on her back and the scent of beechwood dust in the air, Duscha relaxed. The chair could be as old as the early 1900s. She wondered who had sat in it recently. Her father had been a big man. His weight would have made it creak in alarm and been far from comfortable for him. It was definitely a lady's chair. She'd sanded back the ancient varnish on the spindly legs, curved back, and armrests. Kneeling, she worked gently on the embossed wooden seat, careful not to compromise its radiating pattern.

"Good morning."

Duscha looked up and had to grin. Honor was way too cute standing there, arms folded, in nothing but the pyjama top that reached mid-thigh. "More like 'good afternoon.' How are you feeling?"

Stepping forward, Honor protested, "It's only nine thirty. And I'm doing okay, thanks to you."

"You're welcome." Duscha stood dusting herself off, trying and failing to take her eyes of the very shapely woman now standing much too close. "You must be cold. Come inside where it's warm and we can talk…" She trailed off when Honor grasped her hands and drew them to her own hips. With Honor's mouth a breath away, Duscha swallowed hard, her heart hurtling. "Now you're not playing fair."

Dark eyes grown huge, Honor moistened her lips. "You know I'm crazy about you. And fair hasn't worked for me so far." She ran her hands up to Duscha's throat, whispering, "How's this working for you?"

An incredulous chuckle escaped Duscha's throat as she bent to the enticing mouth, hot lips opening to greet hers. Fingers tightened in her hair and she crushed the compliant body to hers, hands searching under the pyjama top, finding flesh devoid of underwear. Weak with want, she fumbled her way to Honor's shoulders, easing herself away.

Still holding Honor's shoulders, she said raggedly, "I can't do this. You're gorgeous. Completely adorable. But you're not free." She took a step back. "Come inside and we'll talk." Striding toward the back door, she added, "And put some clothes on!"

Five minutes later, a fully dressed Honor came into the kitchen where Duscha was making coffee. Forlornly, Honor said, "I'd best get going then. Get out of your hair."

Duscha frowned. "What? I'm not trying to get rid of you. You can see I've made you a coffee. Please join me." She led the way to the sofa.

Honor sat looking at the ceiling. "I feel like I've been told off."

"Oh, Lord." Duscha leaned forward. "Okay, cards on the table. Already I care for you sincerely. I'm undeniably emotionally involved, okay? But I have to protect myself from getting hurt any further. This is painful enough as it is. Plus I don't want to be the other woman…don't want to be the reason for your relationship ending."

"You're not. Merrin and I—"

"Please don't explain. You've had a serious clash of opinions over how she handles her inheritance troubles. I get that, but I'm the wrong person to discuss your relationship with. You have friends for that. I can't advise you, I'm sorry."

They sat in silence, sipping coffee as minutes drifted by. Duscha glanced across, saw the wet cheeks and took Honor's free hand, squeezed it tight.

"You're right," said Honor. "I have to get myself sorted. Just to be clear. If I were single, what then?"

"It's not so much about you being single, although I won't share. It's about where your heart is, where your loyalty lies. Who are you close to? Who do you love, really? Only you can answer with total honesty. Then it's a matter of will you live your life accordingly? It's your choice."

Honor stood. Duscha rose automatically. Honor said, "I'll talk to Stuart."

"Good idea. In the meantime, let's continue to keep our distance from each other, only because it's too hard otherwise. Believe me, it's a major effort for me not to just say, 'to hell with it.' With some distance, if little else can be achieved, perhaps we can be friends. Better than nothing?"

Honor looked intently at Duscha, lifted a hand and trailed trembling fingers along Duscha's jaw, a thumb coming to linger at the corner of her mouth. "I don't think we could be just friends. My friends don't know how I taste."

In danger of drowning in Honor's eyes and perilously close to tears, Duscha stepped back, shoving both hands into her pockets. "My lovely, I need you to go away now. I'm hurting, you're hurting. Please get yourself free or whatever you have to do. Just leave me out of it. I'll see you when I see you."

In the late afternoon, Duscha opted for a bath. She had finished sanding the armchair, dusted it down and put on two coats of water-based varnish. In between coats, she had rolled mauve paint onto the walls in the spare bedroom she was using as a study. By the end of the day, two full coats enhanced the room markedly. The antique armchair was looking superb in its new varnish suit.

Now, Duscha was worn out, splattered with paint and starving. With the bath filling, she tossed frozen minestrone in the microwave to defrost, ready to reheat and eat when she was clean. Being an old-fashioned enamelled bath, long and narrow with a slope at one end, it was just big enough for her. A handful of bath salts made the water turn a bluish-green. She tied her hair up and slid her weary body into the steaming hot water. Protesting muscles began to relax. Through half-closed eyes, she evaluated the room.

Revamped sometime in the 1980s, the bathroom was serviceable, if far from luxurious. In one corner was a shower with yellow glass-panelled doors that barely opened and shut. The bath was in the other corner. Against the middle wall was a vanity unit coated in marble-looking laminate peeling at the drawer edges. Above was a small mirror that did the job, just. On the vanity unit, she had put a hairbrush, hand cream, and an acrylic tumbler that contained her toothbrush. The tumbler was adorned with a colourful, comical toucan and a macaw from one or other Disney film, she couldn't recall which. Noelle had chosen it, since they both loved birds. Childish as it was, they had shared it for many years.

Duscha let the tears fall. All day she'd resisted thinking about anything emotionally confronting. Wafting her hands through the water, she wondered what Noelle would think of the mess she was in.

"Serve you bloody right, probably." She had spoken out loud. In the distance, she could hear the microwave beeping. The soup had defrosted.

"Hey, Aunt Lottie! I bet you've got an opinion as well. Where's that happiness you promised me? What about you, great-Aunt Irene? You'll tell me I'm dreaming. What are my chances of finding anything like the love Noelle and I had ever again? Thought as much. Please help me to let Honor go. Help my heart to mend and let's move on. Much appreciated."

In the middle of roughly scraping paint off her knuckles, she heard an ominous thud from her bedroom across the hall. Hands frozen mid-move, she held her breath, listening. In a flash, she knew what it was. The leaping mirror. Shoulders slumping, she bellowed, "Cut it out ladies! I nearly wet myself. Good thing I'm in the bath, ha, ha. Good thing I know you're friendly. Love your sense of humour."

She quickly washed and pulled the plug.

CHAPTER TWENTY-SEVEN

Just before midnight on Saturday, Honor was driving home from the Canberra Bush Dance at the Yarralumla Woolshed. She had left the LGBTI event in full swing, well before it was due to wind down at one o'clock the following morning. But she was dog-tired, and eager to get home and off the road before too many drunks made driving a health hazard.

She had met up with Stuart for a late afternoon coffee at The Republic Café in Civic. The centre of the city was a pedestrian mall, wall-to-wall with cafés fully occupied by Canberrans winding down and catching up with loved ones. They had talked for hours before making their way to the dance with Stuart's friend, Adam and his boyfriend, Sang.

The dance had a live bush-band, with an experienced caller bellowing steps and moves to the crowd. It was too noisy for all but the briefest conversation. She had spent most of the evening pretending to drink a bottle of light beer, while hundreds of bodies line-danced at manic speed around the packed dance floor. Outside, people had hung around in their western gear, chatting, eating, and taking a breather. There were women about, but they were hugely outnumbered by teenage boys and men. She hadn't spotted anyone she knew, inside or out. Even though she enjoyed people-watching and had to grin at the guys making absolute loons of themselves in their checked shirts, jeans, and boots, she'd had enough well before midnight. She'd made her excuses to a very sweaty, exuberant Stuart and left him to it.

She steered the ute into a left turn off William Hovell Drive and onto Drake-Brockman. Nearly home. Something Stuart had said in the café that afternoon still niggled at her. She had told him what happened in Adelaide and about the road trip back to Duscha's house. Then he had taken her completely by surprise with a forthright reply to what she thought was the most difficult question.

"Let's say I leave Merrin. Where's she going to go? What's she going to do? She has nothing and no one. How will I live with myself if I chuck her out on the street? I don't think I can do it, Stu. I can't."

Hairy hands clasped together and thumbs twiddling in circles, he said, "In case you haven't noticed, you don't owe her anything. You have looked after her for years. Carried her, in fact. So she did the business's books. And? You could have easily paid someone, no strings attached. Apart from appeasing your conscience if you stay with her, what's in it for you?"

Stunned into silence, she'd just looked at him.

"You're in love with Duscha who says she loves you back. Unless you can say the same about you and Merrin, difficult as it may be, it's time to move on. Honesty requires it. Get real, Honor. You owe it to all concerned."

At that moment, Adam and Sang had appeared at their table, ending their conversation. Not that she'd had an even remotely coherent come-back to "what's in it for you?"

She turned into the driveway, pressing the remote for the double garage door. As the door rose, her skin chilled. The ute motored in at a crawl. Engine off, she peered at the empty parking bay alongside. Merrin's Mazda hatch was missing.

At first she thought they'd been burgled. The television was gone. Some décor objects had mysteriously grown legs and walked. Cupboards in the lounge room hung ajar. She hurried to the office, only to find the computer equipment safely in place. But Merrin's jigsaw collection had disappeared. Spooked, she hovered in the hallway, listening for the slightest noise out of place. Nothing. The house seemed strangely empty—more like emptied.

In the bedroom, she opened wardrobe doors, by now unsurprised to discover Merrin's clothes missing, the chest of drawers hollow. She strode around the room and then checked the rest of the house. On the hall phone table, she found a folded sheet of white copier paper bearing a scribbled note:

> 'I don't want anything to do with a GUTLESS TRAITER like you. I have taken all my stuff. Don't contact me. Don't try to find me. I feel sorry for you. M.'

She read it twice. "It's spelled with an *o*. Traitor with an *o*. Crap."

A sinking sensation had her lean on the table to brace unsteady legs. With a sour taste rising in her throat, she gave a mirthless grunt. *A traitor. Why is it that people accuse others of what they themselves are doing? Here was the pot calling the kettle black.*

She threw the note down and tugged her mobile from a back pocket. Staying in the house alone was not an option. She dialled her night-owl father's number, figuring it was highly likely he would still be up. "Hi Dad. May I come and stay the night at your place? No, I'm okay. Just need to see you. On my way."

* * *

Dewdrops on naked rose bushes fractured the morning sun's rays on their way into the dining room. At the table, Denholm bit into a second toasted crumpet. Buttery honey oozed at the corner of his mouth. He caught it with an index finger and licked it off. "Have you any idea where she might have gone?"

Honor eyeballed him over a mug of tea, shaking her head.

Still chewing, he said, "Do you two ever discuss anything important? I admit I'm surprised it was she who left. If I were you, I'd be thanking my lucky stars I got off so lightly."

"You're not helping. I'm worried about her."

He snorted, scratching his nose. "We can find her if you insist. One phone call. Easy. As a matter of fact, this is all too easy. Why would she walk away from a gravy train like you? Moral outrage, my arse. I smell a rat."

"Give it a rest." Jaw clenching, she glared at him. "Her mother's just died. She's been disinherited and has walked away with little more than the clothes on her back. How can you be so hardnosed?" She put the mug down too firmly. "I need to know she's okay."

Eyebrows disappearing into his hairline and nodding sagely, he said, "All right. I'll have her found. On one condition." He paused, mouth downcast. "Don't you roll your eyes at me, young lady. Check the whole house and see if anything is missing. I want your books audited, bank accounts examined and your personal computer forensically investigated. I want absolute proof that all is as it should be. Then and only then, I'll have her found. Deal?"

"Oh, come on, Dad! What BS is this? It would be a complete and utter waste of time." She shook her head, staring out at the roses. Silence yawned between them. And then the password incident with Merrin occurred to her—she had thought it best left unmentioned. "Would it take long?"

"I'll have people pick up what they need from your house this afternoon. Be done in a couple of days." He came to stand behind her, hands resting warmly on her sagging shoulders. "Go home, my soft-hearted angel. I love you to Pluto and back. Don't ever forget it, even when we fight. Especially when we fight."

She covered his right hand with her own. "My house doesn't feel good. Feels like it's been ransacked…violated. May I come back tonight, stay a few days?"

"Aw, angel. Of course. Pack a bag and stay as long as you like. You'll cook for us, eh?" He bent and cheekily pecked the top of her head. "All right!"

* * *

It was late Thursday afternoon when the police report was delivered to Denholm's doorstep. He scanned its pages and picked up the phone. A call to the bank immediately blocked transactions on the Landladies' business account. Another call sent police hurrying to triangulate Merrin's mobile phone, finding her, wherever she was. Yet another call went to the family solicitor. The last call was a text message to his daughter, urging her to come home as soon as she could.

"Thirty-six thousand dollars?" Honor's voice was an incredulous squeal. "How did she manage that?"

Sitting next to her on the sofa, Denholm said, "With help from someone a whole lot smarter than her. Someone who thought they were clever enough to get way with creating false suppliers and surreptitiously skimming the Landladies' accounts over the past ten months."

Honor's eyes were huge. "I'm gob-smacked. After all I've done for her."

"There's a kernel of truth in the old saying, 'no good deed goes unpunished.' The forensic accountant found that, in effect, Merrin was running two sets of books. One to pull the wool over your eyes, and another that showed a trail of illicit transactions, very carefully concealed. You're fortunate enough to know people in high places." He jiggled his eyebrows at her, not bothering to conceal a self-righteous grin. "Told you so."

She shook her head and rested her eyelids. "Yes, your Excellency."

"We know where she is, by the way." He gently poked her arm. "Do you still want to know?"

"I do need to know she's safe."

"In a rental in the Belconnen area. It was leased to one Lance Roach two months ago. He left his wife to shack up with Merrin. They've been planning this for some time."

"What?" Eyes sprung open, she gaped at him. "That pasty ponce? She left me for that slimy—"

"She left you for the money. And whatever else he's got that you haven't. My people said he's close to expert at digital fraud. Almost got away with it. The police will have picked up both of them for questioning by now."

Honor leaned forward, arms folded onto her knees. "I'm struggling to believe any of this. I really am."

Denholm rubbed a hand between her shoulder blades. "The trouble with you is you choose to always see the best in people, too often to you own detriment. We live and learn. And, as I've already said, you've had a lucky escape." Her doubt-filled eyes glanced back at him. "I mean it. You're worth much, much more than thirty-six grand, both financially and as a partner." He clasped her shoulders and drew her to his chest. "By making off with her ill-gotten gains, which will be confiscated as proceeds of crime, plus earning herself a conviction, she'll end up with a hundred percent of nothing. It's very shortsighted. Bloody stupid. Silly woman. Silly, silly woman. She never was worthy of you."

"Please, not that tired cliché. Look, I cared about her… thought she cared about me. I'm really thrown by this underhanded behaviour. It's sickening to realise you've been white-anted. I hate this…hate the idea of having to be suspicious of my partner. I feel a right twit!"

"Don't be too hard on yourself. The lesson is: whoever controls the money has your success or failure in their hands. In a partnership, all parties need to know the facts."

She tugged her plait forward, curling it around her fingers. "What gets me is that I deliberately gave her responsibility so she could be involved and feel better about herself. I chose to trust and have faith in her. When I think about all the time and effort I invested into our relationship, I could kick myself."

"We all make mistakes, my girl. You've learned the hard way, but it could have been a far worse outcome. Fact is, it's all okay. Landladies will be okay. You don't have to worry." He hesitated before asking, "Was her name on the house title?"

"I bought it before I met her, remember? We never got around to amending it. Maybe I'll rent the house out for a while. Then I can think about what I want to do with it. I don't feel like living there alone again. Is it okay if I stay a while?"

"It would be my pleasure to have you here." He tweaked her plait. "Just be careful who you bring home. No Merrin types allowed."

She groaned loudly. "Hardly! I'm still reeling. As it happens, I've met someone you might like, but I don't think she's talking to me."

He leaned away, catching her sheepish look. "This *is* news. How about I take you for a slap-up surf 'n' turf dinner at the club? My shout. On condition that you tell me all about what's-her-name. Hop to it, my girl. Get your glad-rags on and let's go!"

CHAPTER TWENTY-EIGHT

An immaculately dressed Duscha waited patiently for Roxanne. In Fielding & Atkinson's meeting room, she sat with a sandy-haired, quietly spoken man who occupied the head of the table, busily keying in notes on a laptop. Jim had selected Mike Azzopardi, Community Advocate, to mediate between her and Roxanne about the disputed inheritance. Straightening her charcoal suit jacket over a crisp lemon shirt, Duscha checked her shoe polish, choosing to chill rather than ponder what might come of it all.

When her virtual twin walked in, Duscha promptly stood smiling and held out her hand. "Hello Roxanne. Pleased to meet you."

Toe to toe, with eyes on a remarkably similar level, Roxanne cocked her head with ill-concealed surprise. It dawned on Duscha that her half-sister had had no idea what she looked like. They barely shook hands. Po-faced, Roxanne sat across from Duscha.

Mike glanced from one to the other and said, "Thank you both for agreeing to be here. My role as a neutral party is to facilitate understanding between you. I have no vested interest in any specific outcome. You may simply choose to discuss the issues by making statements or asking questions. Please keep it simple and factual to avoid confusion or confrontation. If you have legal questions, I will clarify where I can. Since it was you who instigated this meeting, what is it you want to achieve today, Duscha?"

She half-smiled at him. "I want to give Roxanne the opportunity to explain why she thinks our father should have disinherited me. She may have very good reasons of which I am unaware. With fresh understanding, we may be able to avoid going to court, which would save us both a great deal of time and money."

Roxanne said curtly, "Reasons? Are you being deliberately thick? I am *my* father's only daughter. *You* should never have been born!"

Mike said, "Excuse me, but the paternity test proves that Duscha is your father's bona-fide daughter and therefore, your half-sister. Please keep to the facts."

Duscha looked at him. "Perhaps Roxanne has other ideas as to what constitutes a daughter? I'm willing to hear them." She turned to scrutinise Roxanne. "I'd really like to know why you are his only daughter."

Roxanne leaned forward across the table. "You have no idea, do you? What he was like as a father. Let me tell you he was no saint. Always too busy for my mother or me. Always late coming home, preoccupied with planning some grandiose development that took all his time." She poked herself in the chest. "It was *me* who looked after my mother when she fought with depression and booze. *I* was the one doing all the parenting. *I* was his family until I got married and had my own kids. And what are you? You don't even have a family!"

"What are you talking about?" Duscha's heart sank. "Of course I have a family."

"Bullshit. You're one of those. Like Aunt Charlotte. Just what you deserve for his behaviour. Shaming my mother like that. Bastard."

Mike looked nonplussed. "We seem to have gone off topic somewhat. Duscha, do you understand Roxanne's argument?"

Duscha regarded Roxanne who sat in seeming triumph, eyes glittering rocks. "Let me see if I've got this right. Because she did all the hard yards as our father's long-suffering daughter, she deserves to inherit and I don't. And because gay people like me and Aunt Charlotte allegedly can't have families, even when we do, then I don't deserve to inherit. I think that covers it."

Eyebrows raised, he nodded. "Fair enough. Before I sum up, is there anything else you want to ask?"

"No." Duscha examined the ceiling for a moment and then locked a steely gaze with Roxanne. "But I would like say to Roxanne that she has my sympathy for having to put up with his shortcomings. It seems he was self-absorbed and unpredictable. In contrast, his sister—our Aunt Charlotte—described him as a life-saving rogue. That type of personality is difficult to live with. We all have our masks and you didn't like the one he wore for you. But he had the business vision, carried out the work and made the money. It was his to do with as he so chose. And we are obliged to honour his wishes, whether we like them or not." She glanced at Mike. "I think we're done here."

"Very well. Roxanne, thank you for coming and having your say. In all probability, nothing you have argued would substantially change a judge's determination, should you proceed with contesting your father's will. That is my informed opinion. You may wish to obtain further legal counsel." He closed his laptop.

With a shrug, Roxanne got to her feet. As she turned to go, she caught Duscha's eye and nodded slightly. She walked out, head bowed.

Mike muttered, "You were very restrained."

"She was determined to hate me and be in the right." Duscha exhaled heavily. "What she said is relatively tame. I could have acted outraged and offered lessons in civility, but my mother taught me to never argue with a fool. I suspect trying to educate her would only have escalated things. So, I offered sympathy and gave her an out. A way to be right and save face at the same time. It's worth a punt."

Mike shook her hand. "I get where you're coming from. It's been a privilege, Duscha. Good luck."

On the way home, Duscha stopped by the local supermarket to buy flat rice noodles for the *pad Thai* she planned to make for dinner. She found herself immobile in front of a wall of noodle packets, mulling over Roxanne's slurs and insults.

Because of her eye shape and absent father, she'd been called a "Mongoloid bastard" countless times in primary school. At high school, "lezzo" had been tacked on to the old moniker. She'd found the best policy was to either ignore the name-calling, or trot out a pithy reply, such as, "Yeah, I'm crazy as! Scared? Drink concrete and toughen up!" University had been a welcome escape.

She'd spent most of her adult life resisting the pressure to be something she wasn't. These days, most people paid no attention to who she might love or lie down with. Roxanne was an anomaly: a privileged, entitled social conservative who hated to share her elevated position with those she considered to be lesser beings. There was money in that perspective. Given half a chance, Roxanne would cash in. But this time the law was firmly on Duscha's side. Mike had made that abundantly clear.

She crouched down and found a packet of a favourite brand of dry noodles on the lowest shelf. Under her breath, she muttered, "Pour yourself a tall glass of quick set, Roxie. Drop it now, because you've already lost this one. The world has moved on. Try to keep up!"

Duscha slid the noodles into a bowl of warm water to soak while she chopped vegetables—a meditative activity that she rarely hurried. In the tranquillity and comfortable silence of this old house that had witnessed heaven-knew-what, she contemplated the other women who had lived and loved within its walls: Irene and Ruby, Charlotte and Sylvia. Were their lives markedly more fraught than hers? Were they as passionate and fulfilled as hers had been, and would be into the unknown years ahead? How well had they handled living in a world dominated by heterosexuals?

Piling up julienned carrots, Duscha smiled. Obviously, they had lived and loved, regardless, by staying true to their essential nature. Given society's doubtless opposition, their courage was nothing short of heroic. And she, Duscha, would follow in their footsteps with equally good grace through more enlightened times.

Finely slicing spring onions on the diagonal, she said aloud, "Hey, Aunt Charlotte? I'm loving the house. Thanks again!"

CHAPTER TWENTY-NINE

Canberra, May 1999

On the back patio, Charlotte Coxall slumped in her scruffy old bentwood chair, soaking up the autumn afternoon's sun. The mulberry's leaves were a sea of gold beneath the majestic tree. Others might call it "a right mess," but Lottie thought them utterly gorgeous. She'd always left the leaves to settle and disintegrate wherever they felt like.

Charlotte had pleurisy. And not for the first time. She was prone to chronic bronchitis, the legacy of too many nicotine bonbons in the 1960s and 70s. That was a time when many of her fellow nurses also smoked, not to mention the doctors. She'd given up by 1982, but the bronchitis persisted. Only last year, she'd had full-blown flu that morphed into pleurisy and a hospital stay at Christmas. Not that she much cared. Sylvia died in a traffic accident in 1994. On an early morning trip to visit Aunty Beryl in Goulburn, Sylvia's Subaru had been hit head-on by a fatigued Sydney truckie who bounced his Scania across the median strip, just north of the Sutton Road overpass. Since then, Charlotte had been largely going through the motions.

Christmas without Syl was truly horrible: a gruelling, solitary agony to be endured until New Year.

Now sixty-six years old and noticeably delicate, she'd learned the stabbing pains in her chest were minimised only by shallow breathing, which meant she couldn't do much of anything. Her doctor thought she might have a pulmonary embolism, and wanted her in hospital again, pronto. But she wasn't ready to sign in just yet. She had a decision to make…a dilemma to nut out that wouldn't solve itself with her death.

Aunt Irene's jewellery. The safest and most logical thing was to bequeath it to Cliff and thereby absolve herself of all responsibility. If he sold it off and built houses out of the proceeds, did it really matter? She couldn't help but think that it did. It would be far more in the spirit of Aunt Irene's bequest to her back in 1960 if she passed it on to Cliff's daughter, Duscha, when the time came.

A tickle started and she coughed, phlegm rattling up her throat. She caught it in her cotton hankie, breathing a sigh of relief when the bout subsided.

The dream was what drove her. For weeks now, any number of mornings at precisely six a.m., she had woken from a vivid dream in which she saw Duscha's tousled blond head bent over The Letter. She had already written and rewritten it several times to get the wording just right. The Letter would be in the hidden toolbox, which meant Duscha would have to find it. Should she trust the dream?

If she decided not to and just gave the jewellery to Cliff, its pecuniary fate was virtually sealed. She knew he wouldn't be able to resist its cash value. On the other hand, if she did hide the toolbox and Duscha never found it? That would be a pity. But logically, a stranger would find it one day. It wouldn't be lost forever.

If she did trust the dream and Duscha found the toolbox, then all would be well. And happiness would prevail amongst the ancestors in spirit: Irene and Ruby, herself and Sylvia.

Lottie had made up her mind. She levered her frail frame up from the protesting chair and toddled indoors. Giddy at the bedroom door, she stopped to draw breath.

The small hole in the wall next to the chimney was ready and waiting. The toolbox would go back where Aunt Irene had first hidden it. A description of its whereabouts had been written in a letter given to Charlotte when she inherited the house—she'd never understood the need for subterfuge. And the chocolate box with Sylvia's letters and The Letter would nestle snugly on top. Once the space was filled, she wedged the plywood cover into place, glued over a protective sheet and re-glued the wallpaper to conceal it. She could manage that. Just.

Lottie regarded her reflection in the deco mirror. Aunt Irene had once told her it had been bought especially for the house, the year she and Ruby moved in. The woman who looked back at her now was quite frightening. Without a shadow of doubt, she was painfully thin, not long for this world.

To the mirror, she said, "I look bloody awful, thanks very much."

Over her left shoulder, she glimpsed a shadow in the mirror…an outline of a pony-tailed girl. She whispered, "Oh, Syl. It won't be long now, best beloved. Not long now. We'll be together again soon. Can hardly wait. But first, I have to say this."

She cleared her throat and intoned, "Spirit of number twenty-four, please grant me this last favour. Make perfectly sure that Duscha finds what is rightfully hers. Do whatever it takes. It's over to you and I know you can do it. I'm counting on you. And I know you won't let me down. Thanks."

CHAPTER THIRTY

Late one afternoon, Duscha was rolling the last square of fresh green paint on the bathroom wall. She could hear Stuart hammering intermittently. He'd replaced the top of the doorframe in her bedroom and most of the base plate running beneath the timber-framed walls where they'd been eaten out by the white ants. Now he was busy fitting the new tongue-and-groove floorboards. It was a slow and painstaking task requiring every plank to be cut to size, levered into position and nailed to the original floor joists.

Just as she placed the roller in the tray and stood up to admire her work, she heard a crash, the sound of breaking glass and Stuart bellowing obscenities. She bolted down the hall. On the bedroom floor, Stuart was on his knees surrounded by wicked-looking shards of mirror glass. The mirror's octagonal timber backing board was lying across the floor joists, askew, yet still in one piece.

"Jeez, Duscha. I am God-awful sorry. But I was nowhere near it, I swear!" He looked up at her pleadingly. "I'm down here nailing by the chimney and the bastard thing near crowned me!"

"Are you hurt?"

"Yeah, nah." He sat back on his haunches. "Would you get the wheelbarrow and some newspaper? We'll have to wrap it all up. And my gloves. They're in my tool bag. Best I don't move."

She was already on her way and soon back with the barrow, plus a pair of gloves for herself. Crouched beside him, she collected the shards he handed over and deftly wrapped them.

He said, "It's gone everywhere. I'll have to go under the floor to get to it all." He dropped his feet between the joists, squatted down and began handing up pieces. "Jeez, what a smash-up. Wouldn't it rot your socks? Hey, I can see the mud tunnel the termites made to climb up the chimney bricks and access the timber frame. This is definitely where they got in. Hang on a tick…what's this?"

"What's what?"

"There's something metal strung under the wall next to the chimney. Looks like an old tin." He ducked out of sight and then stuck up a gloved hand. "Pass me a screwdriver, would you please? The long blue one."

Duscha handed him the screwdriver and he disappeared under the floor. Much scraping and levering later, he re-emerged with an elongated, rusty box. He plopped it noisily on the floorboards, twisting it this way and that, stooping to read its side. "The label says it's a Stanley Fix-Up Set. For Pleasure and Profit." Looking up at her with a grin, he said, "In other words, it's a toolbox. And it's got stuff inside. Maybe it's full of treasure! More likely, clapped out old tools. Here, take it. It's yours to crack open. Now I can finish the floor. Then you'll be able to drop the carpet back in place."

"You mean I'll be able to walk around in here without stumbling over anything? Finally!"

Soon after Stuart left, Duscha finished washing out the painting gear—always a long and tedious job, especially when she had to clean herself up as well before going out. She was expected over at her mother's to help make *pelmeni* and *piroshki* for the Russian Orthodox Church bazaar on Saturday. On the way out, she eyed off the vintage toolbox that she hadn't had time to open. Like a long lost and forgotten nuisance, it cluttered up the kitchen bench. On impulse, she hastily tucked the clumsy thing under her arm and slung it onto the passenger seat in her car.

Three hours later, Duscha and Valeria were putting the last of the two hundred dumplings and small pies into freezer packs of ten, ready for sale at the bazaar. While they had rolled pastry, Duscha had told her mother about the broken mirror and Stuart's find, promising they would open it together when they finished.

Valeria chirped, "Quick, quick! Go get the tin while I put the kettle on for tea. I'm *dying* to have a look."

Duscha took off a faded yellow-daisy apron, now coated in flour, and washed her hands. At the kitchen door, she called back, "Don't get too excited. It's probably full of Aunt Charlotte's rusty wrenches."

With merry eyes, Valeria said, "Who cares? It'll be fun. Hurry up!"

Duscha slid the toolbox onto the dining table where Valeria was pouring tea. Then they sat side by side, sipping tea, both staring at the dilapidated thing. It was quite long, made of durable metal sheeting under the rust, with a thin metal handle on top and two front latches most recently secured sometime last century.

Valeria said, "You're right, it looks underwhelming. Could be full of bones. Or worse. Come on, let's be done with it."

"Stuart told me it was right next to the chimney, probably directly beneath where I found the tin of letters. I just didn't notice it at the time."

"*Now* you tell me. I've got the shivers!"

Duscha grinned, placing a thumb under the nearest latch. "You flick open the right one and I'll do the left. Ready?"

They sprung the latches together and Duscha tugged open the reluctant lid. A layer of once-white scrunched up paper stared back at them. After a long moment, she removed the layer. They peered in—tightly packed parcels of tissue paper filled the tin.

Valeria blurted, "Looks like drugs. Shall we open them?"

"Here goes nothing." Duscha slipped out a small parcel that she carefully unwrapped on the table between them. A gold bar brooch featuring a ruby-eyed kookaburra was laid bare.

"Very cute," said Valeria. "Looks harmless enough. What else is in here?"

For the next twenty minutes of silence, they unwrapped jewellery piece after jewellery piece, some simply elegant, others ornate. Yet more was encrusted with coloured stones. There were necklaces, pendants, brooches, pins, and rings of all shapes and sizes, notably varying in age and style.

At the bottom, Duscha found two sheets of foolscap paper stapled together. It appeared to be an itemised list of the toolbox's contents, presumably typed on a manual typewriter with an antiquated typeface.

"Will you look at these baubles?" said Valeria. "Not my taste. A lot of it is flowery. Elaborate. Old-fashioned. I wonder if any of it is real."

"I have a sneaking suspicion it might be, given Aunt Charlotte's story. The problem is what to do with it? Is it worth anything? Who would know how to value it all?"

Valeria looked askance. "Why would you bother? Most of it looks like tacky costume jewellery to me. Disappointing. Still, it *must* be worth something. That mirror practically committed suicide to get you to discover the hiding place."

"I hadn't thought of that. If its glass hadn't shattered and fallen through the floor, this would never have been found. But now what?"

"Perhaps you could ask Mischa. Let's put it all back, huh? Take it home, my Duschka. You could hide it under the bed… pretend it's worth stealing."

On Michele's advice, Duscha sent an email to a curator at the Powerhouse Museum in Sydney. In the message, she explained the collection likely belonged to her great-aunt Irene Coxall, otherwise known as Mrs. Angus Armfield. She attached a copy of the inventory and two photos: one of a white metal ring with large clear stones and another of the prettiest of the pendants.

She didn't hear back. Preoccupied with finishing the painting before starting her job, Duscha promptly forgot all about it. The Powerhouse Museum's curator obviously had more important things to do than pander to random enquiries from the public.

CHAPTER THIRTY-ONE

On a Friday evening two weeks later, Duscha sat on the sofa nursing a cup of tea and a photo. In the background, meditation music consisting of gently crashing waves and seabird calls lulled her to relax. The room was dark except for a colourful leadlight lamp on a low table beside her and a solitary white candle burning steadily. Given the forecasted cold night, she'd turned on the gas heater. Flames flickered over the fake log fire that was remarkably soothing to contemplate.

It was three years since Noelle died—the lit candle was in memoriam. In her left hand was a photo of the two of them standing together, casually dressed and smiling broadly, a lush vineyard disappearing into the distance behind them. They had stopped for a wine tasting and asked another tourist to take the photo. A nudge taller even than Duscha, Noelle's straight brown blunt-cut was inclined toward her, sunglasses parked on her head, as usual. They were happier times. Duscha was still drawn to admire Noelle's even features and serenely confident smile. Apart from a slim figure, she looked not a bit like Honor. She placed the photo beside the lamp.

Eighteen days had passed since she'd last seen or heard from Honor.

Since then, she'd struggled to fall asleep at night. When she tried to nod off, thoughts of Honor would bubble to the surface. She would berate herself for sending Honor away, for being so emphatic about it. Part of her was aching to hear from her, wished she'd ring, text, turn up…*anything* at all. The silence was deafening, made all the worse by the fact that she had insisted on it. Well, Honor had taken her at her word. She had no one to blame but herself.

The fact remained: she was missing her badly.

Duscha closed her eyes against the flickering faux flames and, once again, felt Honor in her arms, with her muscular back and the swell of her hips, that luscious mouth melting beneath hers. She took herself back to that morning when she woke with an exhausted Honor, dead to the world, curled up and backed into her chest, toasty warm and smelling deliciously of salty woman. It had taken all her resolve not to let nature take its course.

Now, she wished she had. God knows, she wasn't going to get another opportunity like that anytime soon. Maybe not ever again.

She shook her head and let the tears fall wherever they may.

Sniffing, she said aloud, "What kind of noble-minded fool would let someone like her get away? You nutcase! You pompous nob! Look at you. You're a pathetic, weeping wreck. What were you thinking?"

But she knew full well what she'd been thinking. About protecting her heart, still vulnerable from the loss of Noelle. In giving her heart to Honor, she would have made herself "the other woman." Duscha hadn't wanted to make Honor choose. Hadn't wanted the guilt. For them to be together, Honor would have to choose to make it so. She would have to leave her partner for Duscha. How likely was that?

Yet the inconvenient truth was that, with a mind of its own, her heart had already given itself to Honor. It had already happened. Her impetuous heart was way ahead of any clumsy intellectual process. It knew who it loved. It just knew. And now it was hurting, notably as a physical ache under her left breast—an insistent ache that refused to be consoled by any rational argument she might try to feed it. If her heart had had eyes to roll at her, it would have.

"I'm sorry. Please forgive me. I did my best and let you down. Barring a miracle, it's all over. There is nothing else I can do. It's up to Honor now, so please let me forget about her for a while. Give it a rest."

She wiped down her wet cheeks and took the cup to the kitchen. A fish curry she'd made was waiting for her to cook basmati rice, with a pumpkin and broccoli side. She dug out a saucepan and prepared the rest of her dinner.

She had her hands in the sink washing dinner dishes when an unexpected thought popped into her head. If she got lucky… *very* lucky…she might get to love Honor, just as she had loved Noelle. To receive that gift twice in one lifetime would be extraordinary. It hadn't happened yet, but it could. Brightening visibly, she decided to stay as positive as she could.

Busying herself at the kitchen table with the jewellery and her camera, Duscha considered her new job. The first week in the Urban Renewal Division had been hectic, a steep learning curve entailing meeting dozens of new faces and coming to grips with her new role. The second week had been far less stressful.

Only this afternoon, she had decided to take photos to match the pieces with the descriptions on the inventory. If she never heard back from the Powerhouse, she would have to find a qualified expert to value everything for insurance purposes. She had no real clue but figured the collection might be worth some thousands of dollars.

She'd also decided to have the suicidal mirror's glass replaced. A call to a local antique dealer had provided the name of a glazier who had promised to re-create the perfect octagonal shape and fit it to the still-intact timber backing board. Not a cheap exercise, she figured it was well worth being restored to its former glory.

SBS Chill radio playing softly in the background, she laid out individual pieces on sheets of copy paper, positioning them to present at their best. An attractive woman she'd met at work earlier in the week came to mind. She resembled Honor, which had thrown Duscha for a loop momentarily. A smile had turned into a sad grimace, causing the other woman to back off and hurry away. It had occurred to her that she might never see Honor again. Now, she shivered, pushing the thought aside. Dwelling on the worst-case scenario served her not one iota. For now, she was keeping the faith.

Her thoughts drifted to great-Aunt Irene and the old toolbox. What had it meant to the old lady, the one-time jeweller's wife who inherited a chain of shops? She must have created the collection of baubles, more or less valuable. Yet she didn't do it alone. By her side was Ruby Milborne, her erstwhile secretary. If Valeria was right, they were a bona-fide couple who packed up and left bustling Sydney for the peaceful, then small town of Canberra. More critically, far away from prying eyes and society's speculation about the true nature of their relationship. And perhaps away from social condemnation, even harassment. In Canberra, they would have been unknown, therefore able to present themselves as whatever they liked. Sisters, spinsters or widows? Whatever story they had spun, it had obviously worked for them.

Duscha tried to imagine how isolating and difficult their lives would have been. Charlotte and Sylvia had had it hard enough in the 60s, let alone Irene and Ruby in the 20s. They could have been together for a very long time, yet there was no way of knowing the length and breadth of their love. No records existed of relationships such as theirs. Given the odds against them, she wondered how they managed to find each other and make a life together in the first place. In the olden days, queer women were tough creatures. They were determined, committed, and strong. If they meant their relationship to survive for any length of time, they had to be.

CHAPTER THIRTY-TWO

Sydney, January 1919

In the first week of the new year, Irene sat at her oak desk in the front parlour of her house in Bellevue Hill, double-checking the previous month's accounts for each of the three stores. It helped that a firm of bookkeepers monitored the calculations before passing them to her each month. It was not her favourite task, but she had to keep abreast of Armfield's financial position. She was the business's sole owner-manager since Angus had died.

The years of fighting in France had taken a dreadful toll on the Allied forces. In January 1917, Angus had responded to a nationwide call for recruits to form the Sixth Australian Division. Despite being a forty-three-year-old, he was accepted, sent to France and killed that June in a battle for the town of Messines.

Now eighteen months later, Irene was barely keeping up with the long, grinding hours made even more difficult by a new, pervasive anxiety…a deep distress…an underlying dread of a loss too awful to contemplate. Just two months ago in

November 1918, the Armistice had been declared, ending "the war to end all wars." In her quiet hours, she had formulated a plan for the future. All depended on one person who may or may not be alive. That dread deepened when, for the first time in eight years, a postcard failed to arrive last Christmas.

Over a year ago, Ruby's Christmas 1917 postcard had reported that she was in France driving ambulances for the Red Cross. For all Irene knew, Ruby could be dead and buried. No one would know to tell her. The thought made her brain freeze in horror. Daily, she fought back the panic that threatened to overwhelm her. What was she going to do?

She walked to the kitchen at the back of the house. The tin kettle filled, she set it on the Metters wood-fired stove and opened the damper to stoke the fire. Outside the back door, she emptied the porcelain teapot over a blazing-red geranium that loved soggy tea leaves. Teapot rinsed and primed with black tea, she pulled out a wooden kitchen chair and waited for water to boil.

That Christmas 1917 postcard had given an address for Ruby as care of the Red Cross in London. Irene had written back a perfunctory one-pager in January 1918 informing Ruby that Angus had been killed the previous June. Not knowing who might read it, she had been deliberately matter-of-fact. And now she wondered if Ruby had ever received that note.

Seated at the kitchen table, Irene was exhausted. Since Christmas Eve with its ominously empty letterbox, she had barely slept. She admitted to herself that she couldn't go on this way, worrying herself sick. Pulling out hairpins, she let loose her mane and rubbed her scalp to ease some tension. But it served only to undo her and tears fell freely. With no one to see, she let them puddle on the table. What did it matter? She'd lost them both. Angus and Ruby, both gone. With a sob, she buried her face in folded forearms. The kettle whistled.

Blotchy face mopped roughly with a gentleman's kerchief, she grabbed the kettle and sloshed water into the pot. There had to be a limit to her swinging wildly between optimism and pessimism. Only that morning, she had read in the newspaper that shipping from Europe via the English Channel was complete chaos, with troop ships, war ships and supply ships all jockeying for access in and out of ports. It could be that mail was delayed, caught up in the fray. She would give it until the end of the month. And then she could fall apart, but not now. For now, she would drink tea by the gallon, keep the faith and pray for a miracle.

* * *

It was dusk when Ruby thanked the tram driver for directions and stepped down from the vehicle onto Bellevue Road. She was looking for a house on Rivers Street. Having disembarked with hundreds of other passengers when her ship docked at Sydney only an hour previously, she had caught the tram outside the crowded terminal.

White kit bag draped over a shoulder, she paused to peer at a street sign and turned left, urgently scanning house numbers. Here was a two-storeyed home with bay windows and east-facing front verandahs. It looked peaceful and perfectly charming, even in the half-light. She took herself quietly through the gate, sucked in a shaky breath and knocked briskly.

The door opened a few cautious inches. Irene said, "May I help you?"

"For pity's sake, I hope so. A person could die of thirst out here."

A squeal and the door flew wide open. "What the…Ruby?" Irene grabbed her by the lapels and pulled her inside, shut the door and stared at her, face lit with incredulous hope. "Dear, dear girl! How did you get here? Oh, you're nothing but skin and bone."

Ruby pulled loose the kit bag, let it plop to the floor and shrugged her way out of her dilapidated box coat. "By boat and tram. To my great fortune, a West End pawn shop gave me forty-two guineas for your hat pin. I'd carried it sewn into the seam of my coat all these years. It became a wee beaten up but delivered in the end."

Stroking each of Ruby's cheeks, Irene said, "My miracle. I can't believe it's you. That you're here in the flesh. What happened to your hair? It's barely past your ears!"

"A nurse cut it for me. Made it much easier for me to keep clean when I was driving all over the front in France. May I sit down somewhere? I'll tell you everything, all in good time."

Irene grasped a hand, leading the way down the hall. "Dear sweet girl, come into the kitchen. I'll give you anything you need. Anything at all."

"For my stomach, bread and butter and a cuppa cha will suffice. Irene, please stop mucking about. Come here. Please." Ruby stood waiting until Irene stepped into her arms. They clung to each other, rocking gently.

"Oh, Irene. Dear God, you feel so, so good! Would you believe, I've learned all sorts since we parted. Now I'm a certified stenographer and bookkeeper, I would be handy for you to have around, practically speaking."

"Dearest Ruby. Whatever you say."

"But all I really need is to be close to you, to love you until my dying day. I don't expect you to feel the same. You said once that you were fond of me. That would be enough, but if you'd rather I didn't, I have enough money for my passage back."

Irene leaned away, peering at Ruby. "Do you think I'd greet you like this if I were merely fond?" She slipped free to sit by the kitchen table, worrying a thumbnail. "When we met, I was married and honour-bound. If it had not been so, I don't know what I would have done, but in the circumstances, I was in no position to speak of strong feelings. That way, if you met someone else you could think, well, Irene was merely fond, and you would have forgotten about me."

"As if I could ever forget you."

Intent on explaining, Irene said, "To be blunt, if I had left my husband, I would have been severely financially compromised so as to bring nothing but pennies to the party. You would have been better off without me. It sounds harsh, but in this world where men and money rule, it would likely have ruined us both, including any shared feelings. You can see that, can't you?"

Ruby pulled out a chair. "When you explain it that way, I do. You made no promises, and I never took you for a fool. But I suspected you felt *more* than fond, which is the major part of why I came to see you."

Mollified, Irene managed an anxious smile. "I was waiting for your postcard and grew frantic when none arrived. Why did you not send me one?"

Ruby waved one hand in the air. "Because, like as not, it would have travelled on the same boat as me. After the Armistice, Calais was like bedlam, but I fluked a ride back to London, read your earlier message about Angus and bought the only berth I could scrounge on the next boat to Sydney."

Irene rocked her head from side to side. "Well, my plan was to wait for your postcard, find out where you were and then invite you to come and live with me." She reached out to take one of Ruby's hands in her own. "My dear sweet girl, I've never forgotten our one night together. It has fortified me through the most difficult of times. Although I would doubt myself sufficiently to wonder if it were all a dream. But you're here now. The God's-honest truth is that I adore you to heaven and back. I have all along and likely will until my dying day. I didn't think it fair to say while I was not free to honour the sentiment."

Ruby patted her lap. Irene left her chair to sit across Ruby's thighs, one arm around her shoulders. "Goodness, been forgetting to eat have we?"

"I'd lost my appetite." Irene smiled wanly. "For many things. But now? With us to live for, I can't tell you how excited I am to be alive. With you, sweet girl."

"You're so beautiful. Still."

"Heavens above, I'm far from it. In truth, I feel like a hag!"

"You feel like a hag? If it pleases you, may I be your hag?"

Irene let out peals of laughter that ended with her face buried in Ruby's shoulder.

"For the love of God, Irene. Just kiss me!"

Irene covered Ruby's mouth with her own, kiss deepening until they both came up for air, flushed and bright-eyed.

Ruby's voice quavered. "I've prayed for you, imagined us together like this. Let's hope our dying days are eons away, because my lady, you and I have been a long time in the making. And I plan to savour every precious moment from here on in. You're sure I can stay a while?"

With a delighted laugh, Irene kissed Ruby's cheeks. "Yes! Please stay forever. Don't you dare leave…never ever!"

CHAPTER THIRTY-THREE

Duscha was framing the kookaburra brooch through the viewfinder when her mobile chimed.

In case you haven't heard, Merrin dumped Honor for a guy. Thought you should know. I'm happy for you both. Stu.

Duscha sagged onto a chair. She frowned at the message, reading and re-reading it. Thumbs flying, she replied:

Are you 100% sure?

Straight up, no bull! H told me. Go for it.

Aloud, she said, "Whoa, that's totally left field. How did that happen?"

She stared sightlessly at the jewellery scattered on the table. Most of the collection had photographed well by the light of two halogen lamps. Natural light could be better. In the morning, the plan was to take it all out onto the back deck to photograph everything again with indirect sunlight and compare results. But her thoughts were elsewhere, in a race with her lurching pulse. She wondered how Honor was feeling about all that. More importantly, why hadn't she heard from her?

What on earth was going on with her pocket-rocket?

* * *

Under the merciless glare of a winter's sun, Honor hissed out loud when a rose thorn tore across her forearm, just above the glove. She was in the middle of vigorously hacking her mother's roses, under the guise of pruning.

She'd just hung up from an awkward conversation with Stuart. He'd assumed she'd been in contact with Duscha and proceeded to ask how things were going between them. She had told him she hadn't ventured down that road. When pressed, she had explained that she was still adjusting to her relationship's abrupt end, not to mention her ex being charged with fraud. Hesitantly, Stuart had asked if she minded if he passed it on to Duscha. She'd told him she wasn't feeling too good about herself, let alone the whole situation. Right now, she was shocked and saddened, if Duscha really wanted to know. Stuart had wished her well before ending the conversation.

The truth was she wasn't sure how much of the current mess she had brought upon herself. Had she become complacent over the years, effectively letting Merrin down by being too indulgent of her flaws? And she still felt guilty about leaving her in Adelaide to face the family alone. Even though that had been Merrin's choice, it seemed shabby.

More to the point, she was humiliated. That Merrin had left her for that repulsive weasel, Lance, did nothing for her self-esteem. And that Merrin had betrayed her trust with the finances was both embarrassing and infuriating. More than a little bit angry and sorry for herself, she was too busy licking her wounds to handle anything remotely contentious with other people. She was definitely not fit for human consumption, let alone to be any kind of endearing company for Duscha.

Beneath the mortification and guilt, she was seething with anger, best kept to herself until she calmed down. It could be a while before that eventuated.

She positioned the loppers' beaked jaws around the base of a thick rose cane, crunched the arms closed and watched it crash to the ground with a satisfying thud.

CHAPTER THIRTY-FOUR

Duscha had chosen the National Museum of Australia's café as a neutral, very public place for her and Honor to meet for coffee. It was forty-three days since they had last seen each other. Duscha was nervous. It had taken a number of polite text messages enquiring after Honor's health to get a response. And then a few more, carefully worded, to get her to agree to meet this Saturday morning.

The café's soaring windows allowed the climbing sun's warmth to bathe the many tables and chairs. Already half-full of visitors, the area overlooked a glassy Lake Burley Griffin swathed in wisps of mist. It was serenely beautiful on a late-winter's day.

Duscha spotted Honor walking in, scanning as she approached. She caught her breath and stared. Eye-catching at her scruffiest, Honor was compellingly lovely when she dressed well. Duscha swallowed hard and stood up, waiting.

With a soft smile, Honor leaned in and let Duscha peck her cheek. "Good morning. Have you ordered?"

"Not yet. It was getting to be a bun fight for a decent table. May I get you a latte?"

"Yes, please." Honor slid onto a chair and looked up. "And water, if they have it."

Duscha hurried way, sensing rapt attention following her progress. The order placed, she came back with two glasses and a carafe.

Honor poured water, and they each took a sip. "I'm sorry it's been a while. I really wasn't playing hard to get. Sorting things out has been tediously complicated. Just needed some time."

"Understood. It's a process," said Duscha. "With sometimes unexpected feelings involved. I don't need you to explain yourself. How's business, and what else have you been up to?"

"Business is picking up with spring on the way. I'm living at my Dad's place for the moment."

"How's that working for you?"

"He loves someone cooking for him!" Honor chuckled. "But he's easily pleased so it's no real hardship. He'll even prep veggies, which is pretty amazing. I don't think he did such things for my mother. But he's retired now. A gentleman of leisure."

A busy waitress scooted cups of coffee across the table and hurried off before they could thank her.

Honor said, "I've been scrubbing up my house in Higgins on the weekends. I'm considering selling it."

"You don't want it?"

"I don't want to live there by myself. It doesn't feel right."

Duscha caught the melancholy in her voice. "Sure. I had to move house when Noelle died. I stayed where I was for a while, but—"

"No comparison. My partner left me. In the scheme of things, no biggie."

"Yet part of you grieves?"

Honor gave her a searching look. "Surprisingly, yes. It's confusing."

"Understandable. All those hopes and dreams gone out the window. It hurts."

"I hadn't thought of it that way. Makes sense." Honor perked up a little. "Very wise of you. Thank you for your patience."

Duscha shrugged. "What else am I doing with myself? Besides carrying a flame for you."

They both laughed, exchanging hesitant glances. Honor's colour rose and abated. Over coffee, Duscha related how far she'd progressed with the house, that she'd settled into her new job, and how well the spinach and pansies were growing. She'd even harvested spinach and made quiche.

Aware that Honor wasn't exactly emotionally invested in such idle chitchat, Duscha changed it up. She said, "Jim Fielding…my solicitor. He phoned me two days ago. After consulting with any number of legal advisors, my half-sister, Roxanne, has withdrawn her threat to contest our father's will. She's backed off."

Understanding dawning, Honor said, "That's terrific. Well done!"

"I'd like to thank you for the advice to try mediation. Things could have taken a nasty turn for the worse without it. Thanks again."

"You're welcome, but it was the obvious course of action." Tongue firmly in her cheek, Honor said, "I knew you'd charm the pants off her."

Duscha guffawed, and they laughed out loud, catching each other's eye. Then Duscha pushed her empty cup aside and folded her arms on the table. Soberly, she said, "Where to from here?"

Honor studied the backs of her hands. "We could go out. Or just hang out. Get to know each other. Slowly." Then she looked intently into Duscha's eyes. "You know how I feel about you. That hasn't changed. But I don't know who you really are in everyday life. I was starting to when I was helping you paint your house. And it felt good…very good. I'd like a friendship with you as well, the likes of which I've never had with a partner. What do you think?"

"Why not? I figure we're halfway there already." Duscha ducked her head. "By the way, I'm delighted to hear you feel the same about me. You had me worried for a while. And be warned, the everyday me is far from perfect. In fact, I'm perfectly flawed. But I'll do my damnedest to always be kind and honest with you. How does that suit?"

With a shy smile, Honor said, "Perfectly."

"Good. How about we stroll around the museum?" Duscha stood up and shrugged on the black coat that skimmed her booted ankles.

Honor murmured, "That coat suits you all the way down to the ground."

Duscha grinned wickedly. "Walk this way."

* * *

That evening, Honor curled up on the sofa near Denholm who was watching a British cop show on the ABC. Unfocussed eyes saw more in her mind than on the television screen.

She and Duscha had wandered through the museum, stopping to read explanatory plaques at the more interesting displays. They had stood closely, not quite touching. When they walked, Duscha's toasty warm hands had drifted across Honor's shoulders, or left a light touch on her forearm or hand. And, just the once, the small of her back where Duscha's energy imprinted the outline of one hand like a tattoo. Elated, Honor could still sense it penetrating her spine, sparking a fire between her hips that smouldered, just waiting to be fanned aflame.

Her father's ears weren't as young as they used to be. On screen, people ran around shouting, guns blazing and sirens blaring at high volume. But she was oblivious. She smiled to herself, wondering at Duscha's impulse to reach out and touch. Despite long-forgotten schoolgirl fantasies, she'd never dreamed Duscha would be so physically expressive in real life. It was exciting to be admired and appreciated…to be wanted again by someone. Not to mention especially by the worshipped-from-afar, impossible-to-attain, Duscha the Dream. It was certainly doing wonders for Honor's self-esteem. Even more exciting was that being desired aroused desire to be desired even more.

It was intoxicating and compelling. And, incredibly, it might actually happen.

Moistening her lips, she uncurled from the sofa, pecked her father's forehead and took herself off to bed where she could continue to dream in private.

CHAPTER THIRTY-FIVE

Toward the end of their meal at Aubergine, Canberra's top restaurant, Honor savoured the white chocolate mousse. Across the table, Duscha was eating the same dessert, dwelling on each silky mouthful. The restaurant was busy, as was usual for a Friday night.

Honor said, "How was the red mullet?"

"Memorably good. And your barramundi?"

"Sublime."

Only halfway through the delicate mousse, Honor put down her spoon, sat back and looked around. Over the first three courses, they'd mostly talked of work. Nothing indigestible. Since the restaurant was too up-market for a family's budget, the other diners were couples or in small groups. They were a sophisticated crowd of discerning well-heeled locals, and perhaps those marking a special occasion.

"I don't know if you want to know, but—" Honor looked for Duscha's response. "Merrin phoned me, and I was curious enough to find out what she had to say. Apparently, Lance has thrown her under the metaphorical bus. He alleges it was all her idea. She says he talked her into it. She apologised and asked if we could reconcile. And would I help her fight the charges?"

Duscha wiped the corners of her mouth with a white linen napkin. "That's enterprising of her. What did you say?"

Tongue firmly in cheek, Honor said, "I gave it some thought. For a nanosecond. And then I asked her why she did it. She said she thought I could afford it. That I wouldn't notice. Wouldn't miss it. Much. And after all, it's only money. And perhaps we could share it again."

By now Duscha's arms were folded. "I love how people say, 'it's only money' when they're talking about *your* money. Still, it's an interesting point of view. And you said?"

"I said that, princess or pauper, theft was theft and I no longer trusted her. In helping her, there was nothing in it for me. And that I'd see her in court."

"Right." Duscha picked up the spoon and finished her mousse. "Am I the only one who wonders how you ended up with that woman?"

Honor was scraping up every last smear of mousse. "You and everyone who knows me. It kind of just happened. A combination of factors, I suppose. I was alone, she needed me, and it seemed like a good idea at the time. I thought it could work. And it did for a while. I was genuinely fond of her."

"You're a softie, Honor Boyce." Duscha leaned across the table. "Please don't change. Shall we go?"

Outside, they ambled along Barker Street, dawdling to look in shop windows. Duscha followed Honor to the dimly lit parking lot behind the shops where her ute was parked—they had come in separate cars.

When Honor unlocked and opened the driver's door, Duscha said, "I was wondering if you would help me prepare a garden bed for some roses."

"Sure, when were you thinking of doing that?"

"How about tomorrow."

Honor leaned on the ute's open door. "Haven't you seen enough of me?"

"Not by a long shot." Duscha stepped in to put her arms around her. "Thank you for a lovely evening. It was pretty special. You're special."

There was no one around. Honor kissed the welcoming mouth, lost her fingers in the blond hair and strained against Duscha's chest, hearts pounding in unison. Honor marvelled at Duscha's exquisite lips. She trembled, lost in a kiss that defied the need for air. But eventually she had to pull away with a gasp and wrapped her arms around Duscha as close as she could squeeze.

Duscha murmured, "Please come home. Stay with me tonight. Please?"

"You just want me to dig up your backyard in the morning."

Duscha hooted, picked up Honor and swung her around in midair. Their peals of laughter disturbed nary a soul.

"I'm glad your house is a whole lot warmer than outside." Honor watched Duscha lighting votive candles placed strategically around the bedroom. "This is nice. Very romantic."

Duscha grinned at her, blowing out the last match. "That's the idea. It also serves to make my wrinkles less obvious." She took a step to draw Honor into her arms. "Do we need mood music?"

"The sound of your voice and the beating of your heart are music enough for me." Honor tucked curls behind Duscha's left ear. "Let's boogie." She clasped hands behind Duscha's back as they slowly turned in circles on the spot.

Duscha kissed cheeks and throat, whispering, "I adore you, my gorgeous garden nut. You smell delicious. I want to climb into your clothes. It would be easier if you took them off."

Honor giggled. "I'd like to see you try to get into my pants. Three sizes too small, much?" She found Duscha's mouth and kissed her hard, hands dropping to lift Duscha's top up her back. Silently, Duscha helped until they were both undressed.

Duscha pulled back the bedclothes and slipped in.

Honor slid in beside her, pushing her back on the pillow. She leaned in so they stared at each other, mouths close. "I've had countless dreams like this. Is this real?"

"Oh, yes, my lovely. If you doubt it, bite me. Let's make some moves. Some music. Serious noise." She tugged Honor's hot body against her, wrapping them together tightly. A deepening kiss sent Honor's pulse into hyperdrive, her breath evaporating under Duscha's hands, searching for her sweet spot. And finding it. Honor caught her breath, and sank to the sheet, opening to take in Duscha's touch, lost in sensation, oblivious to time… to anything other than Duscha's knowing hands and succulent mouth, intent on pleasure, stroking for surrender.

Against Honor's open mouth, Duscha whispered, "I want you, any way you'll have me. For as long as you so desire." And Honor gave in, crying out into the night, half shriek, half bellow…a haunting cry that faded away to a contented silence.

She wrapped her thighs around Duscha's leg, hip to hip. Into Duscha's pulsing throat, she murmured, "Love your work." Duscha chuckled and caressed her back, holding her tenderly as they relaxed into each other.

Honor said, "I've spent half my life loving you. I do so wish this had happened years ago."

"If it weren't for your mother, it might have."

"Huh? What do you mean?"

Duscha coaxed Honor to put her head on her shoulder. Then she told her. About the scene in the supermarket, and what Honor's mother had said. And how awful she had felt at the time, especially when Janelle was fired.

"In another time and place, without that interference, you and I might have progressively got to know each other. And who knows? We might have ended up together."

"But you wouldn't have partnered with Noelle."

"No. And I don't regret that for a second. And you wouldn't have partnered with Merrin."

Honor raised herself to lean on one elbow. "Definitely not. And that's something I *have* lived to regret, in the end. How strange is all that? I can't believe my mother did such a thing. She never really accepted me as I am, but that was mean, if not downright hateful."

"Was it? From her point of view, she was protecting you from me…from yourself. Like as not, she believed she was doing the right thing. She was being a mother, warning off the enemy. Nothing quite like deluded, righteous straight folk for wrecking queer people's lives."

Honor blurted, "She had no right to make that kind of decision for me!"

"She thought she did. Remember, you were only sixteen. I wasn't the kind of future she pictured for her only daughter. Me or any other female. Where's the wedding? Where are the grandkids? It was a disappointing scenario for a woman of her generation."

"Dear Duscha, I'm terribly sorry. For you and me, both."

"The past is the past. As Shakespeare wrote, "the course of true love never did run smooth." But we're here now, and we can make the most of every precious moment from now on. Deal?"

"Absolutely." She kissed every square inch of Duscha's smiling face, her throat and down to her breasts. Heat rising between them, night closed in, cocooning and protecting them from everything but themselves.

Draped in her dressing gown, Duscha sat on the edge of the bed, leaning down to press her lips between Honor's sleepy eyes. "Good morning. I'm about to put the kettle on before I run through the shower. Do you want tea?"

Honor stretched languidly. "I'll make it. Off you go."

Duscha turned at the door. "Was your father expecting you home last night?"

"I told him about you. He'll have worked it out."

"Oh! I could be in trouble?"

"Doubt it. But I'll call him, just in case."

When Duscha came back from her shower, a mug of tea was waiting for her on the nightstand. Swathed in Duscha's voluminous pyjama top, Honor was propped against the bedhead and drinking tea. Duscha sat beside her.

Honor said, "Dad wants to meet you. We've been summoned to drop in for a cuppa tomorrow at ten a.m."

"Uh-oh. Hang on…does that mean you're staying with me tonight? Woo-hoo!" Duscha slid down the bed and snuggled in, her head on Honor's shoulder. "If you play your cards right, I'll take you to the hardware store to buy rose bushes this afternoon."

"Did you know that every one of those stores is a hotspot for lesbian hook-ups?"

Grinning, Duscha said, "Don't worry, I'll protect you from those dastardly dykes. And never let it be said that I don't show you a good time!"

CHAPTER THIRTY-SIX

The next day, they took their own cars to Denholm's house in Queanbeyan. Understandably, Duscha was stagestruck in meeting the former governor general of Australia. But he was gracious in welcoming her warmly. He asked about her career and family background. Despite the nagging feeling that she was being interviewed, Duscha answered him as frankly as she would most people, possibly more so because he was Honor's father. When she explained how she came to be, Denholm frowned, seeming to become lost in thought.

He said, "Cliff Coxall? That name rings a loud bell. I believe he was involved in a number of redevelopments around Kingston. And the lake foreshore."

"It could be. I haven't lived in Canberra for many years. The house he left me comes down from my aunt and great-aunt. It's small, but delightful. If a bit unkempt. I'm working on it, with Honor's help." She glanced at Honor with a dazzling smile full of undisguised affection.

Wryly, he said, "I appreciate your candour, but I don't mean this to be a re-enactment of the Spanish Inquisition. I'm genuinely interested in people's heritage. I think it says a lot about them."

On a sudden impulse, Duscha blurted, "I'd like to ask your opinion about something. It's a bit of a mystery."

He held up open hands. "How can I help?"

"Well." She glanced back and forth between them. "I haven't had much chance to mention this to Honor, but Stuart found a tin of jewellery hidden under the house. I don't know that it's worth much. That, I'm still trying to find out. What puzzles me is why my relatives would conceal it that way. Why wouldn't they put it in a bank safety deposit box or something similar?"

Denholm made a steeple of his fingers under his chin. "When was this, do you think?"

"Maybe late 1950s? Early 1960s?"

He nodded pensively. "Could be to avoid death duty, which was the law in those days. If the contents had substantial value and the inheritor insufficient cash, it might have forced any inheritor to sell it to pay the tax. People thought up all sorts of wild and woolly tricks to protect their assets. Fortunately, inheritance tax no longer exists."

"So, it would never have been mentioned in a will?"

"Probably not. Knowledge of its existence would have depended on word-of-mouth."

"But I wasn't told about it. If I hadn't stripped the wallpaper or had the termite damage repaired, I would never have discovered it." Duscha shook her head. "I wonder why Dad didn't tell me?"

"Maybe he didn't know about it. This is how things get lost forever. You'll never know, I'm afraid."

"Thank you, sir. That's been very illuminating."

"Call me Denholm. Please."

* * *

Duscha had left Honor and Denholm to their own devices and driven home alone to Ainslie. She and Honor, being otherwise occupied, had never made it to digging up the proposed rose garden. But Honor had promised to get stuck into the task over the next weekend. Back home, Duscha put on washing and vacuumed the house, stopping to check her emails for the first time in days. There was a standout message from one Beata Szabo of the Powerhouse Museum.

> *Dear Ms. Penhaligon,*
> *My apologies for the delay in replying to your email. I have been away on a short sabbatical. Upon researching your inquiry with a colleague at the Art Gallery of New South Wales, it appears that the Armfield's Collection, as it was recorded in 1949, was thought lost long ago. My colleagues and I here at the Powerhouse are thrilled to discover that Mrs. Armfield's nationally significant personal collection is still in existence. The inventory seems identical, with the exception of a few pieces, to the document archived at the AGNSW.*
> *Fortuitously, we are organising an exhibition of early Australian jewellery next year, and would be delighted if we might borrow several outstanding pieces for display. However, you may have plans to auction some or all of the collection through Sotheby's or Christie's here in Sydney. Rest assured, there would be considerable interest from both Australian and international buyers, including galleries and museums that specialise in antique jewellery.*
> *As a curator, I am concerned that you protect and store the collection carefully. With the passage of time, its value has increased considerably. Since you're in Canberra and may not want to transport such pieces to either Sydney or Melbourne for a current valuation, the auction houses would come to you, should that suit.*
> *If I can be of further service, do let me know. Please stay in touch.*
> *Regards,*
> *Beata Szabo*
> *Powerhouse Museum (Museum of Applied Arts and Sciences, Sydney)*

Duscha read the message again and then again. The curator sounded a bit over the top with her talk of auction houses and "considerable value." Curiosity piqued, she wondered about the local antiques dealer who had recommended the mirror repairer. He had an honest reputation. Perhaps she could ask him to have a look? For the moment, she put the whole thing into the mental too-hard basket, as she needed to prepare herself for work the following morning. With distracting memories of the last two nights in bed with Honor running through her head and a satisfied smile that persistently pinned back her cheeks, her chores became a blissful blur.

CHAPTER THIRTY-SEVEN

At the dining table two weeks later, Denholm looked up from the daily paper's Sudoku puzzle. "Spring is the best time of year to put property on the market. Is your house ready to roll?"

Honor sat across from him sewing a button back onto her favourite flannel shirt. A client's rose bush she'd been pruning had caught it and almost torn the front pocket off. "Almost. I'm still thinking about re-carpeting. Some rooms look tired, the lounge room in particular."

"Be careful you don't overcapitalise."

Head bowed in concentration, she smiled to herself. "Yes, I know Dad."

He harrumphed and pencilled in another number. "I quite like your new woman."

"Oh, do you?" She glanced across at him. "Duly noted, Your Excellency. And what is it about her, exactly, that meets with your approval?"

"Well," he drawled. "For starters, she's easy on the eye."

"You're transparent. So predictable."

"What's wrong with remarking upon a passably attractive woman? Really. A fella can't say a thing, these days. Political correctness gone mad."

"I didn't say there was anything wrong with it. I said you were pre-dict-able. That's all."

A louder harrumph. He rubbed out a number and pencilled in another. "I take it that you've settled into some kind of routine from the way you've been spending Friday and Saturday nights at her house. Are you thinking of moving in with her?"

She knotted the thread securing the errant button and cut it off close to the fabric. "Honestly? I don't know if that's on the agenda yet. We're still finding our way around each other. And I don't want to make another mistake, unsurprisingly."

He put down the pencil, sitting back to examine her. "So far, she seems nothing like Merrin, but looks can be deceiving. As charming as she is, have you discussed finances?"

She looked hard at him, steady dark eyes mirroring his. "Not in so many words. Money is hardly a romantic subject."

He growled, "Romance be damned. Pretend I'm your bank manager and you want a loan. Sell her to me."

"Oh, c'mon Dad."

Leaning forward, he folded his arms and stared her down. "You just told me you don't want to make another mistake! So tell me what you *do* know."

"All right." Honor puffed up her cheeks and exhaled loudly. "To the best of my knowledge, she inherited the Ainslie house unencumbered. Her half-sister was disputing a cash lump sum, but she withdrew after mediation."

"How much?"

"Don't know. Sufficient to rile up her half-sister, which suggests it was substantial."

"What about cash socked away as savings?"

Honor fidgeted. "I've no idea and I'm not about to ask. Look, she must have superannuation, but she's always been a renter. Until her father left her the house."

"A sure-fire road to poverty. Anything else?"

"We both heard about her aunt's jewellery. I don't think even she knows what that's worth, but probably not much."

"What about debts?"

Honor perked up. "Now, that I'm clear about. She mentioned in passing that she hates debt. Even pays off her credit card every month, she said. I believe her." She watched and waited as he massaged his cheeks, attention fixed on the newspaper's Sudoku.

"From what you've said, she's at least financially literate." He glanced up at her, eyes narrowed. "What does she know about your finances?"

"That I run my own business. That I have a house in Higgins that I may or may not own outright—I haven't spelt it out. Other than that, nothing."

Squeezing his bottom lip into a 'V' with fingertips, he said, "She hasn't asked?"

"It's likely she has no idea what I'm worth. Most wouldn't, just from looking at me."

Barely listening, he continued, "How about a police check?"

"No! Definitely not! I think she has all she needs. Thereafter, she doesn't much care. Would you leave well alone, please? I hate talking about her like this."

"Damn it girlie, I'm looking out for you. No one else will. And you're too nice for your own good."

"I get it, Dad. I appreciate you're trying to protect me, but I think she's trustworthy. However, I may be horribly biased!" She laughed ruefully.

"As long as you've given some thought to finances, that's all I want you to do." He pencilled in the last three numbers to complete the puzzle. "Got it! Just exactly how biased are you, really? If you don't mind me asking."

Honor examined the ceiling. "Really? I feel like I've loved her all my life."

To her worldly ears the statement sounded trite, and she wondered what he made of it. Yet she felt its truth. For a few moments, uncertainty made her mute. And then, for the first time ever, she told her father about her teenage crush on Duscha. The bare facts didn't take long.

Watching her, he listened intently until she fell silent. With infinite tenderness, he said, "I'm stunned. Really. I had absolutely no idea. Why haven't you told me before?"

"Because." She threw up her hands and let them drop. "Because it's kind of embarrassing. I was so young. And secretly, desperately, hopelessly in love. Depressive and obsessive and ridiculous as well. You weren't around much. By the time you were, I was doing my best to put it behind me. There was no point in telling you. What would I have said? A girl I barely knew broke my heart when I was sixteen? I never imagined I'd be where I am now. It's kind of surreal."

He inclined his head and scratched behind an ear. "Oh, girlie. You've always kept things to yourself, haven't you? Very close. That said, thank you for telling me because now things make more sense. I was thinking it was remarkably full-on between you. The fact is, you two go back a long way."

"We do. She knows how I feel…that I adore her more than I can say, as twee as that sounds. But am I seeing her with teenage eyes or my adult eyes? Do I trust my own judgment? That's another question."

"Ah, you're scared. Once bitten, twice shy. It's okay to be scared. Life without risk is as boring as hell. My girl, you have to follow your gut feeling, but do your homework!" Denholm stroked his chin's evening shadow, loving look upon her. "And listen to those who care about you. What does your mate Stuart say?"

"He's encouraging but doesn't know her that well. She's good with people. And I can talk to her about anything and everything. Absolutely anything. It's quite strange in my experience. We've been discussing, if not our future, *my* future. And yes, you were quite right about Landladies. I can't count on my physical fitness for many more years. She suggested I invest in my brain, as she put it, through landscape design, perhaps with staff to do the physical work. I could tack a landscape architecture degree onto my horticultural qualifications. What do you think?"

"Interesting. Shows initiative. You could study part-time. Or full-time, but what would you do with Landladies?"

"If I went full-time, I'd have to retire Landladies and lose a great deal of goodwill from my bread-and-butter clients. Part-time, I could delegate more to Karen who's my smartest team player. She may be interested in a more supervisory role. For higher pay, of course. Or even a partnership."

"But is it what *you* want?"

She shook out the shirt she'd mended and folded it neatly on her lap. "Garden design has always fascinated me. And I've long been a fan of Edna Walling's pioneering use of Australian natives in the home garden."

"*The* Edna Walling?"

"Yep, the one still famous for her art deco-style garden designs in Victoria. And infamous for being euphemistically described as 'she never married' and someone who 'lived down Trouser Lane.' Who knows if she was actually gay? Anyway, while I love getting down and dirty with plants, the where and how of getting them to grow and look good at the same time is the real challenge. It's highly creative. That excites me."

Denholm folded the newspaper around the crossword puzzle. "I'm glad you're excited. In fact, you're the most excited I've seen you for years. Take your opportunities. If you want to share your future with Duscha, talk to her. Get it out there."

"When it feels right, I will. For the record, she was adamant I sort things out with Merrin before we took our relationship further."

"That's admirable, but don't take too long about it, my girl."

She leaned across the table, whispering, "I've been invited to dinner at her mother's house. This Friday."

He snorted, beginning to chuckle. "Since she's Russian, be afraid…be very afraid!"

"Oh, come on! I'm sure she's charming."

"Good luck with that."

She rolled her eyes as she packed the sewing equipment into its lidded box perched on the chair next to her.

"Dad, when's the next Seahorse Society meeting?"

"Saturday week. Why?"

"You could host a soirée here."

He peered at her over his reading glasses. "I don't think so."

"Why not? I've never met any of your Seahorse friends and I'd love to. Invite them over. It would be a blast."

"Don't be silly. What if the neighbours spotted them? It would be all over town."

She paused to frown at him, shutting the sewing box lid with a loud click. "You can't be serious. It's one of the best known secrets in Canberra."

He huffed and puffed, "What nonsense! Nobody knows."

"That you like dressing up as a woman and hanging out with other guys who do the same? *Everybody* knows!"

"Who? Who knows that I haven't personally told? No one, I wager."

"Duscha's mother does. And a whole bunch of other people. Canberra's a small place. Word gets around, trust me. It's high time you leapt out of the closet."

Face screwed up in dismay, he said, "Duscha's mother? How in God's name would she know?"

"Dunno. Duscha mentioned it because her mother had whispered in her ear about you. People tell people who tell other people. Stop hiding and throw a party. *Really* enjoy yourself!"

She picked up the sewing box and left him sitting at the table, speechless.

CHAPTER THIRTY-EIGHT

Ian Grubb removed the jeweller's loupe from his eye socket. He was sitting at Duscha's dining table where she had laid out the collection. A dainty man with neatly combed mouse-brown hair, he straightened his spotted black and white bow tie and thrust out a diminutive chin.

"Thank you for inviting me to examine these fascinating pieces. A very impressive boutique collection."

Duscha said, "Well, you said you preferred a closer look. Thanks for coming. Any thoughts on value, intrinsically or otherwise?"

"Oh. Well. It's difficult to be precise. Should you put the collection to auction, you would garner interest from both institutions and private collectors. In Australia and from overseas. Buyers will pay what the market will bear, according to their own assessment of what a piece might be worth. Then there's a valuation for insurance purposes. Or do you want to sell the collection as a job-lot or individually? It really depends on what you want to do."

"I'm leaning toward selling, but in the interim, I'd like to insure everything. Add them to my house contents insurance."

He blinked at her. "You really don't want to do that. Not unless you have a well-concealed safe. Even then, it would add considerably to your premiums. All of it should be secured in a bank safety deposit box, or with an independent specialist storage company."

"Is that absolutely necessary?"

Fiddling with the loupe, he took his time to reply. "It's only a recommendation, of course. Given its value, I would if I were you."

"How much are we talking about?"

"Conservatively? A hundred and fifty thousand."

Duscha coughed. "Beg yours…say again?"

"A hundred and fifty thousand. Maybe more at auction. Having looked at everything and made extensive notes, I'll now go back to the office, do some research and give you the best estimate I can for each piece. I've still got the inventory and photos that you emailed to me. As soon as I've finalised the estimates, I'll email the results to you."

Duscha was barely listening to him courteously making arrangements. There were only fifteen items, not including the bar brooch bequeathed specifically to Aunt Charlotte, and therefore to herself. Mentally, she did the simple maths. The average value was ten thousand per piece, which was far more than she had guessed for the whole lot. That put a completely new shine on her unexpected inheritance. Dealing with it had suddenly become much more complicated.

In the middle of ironing shirts that evening, Duscha considered the significance of the antique dealer's valuation. A hundred-and-fifty thousand dollars was a completely unexpected and substantial amount of money. On top of it, her father's cool half million had come through a month ago, having been released from probate after Roxanne's backdown.

Duscha already had a tidy sum in savings accumulated over years of working, but nowhere near six figures. She'd lived modestly, both as a child brought up by her single Ma, and as an adult renter bearing moving company costs far too often. Suddenly she had not a money worry in the world, a change in circumstances to which she was still adjusting. A consultation with a financial advisor was on her to-do list. Shrewdly invested, her future financial needs were well and truly covered. In the meantime, the house repairs had ceased to be a headache and any further renovations were easily affordable.

As usual, her thoughts drifted to her beloved Honor who seemed such a competent businessperson. Yet now Duscha felt that, should anything untoward happen, she could look after them both. And if Honor wanted to take up a post-graduate degree, Duscha could comfortably support her. Between her father, his sister Charlotte and great-Aunt Irene, she and Honor had been set up for a long time. A bubble of pleasure rising in her chest, she grinned to herself as she put the last shirt on its hanger and turned off the iron.

Out loud, she said, "Thank you, house. As Aunt Charlotte rightly said, you are a unique treasure and I'm very happy here. Thank you, my ancestors—Dad, Irene and Ruby, Charlotte and Sylvia. I am exceptionally lucky and richly blessed, because of you. Amazing."

CHAPTER THIRTY-NINE

Duscha was frying French toast for breakfast. With an egg lifter, she fished the last two slices out of the pan and dropped them onto paper towel to drain.

"What do you recommend putting on it?" asked Honor, peering at the spreads in a cupboard.

"You can go sweet or savoury. Or both. I like a slice with cheese, followed by another with golden syrup. You could have sugar drizzled with lemon, which is my mother's favourite. Or honey, jam, or maple syrup. Choose your poison."

"I think I'm spoilt for choice." Honor gathered three jars that she juggled to the dining table. Duscha rummaged through the fridge for cheese slices.

They sat in silence, anointing the still-hot toast with one spread or another. Duscha cut a slice into bite-sized chunks. Hot English mustard topped some cheese, adding to her relish.

Honor said, "Hm, yum. This stuff is addictive!" She reached out, grasped Duscha's free hand and smiled contentedly. Holding hands, they ate and grinned at each other, twice dissolving into delighted giggles over nothing. When they'd finished eating, Duscha leaned over for a kiss…or two…or three.

Duscha said, "It's tempting to do this all day, you gorgeous woman, you. But I wanted to talk to you about my aunt's jewellery. Just to bounce some thoughts around and get your opinion." Stacking plates, she stood up. "Coffee?"

"Let me make it. I think I've actually mastered your machine."

The table cleared, Duscha fetched the toolbox from its hiding place in the study. She laid out the packages according to the inventory. Honor brought the mugs of coffee and sat down beside her.

"I'd like you to look at every piece so you know what I'm talking about. But first, there's a special brooch that I'm not allowed to sell." Duscha unwrapped the bar brooch with the three stones that she passed to Honor. "It was my great-aunt's most treasured possession. Commissioned by her father. Designed and made by her husband before they were married."

Honor held the brooch lightly, turning it this way and that, the stones catching the morning light from the windows. "Do you know when it was made?"

"In 1899, I believe."

"Wow, it's eighteen-carat gold. How cool is this? And I bet the rocks are real. What do you think? An emerald, a diamond, and an amethyst. Green, white and violet. Give women votes." She grinned, dimples deepening. "This is a suffragette collector's dream find. And it's a beautiful thing!"

"Well, that one ain't going nowhere, since I'm honour-bound to keep it. No hardship, I can tell you. Wait until you see the rest of them. They've been valued by that guy who owns the largest antiques shop in Fyshwick." Duscha slid a sheet of paper across the table. "Here's his email. It seems to be in chronological order of estimated manufacture."

The Armfields Collection – Valuation
(for insurance purposes, only)

Pendant – 12k Gold locket, decorated with emu and kangaroo. C. 1860. $2,000

Brooch –18k White gold spray, set with old cut brilliants to 3cts. C. 1870. $12,000

Brooch – 18k Gold, double bar, set with 1 diamond. C. 1890. $2,500

Brooch – 15k Gold bar, set with 4 diamonds. C.1890. $3,000

Brooch – 18k White gold circle, set with diamonds and pearls. C. 1890. $8,000

Pendant – Platinum diamond flower, with detachable brooch. C. 1890. $10,000

Brooch – 14k Rose gold oval, set with a 15ct amethyst. C. 1900. $1,200

Brooch – 15k Gold bar with kookaburra, inlaid with seed pearls, ruby eye. C.1900. $1,800

Brooch – 15k Gold, double bar, set with 1 black opal. C. 1900. $1,500

Ring – Platinum, set with 3ct central marquise diamond, diamond studded mount. C. 1905. $65,000

Pendant - 18k Gold swag & pendant drop, 2 amethysts, 20 emeralds & 80 diamonds. C.1910. $12,000

Pendant – Platinum openwork, set with sapphires and pearls. C. 1910. $2,000

Ring – 18k White gold oval plaque, set with 3 old cut brilliants to 4cts. C.1920s. $30,000

Necklace – Platinum, set with 7 black opals and 5 old cut brilliants. C. 1920s. $20,000

Ring – Platinum, set with 1 golden sapphire, diamond border / shoulders. C. 1930. $15,000

TOTAL = A$186,000

Honor read it through, then looked up at Duscha, eyes luminous. "This looks awesome. Can I see now?"

They unwrapped each item, identified it from the email, had a good look and re-wrapped them meticulously. When they came to the marquise diamond ring, Honor lapsed into stunned contemplation. She said, "It's magnificent. And ridiculously valuable. Put it away!"

When she saw the white gold oval plaque ring, she grimaced. "I don't care how much it's worth. That's ugly."

Duscha smirked knowingly. "My mother would agree. It's not to everyone's taste, that's for sure. Someone once loved it and someone may yet again."

Once they had rewrapped everything and tucked it back in the toolbox, Honor said, "Since all of it belongs to you now, is there anything you would like to keep for yourself? You can pick and choose."

"My feeling is it all belongs in a museum. They're not just pieces of jewellery. They're history...Australian history, to boot."

"You wouldn't keep any of it?"

"Nothing I have to have. And I'm getting nervous about having valuables unsecured in the house. I can either store the whole lot with the bank, or have it sold off by one of the auction houses, who will take their commission, of course. I have to make a decision soon. I prefer to sleep worry-free."

Honor said, "It sounds to me like you've already decided."

"Maybe. What about you? What would you keep?"

Eyeing off the tin, Honor said, "Apart from your great-aunt's special brooch, there isn't anything I would wear. Not even the marquise ring. I mean, it's stunning but it's huge. Too big for my hands. I think you're right. All of it either belongs in a museum or someone's private collection."

"Are you quite sure? I only ask because I noticed you took your time with one of the gold bar brooches."

Honor thought for a moment. "You mean the kookaburra with the ruby eye? I just love kookas…they're amazing birds. It's very sweet."

"That's my gardener. If you would wear it, I'll hold on to it for you. Although it's not especially valuable, it is probably unique."

Dimples deepening, Honor squeezed her hand, "Y'know, I think I would. That would be perfect. Thank you!"

"You're very welcome." Duscha lifted Honor's knuckles to her lips, softly kissing each finger. Then she exhaled heavily, saying, "I wonder what great-Aunt Irene would want me to do. It's too valuable to have the collection in the house, but if I lock it away in a safety deposit box, no one gets to either see or appreciate it. That would be a pity, I feel."

"Does that mean what I think it does?"

"That depends. If I had a thing for antique jewellery, I would be tempted to find a way to securely display and hold on to it. I'm loath to disappoint my great-aunt and her sweetheart, Ruby, but I'm not that keen. If Ian Grubb is to be believed, it's valuable both intrinsically and monetarily to people other than me. Like collectors. And the Powerhouse Museum. The Australian people, truth be told. It's a national treasure that really shouldn't be in private hands anymore."

"I can feel an auction coming on."

"I think so. Let's pack it away and go look for rose bushes. Thanks for your precious help." Duscha planted a lingering kiss on Honor's waiting mouth. Huskily, she said, "You're a darling. Entirely magical. Some days, I can't quite believe you're real. Promise not to vanish in a puff of smoke?"

"If I could, I wouldn't."

After dinner, Honor had nearly finished the dishes when Duscha wandered into the kitchen in her dressing gown, still damp from the shower. She checked the kettle had sufficient water, switched it on and slipped her arms around Honor's waist from behind. Dropping a kiss atop Honor's head, she said, "Fancy a hot drink?"

Honor was down to the last of the cutlery, but she stopped what she was doing to relax back into Duscha's chest. "Hm... cocoa would be nice." She turned her head, meeting Duscha's hungry lips with her own. Kiss deepening to distraction when a wayward hand lingered at one of her breasts, she barely noticed Duscha had unfastened her jeans until a hand slid into her underwear. Giggling, she drew away saying, "Forks. Into the drainer. I kinda have to finish...oh, God—"

Duscha's kiss silenced her protests. She was reduced to clinging to the sink's edge, breath growing more and more ragged. Minutes later and desperate for release, she let Duscha field her weight when her knees buckled.

Still fighting for breath, she turned to lock soapy fingers behind Duscha's neck. With her forehead resting on a handy shoulder, she chuckled feebly, "You criminal. There's a perfectly good bed in this house. What's your excuse?"

"You're delicious and delightful, and I want you in a thousand ways," Duscha said, voice breaking. "Honor, you know I love you. I really think we should live together."

Honor lifted her head. "What brought that on?"

"This...us. Is it too soon?"

"Who's to say otherwise? It's up to us." She focussed on Duscha's mouth. "Right now, all I want is revenge!"

When Honor came back from the bathroom in sleep shorts and a T-shirt, she found Duscha sitting up, holding a letter under the light of the bedside lamp. She slipped between the sheets, propping a pillow behind her.

"What are you reading?"

"My aunty's letter about the jewellery. I do so wish I had had the chance to meet her. I'm sure we would have got along famously. Never mind. There's something else I wanted to show you." Duscha rummaged through the letter tin until she extricated the folded sash, unfurling it in front of them. "This belonged to great-Aunt Irene who wore it during suffrage marches. It's that old."

Honor ran a palm over the fabric with its embroidered lettering. "Feels like silk. Should be extremely strong and last for centuries. Any idea when it was made?"

"Around 1900, I assume. Isn't it something? Try it on."

Honor tugged off her T-shirt and slipped on the sash, draping the lettering between her full breasts. Duscha started to laugh. "I don't think she wore it quite like that!"

"Why ever not? You try it," Honor teased, tugging at Duscha's nightshirt. "Come on."

Grinning, Duscha shrugged off her shirt, caught by surprise when Honor shoved back the bedclothes to sit across Duscha's thighs, face on.

"Well now, what have we here?" said Honor. "Shall we share this silken treasure to do the suffragettes proud?" She removed one sash end, dropping it over Duscha's head. "A bond within the sisterhood. Committed rebels, triumphant in the end." And she leaned in until Duscha was in danger of being lovingly smothered.

Duscha kissed her way out of trouble, then slung Honor sideways onto the bed. Amongst the giggles and manoeuvring of limbs and silk, they ended up side by side, opposing wrists wrapped in the sash, binding them together, free hands caressing where they could. Laughter turned to wanting that became insistent. Gently yet firmly, Honor got the better of Duscha's token resistance…got her ecstatic revenge.

Honor turned out the light and drew Duscha's languid form closer, the sash still in place. Her free hand combed blond hair from a dewy forehead to which she pressed her lips, tasting salt and savouring her love's unique scent. Suddenly aware that her heart was beyond full, she squeezed Duscha's entwined hand harder than she ought. The warm body against her stirred and relaxed again.

In the inky blackness, Honor lay still with eyes open, listening to Duscha's breathing, searing every heartbeat into memory. So far in her life, she had known more of disappointment than happiness. For her, it had been the thing of dreams, never quite within reach. Yet here it was. Who knew what the morrow might bring?

She didn't want to think—she just wanted to *feel*. But Duscha's words of love, entwined with the idea of them cohabiting, drifted into her thoughts. Catching her breath, she considered their implications. Duscha wanted them to live together. She wanted to share her life with her...with *her*.

In the dark, Honor shook her head, incredulous. She had secretly loved this woman all her adult life, never imagining they might actually end up together. And that was about to change because she already knew what she would say. Soon, they would talk. But not now, in this moment of heightened awareness, this "now" of them safely ensconced, with Duscha in her arms for a minute or an eternity. It didn't matter beyond now.

She bent to press her lips to Duscha's sleeping mouth, ever so lightly so as not to wake her. It felt so amazing that she did it again, not risking a third time. She could get used to this. Far into the night, she relished every sensation, moment by precious moment, until exhaustion closed her reluctant eyes.

The silken sash still binding them lightly, she murmured, "Love you. By some miracle, you're really mine. Finally and at last. Love you."

CHAPTER FORTY

It was late afternoon on Christmas Eve and Honor was moving in. In Duscha's kitchen, she dragged the electric wok out of the corner cupboard and lifted it onto the bench. Frowning, she stared at the bulky black appliance, wondering if it was ever used.

"Duscha? Have you got a minute?"

Duscha appeared in the doorway, packing box in her arms. "Just let me put this down in the bedroom. Hang about."

Honor crouched down to peer in the cupboard, checking how much space there might be for some of her gear. It looked pretty tight in a kitchen built in far more basic times.

"What's up, love?"

Honor stood, hands on hips. "I think we need a bigger house. Or, at least a bigger kitchen…not happening anytime soon. Do we really need an electric wok?"

Duscha slung an arm around her shoulders. "I do use it. Admittedly not very often, but—"

"My barbeque has a proper wok burner. We're going to park that on the back deck anyway. Would that work as a replacement for you?"

Duscha sighed. "We'll have to rationalise every area, eh? It could go. Hey, don't worry, we'll sort it out."

Honor stared at the thing, fatigue getting the better of her. The last few weeks had been full-on with her packing up her belongings in Higgins. In mid-November she'd sold her house to a young couple with children. They were keen for a quick settlement and very excited to move in before Christmas, if possible. That put unexpected pressure on her and Duscha. They had discussed her moving in at length. Duscha had said she was delighted, but it was a lot to do in their out-of-business-hours free time.

And the whole of Australia was about to close down for Christmas: all the shops and offices and trades, bar a few supermarkets who would make a killing from last-minute goods or emergency seafood and salad supplies. The week between Christmas and New Year saw everyone racing around in the heat to celebrate with family and friends, sharing presents and eating and drinking vast quantities. Afternoons might be spent playing in someone's pool or passing out to recover after long lunches. For parents, it was exhausting. For small children, it was overwhelming. For singles and the elderly, it was interminable. Everyone resorted to watching films they'd been gifted, or streaming services, or the Sydney to Hobart yacht race. For the truly desperate, there were always the long days of watching the cricket test match on the telly.

This evening, with Duscha in tow, Honor was expected for Christmas Eve drinks at her father's house, along with her brothers and their families. She wasn't much in the mood, but the gathering of the Boyce clan was important to her father, especially in the absence of her mother. On Christmas Day, Denholm would visit his wife in the aged-care facility and, as usual, she wouldn't recognise him. Honor would go with him and her brothers on Boxing Day. It was something they would do with mixed feelings, but they would do it regardless.

Honor and Duscha weren't expected at Valeria's house until New Year's Eve when the Russians traditionally celebrated Christmas. Duscha had said that Valeria's cousins were coming down from Sydney especially, and they would join in with Theo's relatives of Hungarian heritage. It was going to be a massive food-laden celebration that was not to be missed. Cooks were already preparing their favourite dishes for the feast, not wanting to be outdone by each other. Those in the kitchen could only pray that it wouldn't be too hot so they could eat outside, rather than in air-conditioning. Some years the summer heat was stifling, some years it was bearable—it was a meteorological lottery the southern sun usually won. But cooks had to be prepared, either way. Honor was simply thrilled to be invited, knowing she'd be sampling food she'd not tasted before. It was going to be special.

Duscha took Honor's hand. "We've been fetching and carrying for hours. Come and lie down for a while. Let's rest our eyes." She led the way down the hall to the bedroom. They flopped down, side by side. "What time is your dad expecting us?"

"Five thirty for six. It's just drinks…nothing too serious." Honor closed sandpapery eyelids, cuddling Duscha's hand to her chest.

"How you doing, sweet cheeks?"

"Okay, I suppose. We've come a long way in these past few months, haven't we?" Duscha squeezed her hand. "It's hard to pack up after living somewhere for nearly ten years. I've recycled or chucked a surprising amount. In the end, it's only stuff. And hardly what you would call heirloom. But I will miss it."

"Your house?"

Honor opened her eyes. "The garden. I planned and planted it out. And it's only now coming to maturity. I'll miss seeing it develop."

"Do you like your new one?"

"As it happens, I do. It's got good bones, as they say. Someone put much thought into its design. Plus a whole lot of love into caring for it."

"That must have been either Irene or Ruby. Or both. At least initially. Charlotte and Sylvia must have had green thumbs as well."

"They did in the olden days when everyone grew their own vegetables and raised a few chooks."

"We can do that, can't we?"

Honor rolled onto her side, toward Duscha. "I thought chooks were too much of a commitment for you?"

Amused, Duscha flashed a smile. "Oh, I think I might be a bit committed already. My deeply adored and absolutely gorgeous girlfriend just moved in."

"Is that right? Lucky you."

With deliberate sloth, Honor leaned in to kiss Duscha's eyebrows and then both cheeks, on the way to her mouth, where she lingered, tongue-tip wreaking havoc with Duscha's breathing.

Suddenly Duscha drew away. "I forgot to tell you. The Powerhouse Museum sent me a message this morning. Their exhibition that includes all the pieces they bought at the auction will be held on the first weekend of March next year. We could go away for a dirty weekend."

Honor inclined her head, eyes twinkling. "Every weekend with you is a dirty weekend."

"But we can have it in Sydney. Check out the exhibition. Go dining and dancing. What do you think?"

"Sounds great. Can we go sooner…have a practice run?"

Duscha pulled Honor in close. "Of course. From memory, there are a couple of lesbian bars where we can dance. I haven't been there since forever, but we'll find out. I just *love* dancing with you."

"Sure thing. But right now I think we've done enough hard yakka for one day. I need to shower before we head out." Honor extricated herself.

Duscha swung her legs over the side of the bed, and abruptly took Honor's hand. She brought warm knuckles to her trembling lips, lingering in silence. Honor stilled and waited until alarm got the better of her.

"My dear Duscha, is something the matter? What's wrong?"

Blinking away moisture, Duscha drew breath. "Nothing at all. It's just that this will be our first 'together-forever' night tonight. And before we get caught up in the whole Christmas debacle, I wanted to say a few things that I think need saying."

"Um…okay. Are you having second thoughts?"

"No, no, nothing like that."

"Would you put me out of my misery, then?"

Duscha pulled herself together. "I just want to say that I appreciate that you are taking the major part of the risk by moving in with me. You've sold your house and you're taking a chance on us…on things working out in the long term. I also want to say that I haven't been very brave about us, sometimes. I don't know why exactly."

Honor shrugged helplessly. "You were getting over Noelle, I knew that. For the record, I don't think I could have moved into this house if you had lived here with her. That wouldn't have worked."

Duscha smiled faintly. "I understand. Another couple's memories."

"But you're comfortable with me being here now?"

"Very much so." Serenity had returned to Duscha's face. "Now that I've got all that out of the way, there's something else I want to say. To clarify."

Holding her breath, Honor stared into Duscha's bright topaz eyes. "Hit me with it."

"I know that your trust—you allowing me to get close and be part of your inner world—is something you rarely give to anyone. That I've gained your trust and get to love you is something totally priceless."

Honor swallowed, hand over heart. "Is that it? You nearly gave me a coronary, you crazy romantic…you lunatic!" She leaned in, landing a smacking kiss on Duscha's mouth. "For the record, you won my trust by putting your money where your mouth is. Or as one self-help guru asserted, love is a verb. Actions speak louder than words, and you have been good to me…considerate, kind, loving and sharing. That means a great deal in my book. Upon that note, I have a confession to make while I still have the courage. Stay right where you are." She slid off the bed and began rummaging through packing boxes on the floor. "Here it is. Cover your eyes. Just humour me, will you?"

"Seriously?" Duscha sat on the edge of the bed, hands wrapped over her eyes.

"You can look now."

Honor stood before her holding the framed picture of Duscha the Centaur.

Duscha peered at it. And then she began to chuckle, looking back and forth from the picture to Honor who was grinning sheepishly. She spluttered, "Where on earth did you get that?"

"It's a long and embarrassing story."

"Well, hell, *I've* just embarrassed myself. Why should *you* get off scot-free?"

"The point is—" Honor gulped and stammered, "The point is I can barely remember a time when I didn't love you. It feels like I always have. I've harboured that truth for years, even though I tried to live a decent life as contentedly as possible, in spite of it. But you were always there. A presence locked away in my psyche like a jewel that no one knew about. To be with you now, so openly and proudly, is the stuff of dreams. Is that, as you are wont to say, clear?"

"Ah, sweet cheeks, it seems I've been your deepest, darkest secret! I'm duly flattered. But'…" Duscha pointed her chin at the picture. "I still want to know where you got it."

"Um…a friend did it for me. I was twenty-ish at the time. I've cherished it ever since. You've got me through many a dark hour. Or torrid night."

Duscha guffawed as she stood up and swiped the picture out of Honor's hands. "And you reckon *I'm* a romantic fruit loop. Oh, you are so in trouble over this. When? How?"

"If I told you, you might have me locked up. Maybe later… much later. Preferably in the dark of night when you can't see me blushing."

Chortling, Duscha dropped the picture on the bed and took Honor in her arms. They stood hugging each other closely until Duscha spoke.

"Are you happy?"

The simple honesty of it made Honor croak, "Couldn't be more so."

"Me too."

CHAPTER FORTY-ONE

Canberra, 1949

It was early morning out on the driveway of their Hargraves Crescent home. Ruby was packing the car, ready for the trip up to Sydney. Irene stood nearby with Shelly, their Sheltie dog, wringing her hands and making helpful suggestions.

"Dearest, you might stop at Berrima for petrol and a cup of tea. It's such a dusty road. You will take care, won't you?"

"Yes, dear. Of course I will. Stop your fussing."

Ruby had securely wedged her suitcase on top of the toolbox that was behind the passenger seat in their 1938 Austin Big Seven. The tall, dark-green four-door car sported shiny black mudguards. With a top speed of fifty-five miles per hour acquired in a heady twenty-five seconds, it would comfortably manage the five-hour trip from Canberra to the Art Gallery of New South Wales in Sydney. However, the radiator would need topping up regularly because it had a slow leak that had resisted Ruby's repair efforts, so far. The car was a reliable workhorse for their everyday use and remarkably modern. It even had indicators in the shape of elongated yellow arrows that flicked out from the doorjambs.

Irene said, "Are you quite sure you mean to go alone?"

Ruby frowned behind her spectacles. "We've been over this. Only one of us need go. I'll stay at the YWCA for the full four days to save a few bob. And I'll telephone you when I get there. Besides, who else would look after Shelly and the chooks?"

"What if someone tries to rob you when you pull over for a rest? They might make off with the jewellery!"

"For the love of God, Irene. What are the chances of that? And who's going to look for jewels in the toolbox? You really are talking tosh, my dear."

"But Ruby, you're not as young as you used to be. It could all be too much for you."

"We've talked about this, *ad nauseum*. Short of flying, or a police escort, this is the only way to make sure the collection is safe in transit. Do have more faith in me, will you?"

Irene stepped forward to wrap her arms around Ruby's waist that had grown stocky with age. At sixty-seven years old, her hair now quite grey, Ruby still stood tall and strong.

With a sniffle, Irene said, "In case I haven't told you lately, you are much loved."

Ruby chuckled softly. "Your secret's safe with me. Do you trust me with your precious collection?"

"I trust you with every bone in my body, everything I possess—you know that very well! And it's *our* collection built with Armfield's profits. Your taste…your fingerprints are all over it. Our joint legacy to Australian posterity. Godspeed, my dear sweet girl. Come home safely."

Ruby glanced up and down the street, checking for prying eyes. Then she bent to kiss her beloved with whom she had lived joyfully throughout the last thirty years. "I'll be back before you know it, old girl. Don't you worry."

She climbed into the driver's seat, turned on the ignition and pulled the starter button. The 6volt battery protested having to turn over the cold 900cc engine, but she'd cleaned the plugs and tuned the carburettor. It started first time. Clutch in, she crunched the gear stick into reverse and backed out onto the road. In the rear vision mirror, she waved to the woman she had loved for nearly forty years. Who knew how many years remained of their great adventure together? Despite the good, the bad, and the indifferent, she wouldn't have changed a thing. Not a second of it for either love or money. She would savour every remaining moment: every morning, every hug, every passing touch, every loving glance and every goodnight kiss.

CHAPTER FORTY-TWO

Beata Szabo met Duscha and Honor at the entrance to the Powerhouse. Her voluptuous figure enhanced by a fitted harlequin jacket that topped an ankle-length black skirt, she introduced herself and escorted them into the exhibition. Standing in front of a row of display cases, she handed Duscha an exhibition catalogue and a large envelope.

With a faint eastern-European accent, Beata said, "Please take this with our compliments. I'm sorry to say I'm short of time and can't show you around. But there's something I want to draw your attention to. Take a look at that." She turned to wave multicoloured fingernails at a photo mural on the far wall behind the display cases. Duscha and Honor obligingly followed her gesture. The mural was an enlarged image of a row of six or more women in Victorian period costume carrying a "Votes for Women" banner.

"If you look at page five, you'll see the same photo. We have the original in our archive, of which there is a copy in the envelope I just gave you. I thought you might like to have it. According to an annotation on the back, it was published in the

English newspaper, the Daily Mirror, in 1910. The woman in the very centre is your great-aunt, Irene Coxall."

"No! Really?" Duscha was staring, wide-eyed. The women gravitated across the room until they stood with Beata between them and directly in front of the mural. Irene's image was three quarters life-size, yet remarkably clear.

Honor nudged Duscha. "She looks like you. Or you look like her!"

"Oh my! Have a guess who *that* is." Duscha pointed to the edge of the mural where a tall woman in a full-length dark coat, her face ever so lightly blurred, stood gripping a banner post. She must have glanced across toward the middle of the row, just as the photo was taken.

"She's your great-aunt's private secretary, Ruby Milborne," said Beata. "She brought the collection to the Art Gallery for exhibition in 1949, along with the photo which she gave to us for posterity."

"It's not half obvious who she's looking at, is it?" Duscha was captivated.

Beata put a hand on Duscha's shoulder and the other on Honor's forearm. "Ladies, I'm delighted to meet you both. I'll leave you to wander where you will. Please enjoy the exhibition. We at the Powerhouse are thrilled that we could purchase the best of the Armfield's collection from you."

Duscha glanced at Honor. "We're relieved to see the pieces in your care rather than private hands. It's where it belongs...in the hands of the Australian people. I must say it's a total buzz to see the pieces on public display. And I couldn't be prouder of my ancestors for making it possible."

The curator thanked them both and left to go back to her office. Duscha and Honor strolled up and down in front of the mural.

"It's a pity we can't see Ruby's face clearly, although she's got an impressive jaw. I love the peaked cap and fabulous coat. Very striking." Honor drifted over to Irene's image. "Now, *she's* got that challenging look of yours. You know that one you do with just the hint of a smile? She's unnervingly like you."

"Hey, I had to get it from somewhere. Shall we have a quick look around and then go? Since we've seen it all before."

"If you like. Where to next?"

"Into The Rocks down by the harbour. We can find somewhere to have dinner and then front up to Sisters Nightclub."

CHAPTER FORTY-THREE

It was getting late, the club's playlist having slowed down to soft rock. Locked in each other's arms, Duscha and Honor shared the dance floor with five other couples who shuffled equally as languidly.

Duscha loosened her hold. "Do you want another drink?"

"Definitely not. Don't you leave me alone again."

"Why not?"

"Every time you go to the bar, someone else tries to hit on me."

"You could be flattered." Duscha squeezed Honor's shoulders.

"I am, believe me. They have appeal. It's just that they're all so…y'know."

"What?"

Honor squirmed. "It's been a long time since I came to a bar. And they're all…well. Baby dykes. They're all so young! I feel ancient next to these kids."

Smiling broadly, Duscha pretended to drag her off the dance floor. "Come on, old lady. Let's go back to the shack."

In the rented apartment overlooking Sydney Harbour, the women sprawled on the lounge suite to watch the blinking lights of passing boats and traffic crossing the bridge, its silhouette looming to the left. The bridge arched high into the night sky, its ultimate landfall blocked from view by a motley collection of harbour-side buildings. With just a halogen lighting the hallway that led to the bedroom, they were mostly in shadow. The world beyond the balcony glass doors was a dazzling abstract display.

Duscha found one of Honor's hands that she rubbed gently between her two palms, stilling the movement when Honor spoke softly.

"We've been living together for three months already. And I love waking up with you, but I'd like to ask. Are you still happy?"

Duscha studied her.

"With me, I mean. Instead of Noelle."

"Oh, Honor." Duscha found the limpid dark eyes, huge in the gloom. "Believe me, Noelle wouldn't want me to be anything else."

Shaking her head, she turned her attention to the kaleidoscope of lights. "My friends said she was an acquired taste. A bit like oysters. You either love them or you don't. She was pragmatic and up front, very blunt with people. Everyone knew if she liked them or she didn't. To the chosen few, of which I was one, she was forthright and generous."

Duscha caught Honor's intent look. "Before she died, she told me to move on when I could, to not waste my life grieving for her. I know she meant every word. You'll have to trust me on that. Would you do that for me?"

Honor said, "I'd do just about anything for you."

"I know." Duscha leaned over until she was mere inches from Honor's eyes. "And I feel *exactly* the same about you. So please don't compare. And for the record, I am *very* happy. With you. Nobody else. You."

Honor's knuckles came to stroke her cheeks. "I'm sorry. It's not you I question, so much as I sometimes think you could do better."

Duscha pulled a face. "Do you doubt my good taste, girl? You should know by now that I have exquisite taste in women. I simply can't do better than the best. And that, my honey, is you." She nuzzled Honor's throat. "Stuart once told me you were a babe and I had to agree. You smell and taste delicious." And she blew a raspberry beneath Honor's jawline.

Squirming and giggling, Honor said, "Speaking of babes, Irene was a bit of a looker. And wasn't Ruby something? Handsome as. The coat. The cap. The boots. She could park those boots under my bed anytime."

"I thought you loved waking up with me?"

Honor guffawed. "Don't stress—she's dead!"

"Well, *hell*, that's academic. I can protest, as would Irene!" Duscha disentangled herself and stood up. "Can I get you a nightcap?"

"Only if you're having one."

"Won't be a minute…don't go anywhere."

Duscha strode briskly down the hall to the bedroom where she quickly undressed. From the wardrobe, she pulled out her black woollen coat and shrugged it on. A quick rummage found her dress boots into which she slipped naked feet. No rakish cap to complete the picture, but she didn't think Honor would mind.

In no time at all, she stood in front of Honor whose eyes grew huge and smile stretched wide as Duscha opened and shut the coat.

"Oh, wow. You are stunning!" Honor jumped up and slid hot hands inside the coat. "Oh, yes…yes! My darling, this is some nightcap." Voice husky, she murmured, "I get Irene and Ruby rolled into one."

Heat rising between them, Duscha bent to kiss her, tongue teasing Honor forward into a slow dance in front of the window, skin flashing ghostly white beneath the black coat. "I love the way you squeeze yourself into me. Love your phantom kisses in the night…yeah, I'm wise to your secret pashes. Love the way you move. Love that you're so good with your hands."

Honor chuckled softly, a palm cruising across Duscha's inner thigh, the other climbing her back. Duscha's mouth silenced her mirth, breath fanning a cheek.

Duscha whispered, "I love that we found each other again, despite the odds. You are more than enough for me…all that I could possibly want or need. I love that we talk. Intimately. And don't have to talk. I love that we are close friends, close lovers, close—"

One hand lost in Duscha's hair, Honor kissed her hungrily, an ankle wrapping behind Duscha's calves. They were in danger of toppling. Fumbling madly, Duscha shrugged off the heavy coat and they sank to kneel on its bulk. Duscha lay down with an expectant sigh and Honor lifted a booted foot over one shoulder.

City lights a dazzling backdrop, Honor bent to satisfy.

When her pulse slowed to a moderate canter, Duscha dropped a languid hand to Honor's head resting on her hip. "You do realise any number of people in neighbouring buildings could have just watched us."

"Only with handy binoculars and dumb luck." Honor searched out her eyes in the gloom. "Too bad if they did. Must we always be conveniently invisible? I'm proud to be with you. Proud of us."

Duscha smoothed back tendrils loosened from Honor's glossy plait. "You and me, once lost, now found. I vote we be inconveniently visible and proud for a very long time."

"Visible and proud it is. With you forever won't be long enough."

Bella Books, Inc.

Women. Books. Even Better Together.

P.O. Box 10543
Tallahassee, FL 32302

Phone: 800-729-4992
www.bellabooks.com